She could think of nothing but Rule.

Nothing but Rule and what they had shared the summer she was seventeen. Sometimes she thought that communication between them was impossible, but at other times it seemed that no words were necessary. She didn't understand him, but she knew him—knew his pride, his toughness, his dark temper that was no less frightening for being controlled. She had grown up knowing that Rule Jackson was a dangerous man, a threat to her emotions and her heart. Now, after years of running away, she was home, if only for a little while, and some things were still the same. Rule was still the same.

He turned to her. "Not planning on a long visit, are you?"

"No," she replied, her voice flat. She had never stayed long at the ranch since that summer.

"Well, think about it, Cat. It's time you came home for good."

LINDA HOWARD

AGAINST the RULES

MIRA BOOKS

ISBN 1-55166-017-2

AGAINST THE RULES

MIRA and the star colophon are trademarks of MIRA Books.

Printed in U.S.A.

To Royce and Mae,
for obvious reasons

Cathryn wearily dropped her travel bag at her feet and looked around the air terminal for a familiar face, any familiar face. Houston's Intercontinental Airport was crowded with holiday travelers over the long Memorial Day weekend, and after being pushed both backward and forward by people hurrying to make connecting flights, Cathryn stepped back out of the worst of the crunch, using her foot to push the travel bag along. Her flight hadn't been early, so why wasn't someone there to meet her? This was her first visit home in almost three years, so surely Monica could have—

"Cat."

The irritated thought was never finished; it was interrupted by a husky growl in her ear and two hard hands curving around her slim waist, turning her around and pulling her against a lean male body. She had a startled, fleeting glimpse of unreadable dark eyes before they were covered by drooping lids and long black lashes; then he was too close, and her lips, parted in surprise, were caught by the warmth of his mouth. Two seconds, three...the kiss lingered, became deeper, his tongue moving in to take sensual possession. An instant before she recovered herself enough to protest, he released her from the kiss and stepped back.

"You shouldn't do that!" she snapped, her pale cheeks becoming warm with color as she noticed several people watching them and grinning.

Rule Jackson thumbed his battered black hat farther back on his head and regarded her with calm amusement, the same sort of look he'd given her when she was an awkward twelve-year-old, all long arms and legs. "I thought we'd both enjoy it," he drawled, leaning down to pick up her bag. "Is this all?"

"No," she said, glaring at him.

"It figures."

He turned and made his way over to the luggage claim area, and Cathryn followed him, fuming inwardly at his manner but determined not to let him see it. She was twenty-five now, not a scared kid of seventeen; she would *not* let him intimidate her. She was his employer. He was only the ranch foreman, not the omnipotent devil her adolescent imagination had painted him. He might still have Monica and Ricky under his spell, but Monica was no longer her guardian and couldn't command her obedience. Cathryn wondered with well-hidden fury if Monica had deliberately sent Rule to meet her, with the knowledge that she hated him.

Unconsciously watching his lean body as he stretched and claimed the lone suitcase with her name tag on it, Cathryn shut off the rest of the violent thoughts that flooded her mind. Seeing Rule had always done that to her, driven her out of control and made her do things she would never have done except in the heat of temper. I hate him, she thought, the words whispering through her mind, but still her eyes moved over the width of his shoulders and down the long, powerful legs as she remembered....

He brought the suitcase to where she stood and one straight black eyebrow arched questioningly. After making her feel that she had imposed on him by having more than one piece of luggage, he grunted, "Not planning on a long visit, are you?"

"No," she replied, keeping her voice flat, expressionless. She had never stayed long at the ranch, not since that summer when she had been seventeen.

"It's about time you thought about coming home for good," he said.

"There's no reason for me to."

His dark eyes glinted at her from under the brim of his hat, but he didn't say anything, and when he turned and began threading his way through the groups of people Cathryn followed him without saying anything either. Sometimes she thought that communication between her and Rule was impossible, but at other times it seemed that no words were necessary. She didn't understand him, but she knew him, knew his pride, his toughness, his damned black temper that was no less frightening for being controlled. She had grown up knowing that Rule Jackson was a dangerous man; her formative years had been dominated by him.

He led her out of the air terminal and across the pavement to the area where private aircraft were kept, his long legs eating up the distance without effort; but Cathryn wasn't used to keeping up with his strides and she refused to trot after him like a dog on a leash. She maintained her own pace, keeping him in sight, and at last he stopped beside a blue-and-white twin-engined Cessna, opening the cargo door and storing her bags inside, then looking around impatiently for her. "Hurry it up," he called, seeing that she was still some distance away.

Cathryn ignored him. He put his hands on his hips and waited for her, his booted feet braced in an arrogant stance that came naturally to him. When she reached him he didn't say a word; he merely pulled the door open and turned back to her, catching her around the waist and lifting her easily into the plane. She moved to the copilot's seat and Rule swung himself into the pilot's seat, then closed the door and tossed his hat onto the seat behind him, raking his lean fingers through his hair before reaching for the headset. Cathryn watched him, her expression revealing nothing, but she couldn't help remembering the vitality of that thick dark hair, the way it had curled around her fingers....

He glanced at her and caught her watching him. She didn't look guiltily away but held her gaze, knowing that the still blankness of her face gave away nothing.

"Do you like what you see?" he taunted softly, letting the headset dangle from his fingers.

"Why did Monica send you?" she asked flatly, ignoring his question and attacking with one of her own.

"Monica didn't send me. You've forgotten; *I* run the ranch, not Monica." His dark eyes rested on her, waiting for her to flare up at him and shout that she owned the ranch, not he, but Cathryn had learned well how to hide her thoughts. She kept her face blank, her gaze unwavering.

"Exactly. I'd have thought you were too busy to waste time fetching me."

"I wanted to talk to you before you got to the ranch; this seemed like a perfect opportunity."

"So talk."

"Let's get airborne first."

Flying in a small plane was no novelty to her. From her birth she had been accustomed to flying, since a plane was considered essential to a rancher. She sat back in the seat and stretched her cramped muscles, sore from the long flight from Chicago. Big jets screamed as they came in for landings or lifted off, but Rule was unruffled as he talked to the tower and taxied to a clear strip. In only minutes they were up and skimming westward, Houston shimmering in the spring heat to the south of them. The earth beneath had the rich green hue of new grass, and Cathryn drank in the sight of it. Whenever she came for a visit she had to force herself to leave, and it always left an ache for months, as if something vital had been torn from her. She loved this land, loved the ranch, but she had survived these years only by keeping to her self-imposed exile.

"Talk," she said shortly, trying to stem the memories.

"I want you to stay this time," he said, and Cathryn felt as if he had punched her in the stomach.

Stay? Didn't he, of all people, know how impossible that was for her? She slid a quick sideways glance at him and found him frowning intently at the horizon. For a moment her eyes lingered on the strong profile before she jerked her head forward again.

"No comment?" he asked.

"It's impossible."

"Is that it? You're not even going to ask why?"

"Will I like the answer?"

"No." He shrugged. "But it's not something you can avoid."

"Then tell me."

"Ricky's back again; she's drinking a lot, running out of control. She's been doing some wild things, and people are talking."

"She's a grown woman. I can't control her," said Cathryn coldly, though it made her furious to think of Ricky dragging the Donahue name in the dirt.

"I think you can. Monica can't, but we both know that Monica doesn't have much mothering instinct. On the other hand, since your last birthday you control the ranch, which makes Ricky dependent on you." He turned his head to pin her to the seat with his dark hawk's eyes. "I know you don't like her, but she's your stepsister and she's using the Donahue name again."

"Again?" Cathryn sniped. "After two divorces, why bother to change names?" Rule was right: she didn't like Ricky, never had. Her stepsister, two years her senior, had the temperament of a Tasmanian devil. Then she slanted a mocking look at him. "You told me that *you* run the ranch."

"I do," he replied so softly that the hair on the back of her neck rose. "But I don't own it. The ranch is your home, Cat. It's time you settled down to that fact."

"Don't lecture me, Rule Jackson. My home is in Chicago now—"

"Your husband's dead," he interrupted brutally. "There's nothing there for you and you know it. What do you have? An empty apartment and a boring job?"

"I like my job; besides, I don't have to work."

"Yes, you do, because you'd go crazy sitting in that empty apartment with nothing to do. So your husband left you a little money. It'll be gone in five years, and I won't let you drain the ranch dry to finance that place."

"It's my ranch!" she pointed out shortly.

"It was also your father's, and he loved it. Because of him, I won't let you throw it away."

Cathryn lifted her chin, struggling to keep her composure. That was a low blow and he knew it. He glanced at her again and continued. "The situation with Ricky is getting worse. I can't handle it and do my job too. I need help, Cat, and you're the logical person."

"I can't stay," she said, but for once her uncertainty was evident in her voice. She disliked Ricky, but, on the other hand, she didn't hate her. Ricky was a pain and a problem, yet there had been times when they were younger when they had giggled together like ordinary teenagers. And as Rule had pointed out, Ricky was using the Donahue name, having taken it as her own when Cathryn's father had married Monica, though it had never been made legal.

"I'll try to arrange a leave of absence." Cathryn heard herself giving in, and in belated self-protection tacked on, "But it won't be permanent. I'm used to living in a big city now, and I enjoy things that can't be found on a ranch." That much was true; she did enjoy the activities that went on nonstop in a large city, but she would give them up without a qualm if she felt that she could have a peaceful life on the ranch.

"You used to love the ranch," he said.

"That was used to."

He said nothing else, and after a moment Cathryn leaned her head back and closed her eyes. She recognized her complete trust in Rule's capabilities as a pilot, and the knowledge was bitter but inescapable. She would trust him with her life, but nothing else.

Even with her eyes closed she was so aware of his presence beside her that she felt as if she were being burned by the heat of his body. She could smell the heady male scent of him, hear his steady breathing. Whenever he moved the nerves in her body tingled. God, she thought in despair. Would she never forget that day? Did he have to shadow her entire life, ruling her with his mere presence? He had even haunted her marriage, forcing her to lie to her own husband.

She drifted into a light doze, a drifting state halfway between awareness and sleep, and she found that she could recall with perfect clarity all that she knew about Rule Jackson. She had known of him her entire life. His father had been a neighbor, a fellow rancher with a small but prospering spread, and Rule had worked the ranch with his father from the time he was old enough to sit a horse; but he was eleven years older and had seemed a grown man to her instead of the boy he had been.

Even as a child Cathryn had known that there was scandal attached to the name of Rule Jackson. He was known as "that wild Jackson boy," and older girls giggled when discussing him. But he was only a boy, a neighbor, and Cathryn liked him. He never paid much attention to her whenever she saw him, but when he did talk to her, he was kind and able to coax her out of her shyness; Rule was good with young animals, even human ones. Some said that he was better suited for the company of animals, but, for whatever reason, he had a rare touch with horses and dogs.

When Cathryn was eight her world changed. It had also been a time of change for Rule. The same year that her mother died, leaving Cathryn stunned and withdrawn, solemn beyond her years, Rule was drafted. He was nineteen when he got off the plane in Saigon. By the time he returned three years later, nothing was the same.

Ward Donahue had remarried to a darkly beautiful woman from New Orleans. From the first Cathryn didn't quite like Monica. For her father's sake she hid her feelings and did her best to get along with Monica, establishing an uneasy truce. Each of them walked softly around the other. It wasn't that Monica was the stereotypical wicked stepmother; she simply wasn't a motherly woman, not even to her own daughter, Ricky. Monica liked bright lights and dancing, and from the first she didn't fit in with the hardworking ranch life. She tried, for Ward's sake. That was the one thing Cathryn never doubted, that Monica loved her father. For that reason she and Monica existed in mutual if unenthusiastic peace.

The upheaval in Rule's life had been even greater. He had survived Vietnam, but sometimes it seemed as if only his body had returned. His dark, laughing eyes no longer laughed; they watched and brooded. His body was scarred with wounds that had healed, but the mental wounds he had suffered had changed him forever. He never talked about it. He seldom talked at all. He kept to himself and watched people with those hard, expressionless eyes, and soon he became an outcast.

He drank a lot, sitting alone and steadily downing the alcohol, his face closed and stony. Naturally he became even more attractive to women than he had been before. Some women couldn't resist the aura of danger that clung to him like an invisible cloak. They dreamed of being the magic one who could comfort him, heal him and take him away from the nightmare he still lived.

He was involved in one scandal after another. His father threw him out of the house and no one else would hire him, the ranchers and merchants banding together to rid the neighborhood of him. Somehow he still found money for whiskey, and he sometimes disappeared for days, leading people to speculate that he had crawled off somewhere and died. But he always turned up like a bad penny, a bit thinner, more haggard, but always there.

It was inevitable that the hostility against him would escalate into violence; he had been involved with too many women, snarled at too many men. Ward Donahue found him one day lying sprawled in a ditch on the outskirts of town. Rule was battered from the punishment a group of men had decided was his due, and so thin that his bones shone white through his skin. Still silent and intent, his dark eyes glittered up at his rescuer with grim defiance even though he was unable to stand. Without a word Ward lifted the younger man in his arms as if he were a child and placed him in the pickup, taking him to the ranch to be cared for. A week later Rule crawled painfully onto a horse and rode with Ward about the ranch, performing the hard but necessary chore of riding fence, repairing broken fencing and rounding up strays. He was in such pain for the first few days that sweat poured from his body whenever he moved, yet he continued with grim determination.

He stopped drinking and began eating normal meals again. He grew stronger and gained weight, both from the food and from the hard physical work he was doing. He never talked about what had happened. The other ranch hands left him strictly alone except for what contact was necessary during work, but Rule was uncommunicative at the best of times. He worked and he ate and he slept, and whatever Ward Donahue asked of him he would have accomplished or died in the effort.

The affection and trust between the two men was evident; no one was surprised when Rule was made foreman after the previous foreman left for another job in Oklahoma. As Ward said to anyone who would listen, Rule had an instinct for horses and cattle, and Ward trusted him. By that time the ranch hands had become used to working with him and the transition was a peaceful one.

Shortly afterward Ward died of a massive stroke. Cathryn and Ricky were at school at the time, and Cathryn could still remember her surprise when Rule came to take her out of class. He led her outside and there told her of her father's death, and he held her in his arms while she cried the violent tears of fresh grief, his lean callused hand smoothing back her heavy mahogany red hair. She had been slightly afraid of him, but now she clung to him, instinctively comforted by his steely strength. Her father had trusted him, so how could she do less?

Because of that tentative trust, Cathryn felt doubly betrayed when Rule began to act as if he owned the ranch. No one could take her father's place. How dare he even try? But more and more Rule took his meals at the ranch house. He finally moved in completely, settling himself in the corner guestroom that overlooked the stables and bunkhouse. It was particularly galling that Monica made no effort to assert herself; she let Rule have his way in anything concerning the ranch. She was a woman who automatically leaned on whatever man was handy, and certainly she was no match for Rule. Looking back, Cathryn realized now that Monica had been utterly lost when it came to ranch matters, yet she had no other home for herself and Ricky, so she had been locked into a life that was alien to her, totally unable to handle a man like Rule, who was both determined and dangerous.

Cathryn was bitterly resentful of Rule's takeover. Ward had literally picked him up out of the gutter and stood him on his feet, held him up until he could stand on his own, and this was how he was repaid, by Rule moving in and taking over.

The ranch was Cathryn's, with Monica appointed as her legal guardian, but Cathryn had no voice in the running of it. Without exception the men went to Rule for their orders, despite everything Cathryn could do. She tried to do plenty. Losing her father had shocked her out of her shyness, and she fought for her ranch with the ferocity of the uninformed young, disobeying Rule at every turn. At that stage of her life Ricky had been a willing accomplice. Ricky was always willing to break rules, any rules. But no matter what she did, Cathryn always felt that she was no more irritating to Rule than a mosquito he could casually brush aside.

When he decided to branch out into horse breeding, Monica provided the capital over Cathryn's vociferous opposition, dipping without argument into the funds set aside for the girls' college educations. Whatever Rule wanted, he got. He had the Bar D under his thumb...for the time being. Cathryn lay awake at night and thought ahead with relish to the day when she would be of age, savoring in her mind the words she would say when she fired Rule Jackson.

Rule even extended his domination to her personal life. When she was fifteen she accepted a date with an eighteen-year-old boy to attend a dance. Rule found out about it and called the boy, quietly informing him that Cathryn wasn't old enough yet to date. When Cathryn discovered what he had done she lost her temper, goaded into action and recklessness. Without thinking, she hit him, her palm slamming across his face with a force that numbed her arm.

He didn't speak. His dark eyes narrowed; then, with the swiftness of a snake lashing out, he grabbed her arm and hauled her upstairs. Cathryn kicked and scratched and yelled every inch of the way, but it was a useless effort. He handled her with ease, his strength so much greater than hers that she was as helpless as an infant. Once they reached her room, he jerked her jeans down and sat on the bed, pulled her across his lap and gave her the spanking of her life. At fifteen Cathryn had just begun shaping from adolescence into the rounder form of womanhood, and the embarrassment she suffered had in some ways been worse than the pain inflicted by his callused palm. When he let her go she scrambled to her feet and repaired her clothing, her face twisted with fury.

"You're asking me to treat you like a woman," he said, his voice low and even. "But you're just a kid and I treated you like a kid. Don't push me until you're old enough to handle it."

Cathryn whirled and went flying down the stairs in search of Monica, her cheeks still wet with tears as she screamed that he should be fired, *now*.

Monica laughed in her face. "Don't be silly, Cathryn," she said sharply. "We need Rule...*I* need Rule."

Behind her Cathryn heard Rule quietly laughing and felt his hand stroke her tumbled mahogany red hair. "Just settle down, wildcat; you can't get rid of me that easily."

Cathryn had jerked her head away from his touch, but he had been right. She hadn't been able to get rid of him. Ten years later he was still running the ranch and it was she who had left, fleeing from her own home in panic that he would reduce her to the position of mindless supplicant, with no more will of her own than the horses he so easily mastered.

"Are you asleep?" he asked now, drawing her back to the present, and Cathryn opened her eyes.

"No."

"Then talk to me," he demanded. Though she wasn't looking, she could visualize his sensually formed mouth moving as he said the words. She had never forgotten anything about him, from the slow way he talked to the dark, slightly hoarse tone of his voice, as if his vocal cords were rusty from lack of use. He gave her a swift glance. "Tell me about your husband."

Cathryn was startled, her dark eyes widening. "You met him several times. What would you want to know about David?"

"A lot of things," he murmured easily. "Such as if he asked you why you weren't a virgin when he married you."

Bitter, furious, Cathryn choked back the words that tumbled to her lips. What could she say that he wouldn't use against her? It's none of your business? He would only reply that it was more his business than it was any other man's, considering that he had been the one responsible for the loss of her virginity.

She tried not to look at him, but against her will she turned to him, her eyes wide and vulnerable. "He never asked," she finally said in a quiet voice. Rule's profile was etched starkly against the blueness of the sky, and her heart lurched; it brought painfully, vividly to mind that summer day when he had bent over her with the hot molten sun and brazen sky behind him, outlining him like a graven image. Her body tightened automatically in remembered response and she tore her gaze away from him before he turned and saw the rawness of her pain mirrored in her eyes.

"I would have asked," he rasped.

"David was a gentleman," she said pointedly.

"Meaning I'm not?"

"You know the answer to that as well as I do. No, you're not a gentleman. You're not gentle in any way."

"I was gentle with you once," he replied, his dark eyes moving over her with slow relish, tracing the curves of her breasts and hips and thighs. Again the hot tightening of her body warned her that she wasn't indifferent to this man, had never been, and pain bloomed in her.

"I don't want to talk about it!" As soon as the words left her mouth she wished they could be unsaid. The ragged panic in her tone made it evident to anyone with normal intelligence that she couldn't treat that long-ago incident with the indifference that the years should have brought, and Rule was more intelligent and intuitive than most. His next words proved it.

"You can't run forever. You're not a kid now, Cat; you're a woman."

Oh, she knew that! He had made her a woman when she was seventeen, and the image of him had tormented her since, even intruded between her and her husband and cheated David out of the devotion that had been his due, though she would have died rather than let him guess that her response to him hadn't been all it should have been. Nor could she tell Rule how deeply he had affected her life with what to him could have been only a casual coupling.

"I didn't run away," she denied. "I went to college, which is entirely different."

"And came home on visits as seldom as you could," he said with harsh sarcasm. "Did you think I'd attack you every time I saw you? I knew you were too young. Hell, I didn't mean for it to happen anyway, and I was going to make damned sure the opportunity never came up again, at least until you were older and had a better idea of what it was about.''

''I knew what sex was!'' she defied, not wanting him to guess how totally unprepared she had been for the reality of it, but her effort was useless.

''You knew what it was, but not what it was like.'' The hard, stark truth of his words silenced her, and after a minute he said grimly, ''You weren't ready for that, were you?''

She drew a shuddering breath, wishing she had pretended to be asleep. Rule was like a blooded stallion: when he got the bit between his teeth there was no stopping him. ''No,'' she admitted raggedly. ''Especially not with you.''

A hard smile curved his grim mouth. ''And I took it easy on you. You really would have been scared out of your dainty little pants if I'd let myself go the way I wanted to.''

Twisting agony in her midsection made her lash out at him, hoping futilely that she could hurt him as he had hurt her. ''I didn't want you! I didn't—''

''You wanted it,'' he interrupted harshly. ''You were in a redheaded temper and fighting me just for the sake of fighting, but you wanted it. You didn't try to get away from me. You lit into me and tried to hurt me in any way you could, and somewhere along the line all that temper turned into wanting and you were wrapped around me like a vine.''

Cathryn winced away from the memory. ''I don't want to talk about it!''

Without warning he erupted into fury, into that deadly temper that smart people learned how to avoid. ''Well, that's just too damned bad,'' he snarled thickly, switching the controls to automatic pilot and reaching for her.

She made an instinctive, useless effort to ward off his hands, and he brushed her fingers away with laughable ease. His fingers bit into her upper arms as he hauled her out of her seat until she was lying sprawled against him. His mouth was hard, hot, well remembered, the taste of him as familiar as if she'd never gone away. Her slim hands curled into fists and beat ineffectively at his shoulders, but despite her efforts at resistance she found that nothing had changed, nothing at all. A hot swell of sensual excitement made her heart beat faster, made her breath come in panting gasps, her entire body quiver. She wanted him. Oh, damn him, how she wanted him! Some curious chemistry in her makeup made her respond to him like a flower to sunlight, twisting, seeking, even though she knew he was no good for her.

His tongue probed slowly into her mouth and her hands ceased their beating to suddenly clasp his shoulders, feeling the hard muscles under her palms with instant delight. Pleasure was filling her, pleasure comprised of the taste and feel and smell of him, the slightly rough slide of his cheek against hers, the intimacy of his tongue on hers that vividly recalled a hot summer day when no clothing had been between them.

His anger was gone, turned into desire that glittered plainly in his dark eyes when he lifted his mouth just the fraction of an inch necessary to demand, "Did you ever forget what it was like?"

Her hands slipped up to his head, trying to pull him across that delicious, intolerable tiny space to her own mouth, but he resisted and her fingers wrapped in his silky, vibrant dark hair. "Rule," she muttered huskily.

"Did you?" he insisted, and drew his head back when she tried to raise her own to allow her mouth to cling to his.

It didn't matter; he knew anyway. How could he not know? One touch and she melted against him. "No, I never forgot," she admitted in a whisper of sound that slid away into nothing as at last his mouth came down and crushed hers and she drank again of the sweet-tart freshness of him.

It was no surprise when she felt his long fingers close over her breast, then slide restlessly down her ribs. The thin silk of her sleeveless summer dress was no barrier to the heat of his hand, and she felt burned as his touch sleeked down her body to stop at her knee, then began a slow, stroking journey up her thigh, lifting her skirt, exposing her long legs. Then abruptly he halted, shuddering with the effort it cost him, and he removed his hand from her leg. "This is no place for making love," he whispered hoarsely, lifting his mouth from hers and sliding his kisses to her ear. "It's a miracle we haven't already crashed. But I can wait until we're home."

Her lashes lifted to reveal dazed, slumberous dark eyes, and he gave her another hard kiss, then shifted her back into her own seat. Still breathing hard, he checked their position, then wiped the sweat from his forehead and turned back to her. "Now we know where we stand," he said with grim satisfaction.

Cathryn jerked herself erect and turned her head to stare out at the sweeping ranchland below. Fool! she berated herself. Stupid fool! Now he knew just how powerful the weapon he had against her was, and she had no illusion that he would hesitate to use it. It wasn't fair that his desire for her didn't leave him as vulnerable as she was, but the basic fact was that his desire was simply that, desire, without any of the accompanying emotions or needs that she felt, while the mere sound of his voice submerged her into so many boiling needs and feelings that she had no hope of sorting them out and understanding them. He was so deeply associated with all the crises and milestones of her life that even while she hated and feared him, he was so much a part of her that she couldn't fire him, couldn't kick him out of her life. He was as addictive as a drug, using his lean, hard-muscled body and educated hands to keep his women under control.

I won't be one of his women! Cathryn vowed fiercely, clenching her fists. He had no morals, no sense of shame. After all her father had done for him, as soon as Ward was in the grave, Rule had taken over. Nor was that enough. He had to have the ranch and Ward's daughter too. In that moment Cathryn decided not to stay, to return to Chicago as soon as the holiday was over. Ricky's problems were not hers. If Rule didn't like the way things were, he was free to seek employment elsewhere.

Then they were circling over the sprawling, two-story frame house to signal their arrival to the ranch, and Rule banked the plane sharply to the left to line up with the small runway. She felt stunned at how little time it had taken to reach the ranch, but a glance at her watch told her that more time had elapsed than she'd thought. How long had she been wrapped in Rule's arms? And how long had she been lost in her thoughts? When she was with him everything else seemed to fade out of her awareness.

A dusty red pickup came bouncing across the field to meet them as Rule took the plane in for a smooth, shallow landing; they touched down so lightly that there was scarcely a bump. Cathryn found herself looking at his hands, strong and brown and competent whether they were flying a plane, mastering a fractious horse or soothing a flighty woman. She remembered those hands on her body, and tried not to.

_____ *Chapter Two*

As Cathryn went up the three steps to the porch that ran the width of the house she was surprised that Monica didn't come out to greet her. Ricky didn't come out, either, but she hadn't really expected Ricky. Monica, on the other hand, had always at least kept up appearances and made a big show of affection when David was alive and visited with her. She opened the screen door and went into the cool dimness; Rule was right behind her with her luggage. "Where's Monica?" she asked.

He started up the stairs. "God only knows," he grunted, and Cathryn followed him with rising irritation. She caught him as he opened the door of the bedroom that had always been hers and went inside to drop the bags by the bed.

"What do you mean by that?" she demanded.

He shrugged. "Monica ranges far and wide these days. She's never been too keen on the ranch anyway. You can't blame her for hunting her own amusements." He turned to leave and Cathryn followed him again.

"Where are you going?" she asked sharply.

He turned back to her with exaggerated patience. "I've got work to do. Did you have anything else in mind?" His eyes strayed to the bedroom door, then back to her, and Cathryn set her jaw.

"I had finding Monica in mind."

"She'll show up before dark. I noticed that the station wagon is gone, and she hates driving after dark, so she'll be here by then unless she has an accident."

"You're so concerned!" Cathryn lashed out.

"Should I be? I'm a rancher, not a chaperon."

"Correction: you're a ranch *foreman.*"

For a moment his eyes flared with temper; then he damped it down. "You're right, and as the foreman I have work to do. Are you going to stay here and sulk, or are you going to change clothes and come with me? There've been a lot of changes since the last time you were here. I thought you might be interested, *boss.*" He stressed the last word slightly, his eyes mocking her. He was the boss, and he knew it; he had been for so many years that many of the ranch hands had been hired since Ward's death and had no loyalty to a Donahue, only to Rule Jackson.

She wavered for a moment, torn between her reluctance to spend any time in his company and her interest in the ranch. The years she had spent away had been an exile and she had suffered every day, longing for the vast spaces and the clean smell of the earth. She wanted to see the land, reacquaint herself with the things that had marked her earliest days. "I'll go change," she said quietly.

"I'll wait for you at the stables," he said, then let his eyes drift down the length of her. "Unless you'd like some company while you change?"

Her fierce "No!" was automatic, and he didn't act as if he had expected any other answer. He shrugged and went down the stairs. Cathryn returned to her room and closed the door, then twisted her arms up behind herself to unzip the dress and take it off. For a moment she

thought of Rule helping her with the zipper; then she
shivered and wrenched her mind away from the treach-
erous idea. She had to hurry. Rule's patience had a time
limit.

She didn't bother to unpack. She had always left most
of her jeans and shirts there at the ranch. In Chicago she
wore chic designer jeans; on the ranch she wore faded,
worn jeans that were limp from use. She sometimes felt
that when she changed clothes, she changed personali-
ties. The chic, polished wife of David Ashe again became Cathryn Donahue, raised with the wind in her
hair. As she stamped her feet into her boots and reached
for the tan hat that she had worn for years, she became
aware of a sense of belonging. She pushed the thought
away, but pleasurable anticipation remained with her as
she ran down the stairs and made her way out to the
stables, pausing in the kitchen to greet the cook, Lorna
Ingram. She was friendly enough with Lorna, but was
aware that the woman looked on Rule as her employer
and that that precluded any closeness between them.

Rule was waiting for her with outward patience,
though his big-boned chestnut nudged him in the back
and shifted nervously behind him. He also held the reins
to a long-legged gray gelding, a horse Cathryn didn't
remember having seen before. Having been around
horses all of her life she had no fear of them and rubbed
the animal's nose naturally, letting him learn the smell
of her while she talked to him. "Hi, fella, you're a
stranger to me. How long have you been here?"

"A couple of years," answered Rule, tossing the reins
to her. "He's a good horse, no bad habits, even-
tempered. Not like Redman here," he added ruefully as
the chestnut nudged him again, this time with enough
force to shove him forward several steps. He swung up

into the saddle without offering to help Cathryn, a gesture she would have refused anyway. She was far from helpless on a horse. She mounted and urged the gray into a trot to catch up with Rule, who hadn't waited.

They rode past the stables, and Cathryn admired the neat paddocks and barns, several of which hadn't been there during her last visit. Money on the hoof either grazed without paying attention to them or sent soft, curious nickers their way. Playful, long-legged foals romped over the sweet spring grass. Rule lifted his gloved hand to point out a structure. "That's the new foaling barn. Want to take a look at it?"

She nodded and they swung the horses' heads in that direction. "There's only one mare due right now," he said. "We're just waiting on her. The last few weeks have been busy, but we have a break now."

The stalls in the foaling barn were airy and spacious and scrupulously clean; as Rule had said, there was only one occupant now. There in the middle of a large box stall stood a mare in a posture of such utter weariness that Cathryn smiled in sympathy. When Rule held out his hand and clicked his tongue, the mare walked to him with a heavy tread and pushed her head over the stall to be petted. He obliged her, talking to her with that special crooning note in his voice that soothed even the most nervous of animals. When she had been younger Cathryn had tried to duplicate the tone and its effect, but without result.

"We're one of the best horse-breeding farms in the state now," Rule said without any evidence of pride, simply stating fact. "Buyers are coming from every state, even Hawaii."

When they resumed their ride Rule didn't say much, letting Cathryn see for herself the changes that had been made. She was also silent, but she knew that the operation she saw was well run. The fences and paddocks were in excellent shape; the animals were healthy and spirited with no signs of ill-use; the buildings were strong and clean and wore fresh coats of paint. The bunkhouse had been added to and modernized. To her surprise, she also noticed several small cottages to the rear of the ranch house, some distance away but within a comfortable range. She pointed to them. "Are those houses?"

He grunted an affirmative answer. "Several of the hands are married. I had to do something or have some good men a long way off if I needed them during the night." He slanted a dark glance at her, but Cathryn had no objection to the houses; it seemed a logical move to her. Even if she had an objection she wouldn't have voiced it, not wanting to start an argument with him. Not that Rule argued. He simply stated his position and backed it up. Without looking at him she was aware of the power of his body, his long, steely-muscled legs that controlled half-ton horses with ease, the dark-fire gaze that made people back away.

"Want to ride out and see the cattle?" he asked, and without waiting for her answer headed out, leaving Cathryn to follow or not. She followed, keeping the gray's head just even with the chestnut's shoulder. It was a brisk ride to the west pasture where the white-faced Herefords were grazing, and it made her predict ruefully that she would regret all of this in the morning. Her muscles weren't used to so much activity.

The herd was small—astonishingly so. She said as much to Rule, and he drawled, "We're not in the cattle business anymore. What we raise is for our own use mostly. We're horse breeders now."

Stunned, Cathryn stared at him for a moment, then shouted, "What do you mean? This is a cattle ranch! Who gave you the authority to get rid of the cattle?"

"I don't need anyone to 'give' me any authority," he replied sharply. "We were losing money on the cattle, so I changed operations. If you had been here, I'd have talked it over with you, but you didn't care enough to visit."

"That's not true!" she yelled. "You know why I didn't visit more often! You know it's because of—" She cut herself off abruptly, sick with emotion but still stopping short of admitting her weakness to him.

He waited, but she said nothing else and he turned Redman's head back to the east. The sun was dipping low, but they kept to a leisurely pace, not talking. What was there to say? Cathryn paid no attention to their exact location until Rule reined in his horse at the top of a gentle rise and she looked down to see the river and a clump of trees, the wide sheltered area where she had swum naked that hot July day, and the grassy bank where Rule had made love to her. Though aware that he was watching her with sharp intensity, she couldn't prevent the healthy color from leaving her cheeks. "Damn you," she said in a shaky voice, leaving it at that, but she knew that he would catch her meaning.

He removed his hat and raked his fingers through his hair. "What are you so upset about? I'm not going to attack you, for heaven's sake. We're going to walk the horses down there and let them have some water, that's all. Come on."

Now the color flamed into her cheeks and she seethed at how easily he had made her make a fool of herself. She took a tight hold on her self-control and followed him down the slope to the river with no hint of her agitation showing on her face, but every inch of her body remembered.

It was here that he had found her skinny-dipping and harshly ordered her out of the water, threatening to haul her out if she didn't leave it willingly. She had stomped out of the river, outraged at his high-handed attitude, and waded right into battle without once considering the possible consequences of attacking a man while she was totally nude. What had happened had been more her fault than Rule's, she admitted now with more maturity than she had been capable of eight years earlier. He had tried to hold her off and soothe her out of her temper, but his hands had slipped over her bare wet flesh, and he was all man, so blatantly virile that his masculinity was like a flashing neon sign to every woman who saw him. When he ground his mouth harshly against hers, stopping her screams of fury, she had changed in one heart-stopping instant from white hot fury to the dark blaze of desire. She had no idea how to control her own responses or exactly what responses she was arousing in him, but he had demonstrated the last point in the most explicit way possible.

When he dismounted to let his horse drink, Cathryn followed suit. He noticed the slight stiffness of her movements and said, "You're going to be sore if you don't get a rubdown. I'll take care of you when we get back."

She stiffened at the thought of him massaging her legs and refused the offer more abruptly than she'd meant to. "Thanks, but I can manage it myself."

He shrugged. "It's your pain."

Somehow his easy acceptance of her refusal irritated her even further, and she glared at him as they remounted and began the ride back to the house. Now that he had mentioned it, she was aware of her steadily increasing soreness with every yard they covered. Only pride kept her from requesting that they slow the pace, and her jaw was rigidly set when they finally reached the stables.

He swung out of the saddle and was beside her before she could kick her feet out of the stirrups. Without a word he reached up and clasped her waist, carefully lifting her down, and she knew that he realized just exactly how uncomfortable she was. She muttered her thanks and moved away from him.

"Go on up to the house and tell Lorna I'll be ready to eat in about half an hour," he ordered. "Hurry, or you won't have time to get the horse smell off beforehand."

That thought loosened her stiff muscles, and it wasn't until she was going into the house that she thought to be irritated at the fact that mealtimes had to conform to his schedule. She hesitated, then remembered that, after all, he did the work around there, so it was only fair that he have hot meals. On the heels of that thought came the idea that he could always eat with the other hands; no one had invited him into the main house. He hadn't waited for an invitation, she thought, then sighed, and dutifully passed along his message to Lorna, who smiled and nodded.

Neither Monica nor Ricky presented themselves, so she dashed up the stairs and took a fast shower. Meals on the ranch weren't formal, but she changed into a sleeveless cotton dress rather than jeans, and carefully applied her makeup, driven by some deeply buried feminine instinct that she was hesitant to examine too closely. As she was brushing her dark mahogany red hair into a smooth bell that curved against her shoulders, a brief knock sounded on the door, which promptly opened to admit her stepsister.

Her first thought was that Ricky's last marriage must have been a rough one. The dark hair was lustrous, the dainty body slim and firm, but there was a febrile tenseness about her, and lines of discontent were fanning out from the corners of her eyes and lips. Ricky was a lovely, exotic woman, a younger version of Monica, with her ripe mouth and slanted hazel eyes, her golden hued skin. The effect of that beauty, however, was ruined by the petulance of her expression.

"Welcome home," she purred, lifting a graceful hand, which held a glass with two inches of amber liquid in the bottom. "Sorry I wasn't here to greet you, but I forgot that today was the big day. I'm sure Rule took good care of you." She took a healthy swallow of her drink and gave Cathryn a twisted, malicious grin. "But then, Rule always takes good care of his women, doesn't he? All of them."

Suddenly, uneasily, Cathryn wondered if Ricky somehow knew about that day by the river. It was difficult to tell; Ricky's normal style of conversation tended to be vicious, springing from her own discontent and internal fears. For the time being Cathryn decided to ignore the insinuations in Ricky's tone and words, and greeted her normally

"It's nice to be home again after so long. Things have changed, haven't they? I almost wouldn't have recognized the place."

"Oh, yesss," Ricky drawled, letting the "yes" linger on a sibilant whisper. "Rule's the boss, didn't you know? He has everything going his way; everybody jumps when he says jump. He's not the outcast anymore, sister dear. He's an upstanding—and outstanding—member of our little community, and he runs this place with an iron fist. Or he *almost* does." She winked at Cathryn. "He doesn't have me under his thumb yet. I know what he's up to."

Determined not to react or ask Ricky what she meant, knowing that in her half-drunken state any sensible conversation was impossible, Cathryn took Ricky's arm and gently but firmly steered her to the stairs. "Lorna should have dinner on the table by now. I'm starving!"

As they left the room, Rule approached them and his hard mouth tightened when he saw the glass in Ricky's hand. Without a word he reached out and relieved her of it. For a moment Ricky looked up at him with a kind of tense, pleading fear; then she visibly mastered herself and trailed a fingertip down his shirtfront, tracing a path from button to button. "You're so masterful," she purred. "No wonder you can have your pick of women. I was just telling Cathryn about them . . . your women, I mean." She gave him a sweetly poisonous smile and continued down the stairs, satisfaction evident in the sway of her slim, graceful body.

Rule swore softly under his breath while Cathryn stood there trying to understand what Ricky was getting at and why it was making Rule angry. There was the possibility that Ricky was getting at nothing. She loved to say upsetting things just for the joy of watching the stir. But just worrying about it wouldn't give her any answers. She turned to Rule and asked him directly, "What's she getting at?"

He didn't answer for a moment. Instead he sniffed suspiciously at the contents of the glass he held, then tossed the remainder of the drink back in one swallow. A terrible grimace twisted his features. "God," he choked, his voice strained. "How did I ever drink this stuff?"

Cathryn almost laughed aloud. From the day her father had carried him home, Rule had refused to drink liquor, even beer. His surprised reaction now was somehow endearing, as if he had revealed a hidden part of himself to her. He looked up and caught her grin, and she was startled when his hard fingers slid under her hair and clasped the back of her neck. "Are you laughing at me?" he demanded, his voice soft, "Don't you know that can be dangerous?"

She knew better than most just how dangerous Rule could be, but she wasn't frightened now. An odd exhilaration made her blood tumble through her veins and she tilted her head back to look at him. "I'm not afraid of you, big man," she said in both taunt and invitation—an invitation she hadn't meant to issue, but one that came so naturally that she had voiced it almost before the thought was completed. A second too late, she tried to cover her mistake by throwing in hastily, "Tell me what Ricky meant—"

"Damn Ricky," he growled as his fingers tightened on her neck a split second before his mouth closed on hers. Cathryn was surprised by the gentle quality of the kiss. Her lips softened and parted easily under the persuasive pressure and movements of his. He made a rough sound in his throat and turned her more fully into his arms, pressing her to him, his hand sliding down her back to her hips and arching her into the power of his loins and thighs. Her fingers clenched on his shirt sleeves in response to the heated pleasure that flared deeply within her. She was vividly aware of his male attraction, and everything that was female within her strained to answer the primitive call of his nature. It had never been like this with any other man; she had begun to realize that it never would be, that this was something unique for her. David hadn't stood a chance against the dark magic that Rule practiced so effortlessly.

The thought of David was a lifeline to grasp, something to pull her mind away from the sensual whirlpool he was drawing her into. She tore her lips away from his with a gasp but was unable to move from his arms. It wasn't that he held her captive, but that she lacked the strength to push him away. Instead she let her body lie against him while she rested her head on his shoulder, inhaling the aphrodisiac of his warm male scent.

"It's good," he muttered huskily, bending his head to bite at the delicate earlobe bared by the tilt of her head. "You're not a kid now, Cat."

What did that mean? she wondered with a flash of panic. That he no longer saw any need to keep away from her? Was he warning her that he wouldn't try to keep their relationship platonic? And who was she trying to kid? Their relationship hadn't been platonic in years, even though they had never made love since that day by the river.

From somewhere she dredged up enough strength to pull away from him and lift her head proudly. "No, I'm not a kid. I've learned how to say no to unwanted advances."

"Then mine must be wanted, because you sure as hell didn't say no," he taunted softly, moving his body in such a way that she was eased to the head of the stairs. So that was how a cow felt when being gently but inexorably herded to wherever a cowboy wanted, she thought on a slightly hysterical note. She took a deep breath and briskly composed herself, which was just as well, because suddenly Monica appeared at the foot of the stairs.

"Cathryn, Rule, whatever is keeping you?"

That was Monica—not even a greeting, though it had been almost three years since she'd last seen her step-daughter. Cathryn didn't object to Monica's remote-ness. At least it was honest. She went down the stairs with Rule close behind her, his hand resting casually on the small of her back.

The table wasn't formal. After a long, hot day on the ranch a man wanted a meal, not a social occasion. Cathryn's decision to wear a dress had been an unusual one, but now she noticed that Ricky had also elected to leave off her jeans and instead wore a white gauze dress that wouldn't have been out of place at a party. She knew instinctively that Ricky didn't have a date that night, so she had to be dressing up for Rule's benefit.

Cathryn's eyes strayed to Rule as he sat in the chair where Ward Donahue had always sat. For the first time she noticed that he had changed into dark brown cords and a crisp white shirt, with the cuffs unbuttoned and rolled back to reveal brawny tanned forearms. Her breath caught as she watched him, examined the fea-tures that had so often occupied her dreams. His hair was thick and as silky as a child's, with only a hint of curl; both his hair and eyes were that precise, peculiar shade that was neither black nor brown, but a color that she could define only as dark. His forehead was broad, his brows straight and heavy over a thin, high-bridged nose that flared into spirited nostrils. His lips were chiseled, sensual, but capable of compressing into a grim line or twisting into an enraged snarl. His broad shoulders strained at the white cloth that covered them, while in the open neck of the shirt she could see the beginnings of the virile curls that decorated his chest and arrowed down his abdomen. She knew all of that about him, knew exactly the texture of that hair beneath her fingers. . . .

Slowly she became aware of the amusement in his eyes and she realized that she had been staring openly, practically eating him with her eyes. She flushed and fidgeted nervously with her fork, not daring to look at either Monica or Ricky for fear they had also noticed.

"How was the flight?" Monica asked trivially, but Cathryn was grateful to her and latched onto the gambit eagerly.

"Crowded, but on time, for once. I didn't ask if you had to wait," she said to Rule, deliberately making the effort to converse with him and demonstrate that she wasn't disturbed at having been caught staring at him.

He shrugged and started to say something, but Ricky broke in with a harsh, bitter laugh. "It didn't bother him any," she sniped. "He left yesterday afternoon and spent the night in Houston to make certain he didn't miss you. Nothing's too good for the little queen of the Bar D, is it, Rule?"

His dark face had that closed, stony look that Cathryn always associated with the painful days when he had first come to the ranch, and she had to clench her fists to quell the sudden, powerful urge to protect him. If any man was less in need of protection than Rule Jackson, he was one tough customer indeed. Rule proved that by giving Ricky a smile that was nothing more than a baring of his teeth as he agreed with seeming ease. "That's right. I'm here to give her whatever she wants, whenever she wants it."

Monica said coolly, "For God's sake, can't we have one meal without the two of you sniping at each other?

Ricky, try acting your age, which is twenty-seven, instead of seven."

In the small silence that followed, Monica continued with a statement that must have seemed completely innocent to her, but which hit Cathryn with all the power of a jackhammer. "Rule says that you've come home to stay, Cathryn."

Cathryn shot a furious look at Rule, which he met blandly, but the denial that was on her lips was never voiced as Ricky dropped her fork with a clatter. All heads turned to her; she was white, shaking. "You bastard," she said thinly, glaring at Rule with pure venom in her eyes. "All of these years, as long as Mother had control of the ranch, you've mooned around her and sweet-talked her into doing anything you wanted, but now that Cathryn's twenty-five and has taken over legal control, you drop Mother as if she's nothing more than yesterday's laundry! You used her! You didn't want her or me eith—"

Rule leaned back in his chair, his eyes flat and unreadable. He didn't say anything, just watched and waited, and Cathryn had a sudden impression of a cougar flattening out on a limb, waiting for an unsuspecting lamb to walk beneath it. Ricky must have sensed danger too, because her voice halted in midword.

Monica glared at her daughter and said icily, "You don't know what you're talking about! With your track record in romance, how can you have the gall to either criticize or advise anyone else?"

Ricky turned wildly to her mother. "How can you keep on defending him?" she cried. "Can't you see what he's doing? He should've married you years ago, but he put you off and waited until *she* came of age! He knew she would be taking over the ranch! Didn't you?'' she spat, whirling to face Rule.

Cathryn had had enough. Trembling with temper, she discarded her hold on good manners and slammed her silverware down on the table while she struggled to organize the red-hot words in her mind into coherent sentences.

Rule had no such difficulty. He shoved his plate back and got to his feet. Ice dripped from his tone as he said, "There's never been the slightest possibility that I'd marry Monica." He left on that brutal note, his booted feet taking long strides that carried him out of the room before anyone else could add to the fire.

Cathryn glanced at Monica. Her stepmother was white except for the round spots of artificial color that dotted her cheekbones. Monica snapped harshly, "Congratulations, Ricky! You've managed to ruin another meal."

Cathryn demanded in rising anger, "What was the meaning of that scene?"

Ricky propped her elbows gracefully on the table and folded her hands under her chin in an angelic posture, regaining her poise though, like Monica, she was pale. "Surely you're not as dense as that," she mocked. She looked definitely pleased with herself, her red lips curling up in a wicked little smile. "There's no use in pretending that you don't know how Rule has used Mother all these years. But lately... lately he's realized that you're of age, conveniently widowed, and can have full control over the ranch whenever you decide to take an interest. Mother's of no use to him now; she no longer holds the purse strings. It's a simple case of off with the old, on with the new."

Cathryn gave her a withering look. "You're twisted!"

"And you're a fool!"

"I'd certainly be one if I took anything you said at face value!" Cathryn shot back. "I don't know what you've got against Rule. Maybe you're just soured on men—"

"That's right!" Ricky shrilled. "Throw it up to me because I'm divorced!"

Cathryn wanted to pull her own hair in frustration. She knew Ricky well enough to recognize a play for sympathy, but she also knew that when the spirit moved her, Ricky didn't adhere too closely to the truth. For some reason Ricky was trying to make Rule appear in the worst light imaginable, and the thought irritated her. Rule had enough black marks against him without someone manufacturing false ones. The area had never forgotten how he had acted when he returned from Vietnam, and as far as she knew he had never been reconciled with his father. Mr. Jackson had died a few years ago, but Rule had never mentioned that fact in her hearing, so she supposed that the strain between him and his father had still existed at the time of Mr. Jackson's death.

Unwilling to examine her motives more closely, merely acknowledging the surface desire to set Ricky back on her heels, Cathryn said, "Rule did ask me to stay, but, after all, this is my home, isn't it? There's nothing to keep me in Chicago now that David is dead." With that parting shot she got to her feet and left the room, though with considerably more grace than Rule had exhibited.

She started to go to her room, because she was feeling the effects of travel and her long ride. Her stiff muscles, forgotten during the heat of battle, renewed their appeal for her attention, and she winced slightly as she crossed to the stairs. Pausing with one foot on the first step, she decided to find Rule first, prompted by some vague urge to see him. She didn't know why that should be when she had spent years avoiding him, but she didn't stop to analyze her thoughts and emotions. It was one thing for her to rip up at him; it was something else entirely for anyone else to take that liberty! She let herself out by the front door and walked around the house, directing her steps to the foaling barn. Where else would Rule be but checking on one of his precious horses?

The familiar smells of hay and horses, liniment and leather greeted her as she entered the barn and walked the dark length of the aisle to the pool of light that revealed two men standing before the stall of the pregnant mare. Rule turned as she emerged into the light. "Cat, this is Floyd Stoddard, our foaling man. Floyd, meet Cathryn Ashe."

Floyd was a compact, powerfully built man with leathery skin and thinning brown hair. He acknowledged the introduction by nodding his head and drawling, "Ma'am," in a soft voice totally at odds with his appearance.

Cathryn made a more conventional greeting, but there was no chance for further conversation. Rule said briefly, "Tell me if anything happens," and took her arm. She found herself being led away, out of the circle of light and into the darkness of the barn. She didn't have good night vision, and she stumbled uncertainly, not trusting her footing.

A low chuckle sounded above her head and she felt herself pulled closely against a hard, warm body. "Still can't see in the dark, can you? Don't worry, I won't let you run into anything. Just hold on to me."

She didn't have to hold on to him. He was doing enough holding for the both of them. To make conversation she said, "Will the mare foal soon?"

"Probably tonight, after everything quiets down. Mares are usually shy. They wait until they think no one's around, so Travis will have to be really quiet and not let her hear him." Amusement in his voice, he said, "Like all females, they're contrary."

Resentment on behalf of her sex flared briefly, but she controlled it. She realized that he was teasing her, hoping to make her react hotly, thereby giving him a perfect reason for kissing her again—if he even needed a reason. When had he ever let a little thing like having a reason stop him from doing anything he wanted? Instead she said mildly, "You'd probably be contrary, too, if you were faced with labor and birth."

"Honey, I'd be more than contrary. I'd be downright surprised!"

They laughed together as they left the barn and began the walk back to the house. She could see now by the faint light of the rising moon, but he kept his arm around her waist and she didn't protest. A silent moment went by before he murmured, "Are you very sore?"

"Sore enough. Got any liniment I can use?"

"I'll bring a bottle to your room," he promised. "How long did you tough it out with Monica and Ricky?"

"Not long," she admitted. "I didn't finish eating, either."

Silence fell again and wasn't broken until they had neared the house. His hold on her tightened until his fingers bit into the soft skin at her waist.

"Cat."

She stopped and looked up at him. His face was completely shadowed by his hat, but she could feel the intensity of his gaze. "Monica isn't my mistress," he said on a softly exhaled breath. "She never has been, though not for lack of opportunity. Your father was too good a friend for me to jump into bed with his widow."

Apparently the same restriction didn't apply to Ward's daughter, she thought, stunned into momentary speechlessness by his bold statement. For a moment she simply stared at him in the dim, silvery light as she stood there with her face tilted up to his. Finally she whispered, "Why bother to explain to me?"

"Because you believed it, damn you!"

Stunned again, she wondered if she had automatically accepted, without really thinking about it, that Rule had been Monica's lover. Certainly that was what Ricky had been getting at earlier, but something in Cathryn violently rejected the very thought. On the other hand, she instinctively shied away from handing him a vote of confidence. Torn between the two, she merely said, "Everything pointed to it. I can see why Ricky is so convinced. Whatever you wanted, you only had to mention it to Monica and she made sure you got the money to do it."

"The only money I ever got from Monica was for the ranch!" he snapped. "Ward trusted me to run this ranch for him, and his death didn't change that."

"I know that. You've worked for this ranch as hard—harder—than any man would for his own spread." Obeying another instinct, she put her hand on his chest, spreading her fingers and feeling the warm, hard flesh beneath the material of his shirt. "I resented you, Rule. I admit it. When Dad first died it seemed like you were bulling in and taking over everything that had been his.

You took the ranch, you moved into his house, you organized everything about our lives. Was it so impossible to think that you might have taken over his wife, too?'' God, why had she said that? She didn't even believe it, yet she felt driven to somehow lash out at him.

He went rigid and his breath hissed between his teeth. ''I'd like to turn you over my knee for that!''

''As you've said several times, I'm all grown up now, so I wouldn't advise it. I won't take being treated like a child,'' she warned, her spine stiffening as she remembered that long-ago incident.

''So you want me to treat you like a woman, then?'' he ground out.

''No. I want you to treat me like what I am . . .'' She paused, then spat out, ''Your employer!''

''You've been that for years,'' he pointed out harshly. ''But that didn't stop me from spanking you, and it didn't stop me from making love to you.''

Realizing the futility of standing there arguing with him, Cathryn jerked away and started for the house. She had taken only a few steps when long fingers closed over her arm and pulled her to a halt. ''Are you always going to run when I mention making love?'' His words were like blows to her nervous system, and she quivered in his grip, fighting the storm of mingled dread and anticipation that confused her.

''You didn't run that day by the river,'' he reminded her cruelly. ''You were ready and you liked it, despite it being your first time. You remind me of a mare that's nervous and not quite broken, kicking your heels at a stallion, but all you need is a little calming down.''

''Don't you compare me to a mare!'' The furious words burst out of her throat and she was no longer confused; she was clearheaded and angry.

"That's what you've always brought to mind—a long-legged little filly with big dark eyes, too skittish to stand under a friendly hand. I don't think you've changed all that much. You're still long legged, you've still got big dark eyes, and you're still skittish. I've always liked chestnut horses," he said, his voice sliding so low that it was almost a growl. "And I've always meant to have me a redheaded woman."

Sheer rage vibrated through her slender body, and for a moment she was incapable of answering. When she was finally able to speak, her voice was hoarse and shaking with the force of her temper. "Well, it won't be me! I suggest you go find yourself a chestnut *mare....* That's more your type!"

He was laughing at her. She could hear the low rumbling sound in his chest. She raised her clenched fist to hit him, and he moved with lightning reflexes, catching her delicate fist in his big, hard palm and holding it. She tried to jerk away, but he pulled her inexorably closer until she was close enough that their bodies just touched. He bent his head until his breath feathered warmly over her lips, and with the lightest of contacts he let his mouth move against hers as he said, "You're the one, all right. You're my redheaded woman. God knows I've waited long enough for you."

"No—" she began, only to have her automatic protest cut short as he moved forward the tiny bit that was needed to firm the contact between their mouths. She shivered and stood still under his kiss. Since that morning when he had kissed her at the airport it seemed that she had done nothing but let him kiss her whenever he pleased, a situation that she had never even dreamed would develop. With a shock she realized that his behavior all day had been distinctly loverlike, and for the first time she wondered what lay behind his actions.

Her lack of response irritated him and he drew her roughly nearer, his mouth demanding more and more until she gave a muffled groan of pain as her muscles protested against the handling she was receiving. Immediately his arms relaxed and he raised his head. "I forgot," he admitted huskily. "We'd better go in and get you taken care of before I forget again."

Cathryn started to protest that she could take care of herself but bit the words back, afraid of prolonging the situation. With counterfeit docility she suffered the possessive arm that lay around her waist as they entered the house. There was no sign of either Monica or Ricky, for which she was profoundly grateful, as Rule went up the stairs with her, his arm still around her. She could imagine the comments either of them would have been likely to make and which she felt oddly incapable of handling just then.

Rule unsettled her; he always had. She had thought herself mature enough now to face him with calm indifference, only to find that where he was concerned she was far from indifferent. She hated him, she fiercely resented him, and underneath all of that lay the burning physical awareness that had haunted her during her marriage to David and made her feel as if she were being unfaithful . . . to Rule, not her own husband! It was stupid. She had sincerely loved David and suffered after his death, and yet... She had always been aware that, while David could take her to the moon, Rule had made her reach the stars.

To her surprise Rule left her at her bedroom door and continued down the hall to his own room. Not questioning her good luck, Cathryn quickly entered her room and closed the door. She longed for a soak in a tub of hot water to ease her protesting muscles, but the only bathroom with a full tub, instead of a shower stall, was down the hall between Rule's bedroom and Monica's, and she didn't want to risk an encounter with either of them. Sighing in regret, she began unbuttoning her dress. She had slipped three of the buttons loose when a brief hard knock on the door, a knock which preceded Rule by only a split second, had her whirling around in a startled movement that made her wince with pain.

"Sorry about that," Rule muttered. "Here's the liniment."

She reached out for the bottle of clear liquid and saw his eyes drop to the unbuttoned neckline of her dress. In instantaneous reaction she felt her breasts tighten and grow heated in that bitter, uncontrolled response she had to him. She drew a ragged, protesting breath, and his eyes lifted slowly to her face. His pupils were dilated, his skin taut as he sensed, like a wild animal, the way it was with her. For a moment she thought that he was going to heed the primal call; then, with a stifled curse, he shoved the bottle into her hand.

"I can wait," he said, and left as abruptly as he had entered.

Cathryn felt as if her legs were going to collapse beneath her and she moved to the bed, sinking gratefully onto the white chenille bedspread. If that wasn't a close call, she didn't know what was!

After carefully rubbing her legs and buttocks with the pungent liniment, she put on her nightgown and crawled stiffly into bed, but despite her weariness she was unable to sleep. Everything that had been said that day drifted through her tired mind with maddening persistence.

Rule. Everything came back to him. Cathryn thought she knew enough about men in general, and Rule in particular, to recognize passion, and Rule did nothing to hide his arousal when he kissed her. But Rule was a complicated man, and she didn't feel that he was motivated solely by simple lust. He was like an iceberg only allowing a small bit to show. He kept most of himself submerged, hidden from view, and she could only guess at his motives. Was it the ranch? Was Ricky right after all in her assessment? Was he trying to make the ranch legally his by marrying the owner?

She drew her thoughts up sharply. Married! What made her think that Rule would ever consider marriage? She was beginning to understand that he could control her easily enough by other means, and the realization was sharply humiliating. Unless he did want the ranch legally...? He was a man with a dark past; who could guess at the importance of the ranch to him? She could well imagine that to him it represented his salvation, both physically and emotionally.

Whatever happened, she didn't want to let herself become embroiled with him. And whatever his motive, she was certain that she wouldn't be able to shield herself from harm. She was so frighteningly vulnerable to him....

Chapter Three

Cathryn had intended to get up early, but her intentions weren't strong enough to do the job and it was after ten when she rolled over groggily and pushed her hair out of her face to peer at the clock. She yawned and stretched, cutting the motion short with a wince of pain. Easing gingerly out of the bed, she decided that she wasn't as sore as she had feared she would be, but she was still sore enough. As Rule would have been out of the house for hours by now, she felt safely able to have that hot bath, and she gathered up her clothes, then beat a path to the bathroom.

An hour later she felt considerably better, though still stiff. She rubbed the liniment into her muscles again, then decided to ignore the pain. Despite the night's uncomfortable beginning, the long sleep had completely refreshed her and her dark eyes were sparkling, her cheeks delicately pink. Her hair was pulled back on each side with a matching pair of tortoiseshell combs, giving her the look of a teenager. For a moment as she looked in the mirror she had a disturbing sense of looking into the past, as if the reflection she saw was that of the young girl she had been on a hot summer day, gleefully planning on a ride to the river. Had she smiled that way? she wondered as her lips curved in a faint smile of secret anticipation. Anticipation of what?

She studied the face in the mirror, searching for an answer. The delicate features revealed nothing; she saw only the elusive smile, a certain mystery in the dark eyes. Her coloring was unusual, inherited directly from her father; dark fire in her hair, a shade neither red nor brown but with the sheen of mahogany; dark eyes, not as dark as Rule's, but a soft deep brown. Her skin, thankfully, had no freckles. She could tan lightly, but had never been able to acquire a deep tan. What else was there? What else would attract a man's attention? Her nose was straight and dainty, but not classical. Her mouth looked vulnerable, sensitive; her facial bones were delicate, finely drawn. Fairly tall, slender and long-legged, with narrow hips, a slim waist and rather nice, round breasts. She didn't have voluptuous curves, but she did have the long, clean lines of good breeding and a certain grace of movement. Rule had compared her to a long-legged filly. And Rule had always wanted a red-haired woman.

No great beauty, the young woman in the mirror, but passable.

Passable enough to hold Rule Jackson's interest?

Stop it! she told herself fiercely, turning away from the mirror. She didn't want to hold his interest! She couldn't handle him and she knew it. If she had any sense at all she'd take herself back to Chicago, continue her rather boring job and forget the nagging, incessant ache for the home where she had grown up. But this was her home, and perhaps she didn't have any sense. She knew every plank in this old house, had never forgotten anything about it, and she wanted to stay there.

She went downstairs to the kitchen. Lorna turned from the stove as she entered and gave her a friendly smile. "Have a good sleep?"

"Marvelous," Cathryn sighed. "I haven't slept this late in years."

"Rule said you were worn out," said Lorna comfortably. "You've lost some weight, too, since your last visit. Are you ready for breakfast?"

"It's almost lunchtime, so I think I'll wait. Where is everyone?"

"Monica is still asleep; Ricky went out with the men today."

Cathryn lifted her eyebrows questioningly, and Lorna shrugged. She was a big-boned woman in her late forties or early fifties, her brown hair showing no trace of gray, and her pleasantly unremarkable features revealed only contentment with her life. Acceptance was in her eyes as she said slowly, "Ricky's having a rough time right now."

"In what way?" Cathryn asked. It was true that Ricky seemed even more highly strung than before, as if she were only barely under control.

Again Lorna shrugged. "I expect she woke up one day and realized that she doesn't have what she wanted, and she panicked. What has she done with her life? Wasted it. She has no husband, no children, nothing of any importance that she can say belongs to her. The only thing she's ever really had is her looks, and they haven't gotten her the man she wanted."

"She's been married twice," said Cathryn.

"But not to Rule."

Shocked, Cathryn sat silently, trying to follow Lorna's reasoning. Rule? And Ricky? Ricky had always alternated wildly between rebelling against Rule and following him with slavish devotion, while Rule had always treated her with stoic tolerance. Was that the basis for Ricky's sudden outbreak of hostility? Was that why she didn't want Cathryn to stay? Once again Cathryn had the uneasy thought that somehow Ricky knew that Rule had made love to her when she was seventeen. It was impossible, but yet...

It was all impossible. Ricky couldn't be in love with Rule. Cathryn had known what it was to love, and she could see none of the signs in Ricky, no gentling, no caring. Her reactions to Rule were a mixture of fear and hostility that bordered on actual hate; that, too, Cathryn understood all too well. How many years had she stayed away because of those same feelings?

Agitated, she felt a sudden, powerful need to be alone for a while, so she said, "Does Wallace's Drugstore still stay open on Sundays?"

Lorna nodded. "Are you thinking of driving into town?"

"If no one else needs the car, I will."

"Nobody that I know of, and even if they did there's other means of going," Lorna said practically. "Would you mind picking up a few things?"

"I'll be glad to," Cathryn replied. "But to be on the safe side, write everything down. No matter how careful I try to be, I always forget one item unless I have a list, and it's usually the most-needed thing that I forget."

With a chuckle Lorna pulled open a drawer and extracted a notepad from which she tore the top sheet. She handed it to Cathryn. "It's already done. I'm guilty of the same thing, so I always write things down as I think of them. Let me get some money from Rule's desk."

"No, I have enough," Cathryn protested, looking at the list of items. It was mostly first aid things such as alcohol and bandages, nothing very expensive. Besides, anything bought for the ranch was her responsibility.

"All right, but keep the sales receipt. Taxes."

Cathryn nodded. "Do you know where the keys to the station wagon are?"

"Usually in the ignition, unless Rule took them out this morning to keep Ricky from disappearing as she sometimes does. If he did, then they'll be in his pocket, but since Ricky went with them he wouldn't have had any reason for taking the keys."

Cathryn made a face at that information and went upstairs to get her purse. Was Ricky so bad that it was necessary to hide the car keys from her? And what if someone else needed the car? But then, Lorna and Monica would make arrangements beforehand if they needed the car, and in any medical emergency Rule could be located quickly enough. The plane would be faster than a car anyway.

She was in luck. The keys were still dangling from the ignition. She opened the door and slid behind the wheel, looking forward to her little trip.

The station wagon wasn't a new model and it had a rather battered appearance, but the engine caught immediately and hummed with steady precision. Like everything else on the ranch, it was kept in good mechanical condition, another indication of Rule's excellent management. There was no way she could fault him on that score.

She felt pride in the way the ranch looked as she drove down the dusty road that led to the highway. It wasn't a huge ranch or a rich one, though it had done well enough. She knew that Rule had brought new life into it with his horses, though it had been a comfortable place before that. But now the land had the well-tended look that only devotion and hard work could bring.

The town was small, but Cathryn supposed it had everything required by civilization. It was as familiar to her as her own face, never changing much despite the passage of time. San Antonio was the nearest large city, almost eighty miles distant, but to someone used to Texas distances, that didn't seem like a long trip. No one felt denied by the undemanding tenor of life in Uvalde County.

Probably the last scandal in memory was the last one Rule had figured in, Cathryn thought absently as she parked the station wagon against the curb, joining the lineup of dusty pickups and assorted cars. She could hear the jukebox inside, and a smile lit her face as memories washed over her. How many Sunday afternoons had she spent here as a teenager? The pharmacy was located in the back of the building. The front was occupied by a booming hamburger business. Red-topped stools lined the counter and several booths marched down the opposite wall, while a few small tables were scattered about the remaining space. The stools and booths were crowded, while the tables remained empty, always the last to be filled. A quick glance around told her that the majority of the customers were teenagers, just as it had always been, though there were enough adults on hand to keep youthful enthusiasms under control.

She went back to the pharmacy and began gathering the items on Lorna's list, wanting to do that first; then she intended to reward herself with a huge milk shake. The pile in her arms kept growing and became unmanageable; she looked around for a shopping basket and her gaze was met by a young woman her own age who was studying her curiously.

"Cathryn? Cathryn Donahue?" the woman asked hesitantly.

As soon as she spoke Cathryn placed her voice. "Wanda Gifford!"

"Wanda Wallace now. I married Rick Wallace."

Cathryn remembered him. He was the son of the owner of the drugstore and a year or so older than she and Wanda. "And I'm Cathryn Ashe."

"Yes. I heard about your husband's death. I'm sorry, Cathryn."

Cathryn murmured an acknowledgement of the polite phrase as Wanda moved to take some of the precariously balanced things out of her arms, then swiftly changed the subject, still feeling unable to discuss David's death calmly. "Do you have any children?"

"Two, and that's enough. Both boys, and both monsters." Wanda smiled wryly. "Rick asked me if I wanted to try for a girl next time, and I told him that if there was a next time we'd have a parting of the ways. Good Lord, what if I had another boy?" But in spite of her words she was laughing, and Cathryn had a moment of gentle envy. She and David had discussed having children, but put it off in favor of a few years alone; then they had learned of David's illness and he had refused to burden her with a child to raise alone. She didn't understand how he could have imagined that his child would ever be a burden to her, but she had always thought that making a baby should be a mutual decision, so she hadn't pressured him. He had been under enough pressure, knowing that his life was slipping away.

Wanda led the way to the nearest table and dumped everything onto the shiny surface. "Have a seat and let me buy you a soft drink to welcome you home. Rule told us that you're home to stay this time."

Slowly Cathryn sank into an empty chair. "When did he say that?" she asked, wondering if she looked as cornered as she felt.

"Two weeks ago. He said you'd be home for Memorial Day weekend." Wanda went behind the counter to get two glasses brimming with ice and fill them with fountain cola from the machine installed there.

So Rule had let it be known two weeks ago that she was coming home to stay? Cathryn mused. That was when she had called to let Monica know that she was coming home for a visit. Just like that, Rule had decided that she'd stay this time and had spread the news. Wouldn't he be surprised when she got on that plane tomorrow?

"Here you go," said Wanda, sliding the frosted glass in front of her.

Cathryn leaned over to take an appreciative sip of the strong, icy drink, sharp as only fountain cola could be. "Rule's changed a lot over the years," she murmured, not certain just why she said it, but wanting for some reason to hear someone else's opinion of him. Perhaps he wasn't out of the ordinary; perhaps it was her own perception of him that was at fault.

"In some ways he has, in some he hasn't," said Wanda. "He's not wild anymore, but you get the feeling he's just as dangerous as he always was. He's more controlled now. But the way most folks think about him has changed. Rule knows ranching and he's a fair boss. He's president of the Local C.A., you know. Of course, to some people he'll always be as wild as a mink."

Cathryn managed to hide her surprise at that information. In some parts of the West, the Cattlemen's Association was the inner circle of the elite; in other parts, such as here, it was a working group of not-so-big ranchers who tried to help each other. Still, she was stunned that Rule had been elected president, because he wasn't even a ranch owner. That, more than anything, was a measure of his move from scandalousness to respectability.

She gossiped with Wanda for the better part of an hour and noticed that Ricky's name wasn't mentioned at all, an indication of how completely Ricky had alienated the local people. Had Wanda been on friendly terms with the other young woman, she would have asked after her, even if it had been only a day or two since she had seen her.

Cathryn finally noticed the time and began gathering up the items she had scattered over the table. Wanda helped her manage them and walked with her back to the cash register, where her father-in-law checked Cathryn out. "We still have a dance every Saturday night," Wanda said, her friendly eyes smiling. "Why don't you come next time? Rule will bring you if you don't feel like coming on your own, but there's plenty of men who'd like to see you walk in without an escort, especially without Rule."

Cathryn laughed, remembering the Saturday night dances that were such an integral part of the county social life. Most of the marriages and at least a few of the pregnancies of the last fifteen years had gotten their start at the Saturday night dances. "Thanks for reminding me. I'll think about it, though I don't think Rule would thank you for volunteering him for escort duty."

"Try him!" was Wanda's laughing advice.

"No, thanks," muttered Cathryn to herself as she left the coolness of the pharmacy and the heat of the cloudless Texas day hit her in the face. She had no intention of being there for the next dance, anyway. She'd be on that plane in less than twenty-four hours, and by the next Saturday she would be safe in her Chicago apartment, away from the dangers and temptations of Rule Jackson.

She opened the car door and dropped her purchases onto the seat, but stood for a moment allowing the interior of the car to cool somewhat before she got in.

"Cathryn! By God, I thought it was you! Heard you were back!"

She turned curiously and a grin widened her mouth as a tall, lanky man with white hair and sun-browned skin loped along the sidewalk to reach her. "Mr. Vernon! It's nice to see you again!"

Paul Vernon reached her and enfolded her in a hug that lifted her off the ground. He had been her father's best friend, and she had carried on the tradition with his son, Kyle. To Paul Vernon's disappointment the friendship between the two had never matured into romance; but he had always had a soft spot in his heart for Cathryn and she returned the affection, in some ways liking the older man more than she had Kyle.

He replaced her on the ground and turned to beckon another man forward. Cathryn knew him at once as a newcomer, even though she had been away for years. The man who removed his hat politely and nodded at her wasn't dressed in quite the manner a local would have dressed. His jeans were a little too new; his hat wasn't a hat that had been on the range.

Mr. Vernon's introduction confirmed her guess. "Cathryn, this is Ira Morris. He's in the region looking at some livestock and horses; he owns a spread in Kansas. Ira, this is Cathryn Donahue...sorry, but I can't remember your married name. Cathryn is from the Bar D."

"Bar D?" asked Mr. Morris. "Isn't that Rule Jackson's spread?"

"That's right; you'll have to see him if it's horses you want. He's got the best quarter horse farm in the state."

Mr. Morris was impatient. He barely contained his restlessness when Paul Vernon seemed content to linger and chat for a while. Cathryn was in sympathy with his impatience, because she was burning with fury and it was taking a great deal of self-control to hide it from Mr. Vernon. At last he said goodbye and admonished her to come visit soon. She promised to do so and quickly got into the car before he could continue the conversation.

She started the car and slammed it into gear with violent temper; not in years had she been so consumed with white-hot rage. The last time had been that day by the river, but there wouldn't be the same ending this time. She wasn't a naive teenager who hadn't any idea of how to control a man or handle her own desires now. She was a woman, and he had encroached on her home territory. Rule Jackson's spread, indeed! Was that how people thought of the Bar D now? Maybe Rule thought it was his, too; maybe he considered himself so much in control that there was no way she could dislodge him. If so, he'd find out soon that *she* was a Donahue of the Bar D and a Jackson just didn't belong!

The first wave of anger had passed by the time she reached the ranch, but her resolve hadn't faded. First she took her purchases in to Lorna, knowing that the woman would have seen her arrival from the kitchen window. That guess was proved correct when she opened the door and saw Lorna standing at the sink while she peeled potatoes, looking out the window so as not to miss any activity in the yard. Cathryn placed the paper bag on the table and said, "Here are the things. Have you seen Rule?"

"He came in for lunch," said Lorna placidly. "But he could be anywhere now. Someone in the stables should be able to tell you where he's gone."

"Thanks," said Cathryn, and retraced her steps, moving with her free-swinging stride to the stables, her feet kicking up tiny clouds of dust with every step.

The cool dimness of the stable was a welcome change from the bright sun, the smell of horses and ammonia as familiar as ever. She squinted, trying to adjust her eyes to the dimness, and made out two figures several stalls down. In a few seconds she recognized Rule, though the other man was a stranger.

Before she could speak Rule held out his hand. "Here's the boss lady," he said, still with his hand held out to her, and she was so surprised by his words that she stepped into reach of that hand and it curved around her waist, drawing her close to his heat and strength. "Cat, meet Lewis Stovall, the foreman. I don't think you've been here since he was hired. Lewis, this is Cathryn Donahue."

Lewis Stovall merely nodded and touched his hat, but his silence wasn't prompted by shyness. His face was as hard and watchful as Rule's, his eyes narrowed and waiting. Cathryn felt uneasily that Lewis Stovall was a man with secrets locked inside, just as Rule was, a man who had lived hard and dangerously and who bore the scars of that life. But...he was the foreman? Just what did that make Rule? King of the mountain?

She wasn't in the mood for small talk, so she returned the greeting that she had received, a brief nod of the head. It was enough. His attention wasn't on her; he was listening to Rule's instructions, his head slightly dipped as if he were considering every word he heard. Rule was brief to the point of terseness, a characteristic of his conversations with everyone. Except with herself, Cathryn realized suddenly. Not that Rule could ever be termed talkative, but he did talk more to her than he did to anyone else. From the day he had told her of her father's death, he had talked to her. At first it had been as if he had to force himself to communicate, but soon he had been teasing her in his rusty, growling voice, aggravating her out of her grief.

Lewis nodded to her again and left them, his tall body graceful as he moved away. Rule turned her back toward the entrance, his hand still on the small of her back. "I came up to the house at lunchtime to take you with me for the rest of the day, but you had already gone. Where did you go?"

It was typical of him that he hadn't asked Lorna. "To Wallace's drugstore," she answered automatically. The warm pressure of his hand was draining away her resolve, making her forget why she was so angry. Taking a deep breath, she stepped away from his touch and faced him. "Did you say that Lewis is the foreman?" she asked.

"That's right," he said, pushing his hat back a little and watching her with his dark, unreadable eyes. She sensed the waiting in him, the tension.

She said sweetly, "Well, if he's the foreman, then I don't need you any longer, do I? You gave away your own job."

His hand shot out and caught her arm, pulling her back into the circle of his special heat and smell. His mouth was a grim line as he shook her slightly. "I needed help, and Lewis is a good man. If you care so much, then maybe you'd better stay around and do a share of the work too. Ward had a foreman to help him, and that was without the added work of the horses, so don't turn bitchy on me. While you were tucked up in bed, I was up at two o'clock this morning with a mare in foal, so I'm not in the mood to put up with any of your tantrums right now. Is that clear?"

"All right, so you needed help," she admitted grudgingly. She hated to acknowledge the logic of his words, but he was right. However, that didn't have anything to do with what she had heard in town. "I'll concede that. But can you tell me why the Bar D is known as Rule Jackson's spread?" Her voice rose sharply on the last words and temper made color flare hotly in her cheeks.

His jaw was set like granite. "Maybe because you haven't cared enough to stay around and remind people that this is Donahue land," he snapped. "I've never forgotten who this ranch belongs to, but sometimes I think I'm the only one who does remember. I know very well that this is all yours, little boss lady. Is that what you wanted to hear from me? Damn it, I've got work to do, so why don't you get out of my way?"

"I'm not stopping you!"

He swore under his breath and stalked away, his temper evident in the set of his broad shoulders. Cathryn stood there with her fists clenched, fighting the urge to launch herself at him and pound on him with her fists as she had done once before. At last she stormed into the house and was on the way to her room when she met Ricky.

"Why didn't you tell me you were going into town?" demanded Ricky petulantly.

"You weren't here, for one thing, and for another you've never been that crazy about Wallace's Drugstore," replied Cathryn wryly. She looked at her stepsister and saw the brittleness of her control, the shaking of her hands. Impulsively she asked, "Ricky, why are you doing this to yourself?"

For a moment Ricky looked outraged; then her shoulders slumped and she gave a defeated little shrug. "What would you know about it? You've always been the darling of the house, the one who belonged. I could call myself a Donahue, but I've never really been one, have I? You noticed who the ranch was left to, didn't you? What did I get? Nothing!"

Ricky's particular brand of illogic defeated Cathryn; evidently it made no difference to her that Ward Donahue hadn't been her father, while he had been Cathryn's. She shook her head and tried again. "I couldn't have made you feel unwelcome, because I haven't even been here!"

"You didn't have to be here!" Ricky lashed out, her small face twisting with fury. "You own this ranch, so you have a weapon to hold over Rule!"

Rule. It always came back to Rule. He was the dominant male in his territory and everything revolved around him. She hadn't meant to say it, but the words left her mouth involuntarily. "You're paranoid about Rule! He told me that he's never been involved with Monica."

"Oh, did he?" Ricky's slanted hazel eyes brightened suspiciously; then she turned away before Cathryn could decide whether the brightness had been caused by tears. "Are you really gullible enough to believe him? Haven't you learned yet that he won't let anything stand between him and this ranch? God! I can't tell you how often I've prayed that this damned place would burn to the ground!" She brushed roughly past Cathryn and bolted down the stairs, leaving Cathryn standing there mired in a combination of pity and anger.

She would be a fool to believe anything Ricky said; it was obvious that the other woman was emotionally unstable. On the other hand, Cathryn remembered clearly the way Rule had doggedly followed her father's instructions when he had first come to the ranch, working when his body was weak and wracked with pain, his eyes reflecting the wary but devoted look of a battered animal that had finally met with kindness rather than kicks. He too had been emotionally unstable at that time; it was possible that the ranch had assumed an irrational importance to him.

Cathryn shook her head. She was thinking like an amateur psychiatrist, and she had enough trouble sorting out her own thoughts and emotions without taking on someone like Rule. He certainly wasn't uncertain about anything now. If there was anyone on this earth who knew what he wanted, it was Rule Jackson. She was simply letting Ricky's paranoia cloud her own thinking.

All afternoon Cathryn thought of what she had said to Rule earlier, and reluctantly she came to the conclusion that she would have to apologize. No one could ever accuse him of not working, of not putting the ranch first. Whatever his reason, he had driven himself

past the point where lesser men would have broken, not
for his personal gain but for the good of the ranch.
Facing it squarely, she admitted that she had been
wrong and had flared into rage out of sheer, petty jealousy, striking out at him for cherishing the same land
that she loved so deeply. She was wrong, and she felt
small.

When he finally came in to wash before dinner her
heart tightened painfully at the sight of him. His face
was taut with weariness, his clothing soaked in sweat
and overlaid with a thick coat of dust that was turning
to mud on his body, evidence that he was no shirker
when it came to work. She stopped him before he went
up the stairs, placing her slim hand on his dirty sleeve.

"I'm sorry for the way I acted this afternoon," she
said directly, meeting his flinty gaze without flinching.
"I was wrong, and I apologize. This ranch would never
have made it without you, and I...I suppose I envy
you."

He looked down at her, his face blank and hard.
Then he took off his sweat-stained hat, wiping his sleeve
across his moist face and leaving a brown smear of mud
behind. "At least you're not totally blind," he snapped,
pulling his arm from her touch and taking the stairs two
at a time, his lithe body moving easily, as though weariness were a stranger to him.

Cathryn sighed, torn between wry laughter and the
anger that he so easily provoked. Had she really thought
that he would be gracious? As long as he was angry no
apology she could make would pacify him.

Dinner was a silent meal. Monica was quiet, Ricky
sullen. Rule wasn't a conversationalist at any time, but
at least he did justice to the hot meal Lorna had provided for him. As soon as he was finished he excused

himself and disappeared into the study, closing the door with a thud. Ricky looked up and shrugged. "Well, that's a normal evening. Exciting, isn't it? You're used to a big city, to entertainment. You'll go crazy here."

"I've always liked a quiet life," replied Cathryn, not looking up from the peach cobbler she was destroying with delicate greed. "David and I weren't the life of the town." They really hadn't had much time together, she reminded herself painfully. She was glad they had spent it learning to know each other, rather than wasting the precious time they'd had in socializing.

It was still early, but she felt tired. Lorna cleared away the dishes and stacked them in the dishwasher; Monica went upstairs to her bedroom to watch television in privacy. After sulking for a few minutes Ricky flounced upstairs to her own room.

Left on her own, Cathryn didn't linger. On an impulse she opened the door of the study to tell Rule good night, but paused with the words unsaid when she saw him sprawled back in the oversized chair, sound asleep, his booted feet propped up on the desk. Papers scattered on the desk indicated his intention to work, but he hadn't been able to fight off sleep any longer. Again that funny wrenching of her heart caught at her as she watched him.

Vaguely annoyed with herself, she started to back out of the room when his eyes snapped open and he stared at her. "Cat," he said huskily, his voice rough with sleep. "Come here."

Even as her feet carried her into the room, she wondered at her own obedience to that drowsy voice. He swung his feet to the floor and stood up, his hand going out to close around her wrist and pull her close to him. Before she could guess his intent, his mouth was warm on hers, moving hungrily, demanding her sub-mission. A ripple of unwilling pleasure moved up her spine and her lips parted, allowed him to deepen the kiss.

"Let's go to bed," he muttered against her mouth.

For a moment Cathryn sagged against him, her body more than willing; then awareness snapped her eyes open and she pushed belatedly at his heavy shoulders.

"Now, wait a minute! I'm not going to—"

"I've waited long enough," he interrupted, brushing his lips against hers again.

"That's tough! You can just keep on waiting!"

He laughed wryly, sliding his hands down to her hips and pulling her solidly against the power of his loins, letting her feel his arousal. "That's my girl. Fight me to the bitter end. Go on up to bed, Cat. I've got a lot of work to do before I can turn in."

Confused by his dismissal, Cathryn found herself out of the room before she knew what was happening. What *was* happening? Rule wasn't a man to deny him-self...unless it concerned the ranch. Of course, she told herself in amusement. He had work to do. Everything else could wait. And that was just fine with her!

She went into the kitchen to tell Lorna good night, just catching the cook before she went to her own two-rooms-and-a-bath quarters at the rear of the house, converted specifically for her use when Rule had hired her. Then Cathryn climbed the stairs, wincing at the pain in her legs with each step. Another leisurely bath loosened her muscles a bit and she didn't bother with the liniment, though she knew that she would regret it in the morning.

After opening the curtains to let in the moonlight, she tossed her robe over the back of the rocking chair that sat placidly in the corner, then turned out the light and crawled into the familiar bed with a sense of home-coming, of belonging. There was no other place on earth where she felt so peaceful and complete, no other place where she was so relaxed.

But, relaxed or not, she couldn't sleep. She moved restlessly onto her side, her mind turning inexorably to Rule. So he'd waited long enough, had he? Was there no limit to that natural arrogance of his? If he thought she was going to trot obediently to bed and wait for him . . .

Was that what he had meant? Her eyes popped open. Surely not. Not with both Monica and Ricky just down the hall. She tried to remember exactly what he had said. Something about her going on to bed because it would be a while before he could turn in. What did that have to do with her? Nothing. Nothing at all. Un-less . . . unless he meant to come to her later.

Of course not, she reassured herself. He knew that she wouldn't let him do that, and he wouldn't risk rais-ing a ruckus. She closed her eyes again, trying to ig-nore the nagging thought that Rule would risk anything to get what he wanted.

She dozed, but came suddenly awake to the knowl-edge that she wasn't alone. Quickly she turned her head to see the man standing beside her bed, removing his shirt. Her breath strangled in her throat and her heart-beat accelerated, making her body feel warm and flushed, making the thin nightgown she wore seem suddenly restrictive. She gasped for breath, struggling for words as he shrugged out of his shirt and tossed it aside. The colorless moonlight fell across him, starkly illuminating his lean, muscled torso, but leaving his face concealed in darkness. But she knew him, knew the look and smell and heat of him. Vivid images of a hot summer day and his black outline against the brazen sky as he covered her washed over her, swamping her senses with oddly mingled panic and longing. He *had* dared, after all.

"What are you doing?" she was finally able to choke as he removed his boots and socks, then stood to unfasten his belt.

"Undressing," he explained in a low rasp, his voice flat and inexorable. In further, unneeded explanation he said, "I'm sleeping here tonight."

That wasn't what she had meant. She had been asking if he had lost his senses, but Cathryn felt as if all the breath had left her body. She was unable to make a protest, unable to order him to leave. After a long pause while he seemed to wait for her objection, one that didn't come, he chuckled. "Or rather, I'm staying with you tonight, but I doubt we'll be doing much sleeping."

An automatic refusal rose to her lips but remained unsaid; somehow the words wouldn't come, halted by the hot life that flooded into her stunned body, by the wild slamming of her heart against her ribs. She sat up, her eyes locked on his moon-silvered body. She heard the sibilant whisper of a zipper sliding down; then he slid out of his jeans. His hard body was muscled, powerful, his masculinity a potent, visible threat . . . or was it a promise?

The heat in Cathryn began to throb maddeningly and she held out a hand that beckoned even as she warned in a whisper. "Don't come near me! I'll scream!" But the lack of conviction in her words was evident even to herself. Oh, Lord, she wanted him so badly! As he had pointed out to her so often, she was a woman now and she no longer feared his sexual power, but rather wanted to cling to him and warm herself with his fire.

He knew. He sat down on the bed beside her and cupped her cheek in his hard, callused palm. Even in the colorless moonlight she could feel the heat of his gaze as it wandered over her body. "Are you, Cat?" he asked, his voice so low that it was almost without sound. "Are you going to scream?"

Her mouth was too dry to allow speech; she swallowed, yet still she was able to manage only a faint admission. "No."

He drew a deep, shuddering breath into his lungs and the hand on her face trembled. "God, sweetheart, if you've ever wanted to slap a man for what he was thinking of doing, now's your chance," he said roughly, his voice shaking with the force of his desire.

The unsteadiness of his words told her how affected he was by her nearness and the quiet intimacy of her bedroom. That reassured her, gave her the courage to reach out and put her hand on his chest, feeling the rough curl of dark hair against her palm and the sleek warmth of his skin where the hair ended, the taut, tiny buds of his nipples. The sound that rumbled in his throat could have been a growl, but her heightened senses recognized it for what it was—a rough purr of pleasure.

She leaned closer, seeking the delicious male scent of him. "Are you going to do everything you're thinking about?" she asked, her voice shaking.

He was sliding closer too, moving in to nuzzle his mouth against the base of her throat where the skin was throbbing with the pounding of her pulse, his lips feeling the frantic rhythm and increasing it with his touch. "I couldn't," he murmured, his mouth moving against that delicate spot. "I'd kill myself if I tried to live up to those particular fantasies."

Cathryn shuddered with the liquid desire that flooded her and she twined her arms around his shoulders, trembling with a need that she couldn't deny even though she couldn't understand it. This was a mistake, and she knew it, but for now the primitive joy she was drowning in was more than worth the price she would have to pay when sanity returned. She allowed him to stretch her out on the bed and take her in his arms, his nakedness scorching her flesh through the flimsy fabric of her gown. Her head tilted back in invitation and Rule laughed quietly, then gave her what she wanted, his mouth coming down and taking control of hers, parting her lips for the invasion of his tongue.

She could have died content in that moment, delirious with the pleasure of his kisses, but soon the contentment was gone and kisses weren't enough. She twisted restlessly in his arms, seeking more. Again he knew; he sensed the exact moment when she was ready for increased intimacy. His hand went to the neckline of her gown and she went still with anticipation, hardly daring to breathe as she felt his lean fingers deftly slipping open its buttoned top. Her breasts began to throb, and she arched, seeking his touch. He satisfied her need immediately, his hand sliding in to cup and fondle the rich, sensitive mounds, his rough palm seeming to delight in the softness of her.

The groan that followed was his, an inarticulate sound of hunger. His hands pulled at the nightgown with rough urgency and moved it from her shoulders, baring her breasts to the moonlight. His mouth left hers and slid down her body; then his tongue snaked out to capture a taut nipple and draw it into the searing moistness of his mouth. Cathryn gave a strangled cry at the wildfire that leaped along her nerves; then she arched herself into his powerful body, her hands clenching on his shoulders.

He reached down to her ankles and slid his fingers beneath the hem of the gown, then made a reverse journey, a journey that took the hem upward. There was no protest. She was burning, aching, ready for him. She lifted her hips to aid him and he bunched the cloth about her waist, but that was as far as it got. With a hoarse, shaking sound he covered her, kneeing her thighs apart, and Cathryn went still, waiting.

"Look at me," he demanded hoarscly.

Unable to do otherwise, she obeyed him, her eyes locked with his. His face was taut with primitive hunger, releasing the answering hunger in her body that she had tried—and failed—for so many years to conquer. The probing of his maleness found her moist and yielding, and he took her easily, sliding his hands beneath her bottom to lift her into his possessive thrust. Electric pleasure shuddered through her and she gave a faint, gasping cry. This was wilder, hotter than anything she had experienced before. Her eyes began to slide shut and he shook her insistently, whispering from between his clenched teeth, "Look at me!"

Helplessly she did so, her body his as he began to move. Nothing she had known had prepared her for this, for the wildly surging pleasure that didn't wait but almost immediately swept away her control, carrying her swiftly to the peak. He held her tightly to his chest until she was limp beneath him; then he gently lowered her to the pillow. "Greedy," he said in a low, tender drawl. "I know just how you feel. It's been too long, and I can't hold back either."

Still stunned by the force of her ecstasy, she was totally overwhelmed by his passion and need. Nothing made any sense; nothing mattered but the strength of his driving body. She clung to him with the frail tenacity of a slender vine wrapped around a sturdy oak, cradling him within her silky embrace until he too surrendered to pleasure and cried out hoarsely.

Long minutes later he stirred, lifting his heavy weight onto the support of his elbows. He kissed her mouth and eyes, feathering kisses along her lids until they lifted and darkness met darkness, hers soft and vulnerable, his sharp with undisguised triumph. "That took the edge off," he growled, his voice rough and low and vibrant. "But that was a long way from the end of it."

He proved it, making love to her this time with patience and an absorbing tenderness that was even more devastating than his rampaging lust. There was no way she could resist him, no way she even wanted to try. This too had a sense of homecoming, a completion that she had lacked, a satisfaction that she had longed for and tried to deny. Tomorrow she would regret this, but for tonight she had the wild joy of being in his arms.

When the sensual storm had passed he didn't leave her, didn't roll away to fall into isolated sleep; he kept her a willing captive beneath him, his long fingers threaded into her hair on each side of her head as he began a siege of kisses. He didn't speak. His lips feathered kisses over her entire face, slowly, lightly, feeling the contours of her features with his mouth. His tongue teased at her skin, stealing tastes. She made no protest; she didn't even try to resist the erotic appeal of his exploring mouth. She let herself be absorbed in his sexual magic, in the tremors that started anew, feeling them grow stronger as she tightened her hold on him. They were both prisoners, she of his confining, muscled weight, he of the strong, silky bonds of her arms and legs.

When he freed a long, muscular arm and stretched it out to snap on the bedside lamp, she murmured an inarticulate protest at the intrusion of light. The silvery moon magic had wrapped them in a comforting aura of unreality, but the soft glow of the lamp created new shadows, illuminated things that had previously been hidden, and concealed expressions that had been brought out by the stark colorless light of the moon. One thing that couldn't be concealed was the hard male triumph written on the dark face above her. Cathryn became aware of a blooming regret as she began to admit the folly of the night's actions. There were a lot of things she didn't understand, and Rule himself was the largest enigma, a complicated man turned in on himself, but she did know that the hot sensuality between them had only made their situation more complex.

He trapped her face between his hands, his thumbs under her delicate chin as he gently forced her to look at him. "Well?" he growled, his raspy voice sinking into a rumble. He was so close that his warm breath touched her lips, and automatically she parted them in an effort to recapture his heady taste. A shudder of reaction rolled through her, eliciting an answering ripple in the strong body that pressed over her.

She swallowed, trying to gather her thoughts into some sort of coherency, not certain what he was asking, or why. She wanted to give him a controlled, bland response, but there was no control to be found, only raw, unvarnished emotions and uncertainties. Her throat was tight with anxiety as she blurted, "Is this an effort to keep your job as ranch manager?"

His shadowy eyes narrowed until only gleaming slits remained; he didn't reply. His thumbs exerted just enough pressure to raise her chin and he settled more heavily against her, fitting his mouth to hers with sensual precision. Hot tingles twitched into life beneath her skin and she joined the kiss, meeting him with teeth and tongue and lips. Why not? she reasoned fuzzily. It was too late to even try to stifle her responses to him. Rule was an exciting lover on such a basic, primary level that responding to him was as compelling a need as breathing.

At last he lifted his mouth enough to let an answer whisper between them. "This doesn't concern the ranch," he murmured, his lips so close to hers that they brushed hers lightly when he spoke. "This is between us, and nothing else even begins to matter." Suddenly his voice thickened and he said harshly, "Damn you, Cat, when you married David Ashe I was so mad I could have torn him apart. But I knew it wasn't over between us, so I let you go for then, and I waited. He died, and I waited. You've finally come home, and this time I won't let you get away. This time you won't run away to some other man."

Under the lashing fury in his voice she instantly retaliated, digging her fingers into the thick strands of his hair and holding him as he held her. "You make it sound as if there was a commitment between us!" she snapped. "There was nothing besides a stupid, hot-tempered teenager and a man who couldn't control himself. Nothing else!"

"And now?" he mocked. "What excuse do you have for now?"

"Do I need an excuse?"

"Maybe you do, for yourself. Maybe you're still not able to admit that, like it or not, we're a pair. Do you think that hiding your head in the sand will change anything?"

Cathryn shook her head blindly. He was asking for more than she was ready to give. She couldn't say that she loved Rule; she could only admit to herself that the strength of the physical attraction she felt for him was undeniable. To admit to more was to give herself up to his influence, and too many questions and uncertainties remained for her to allow that to happen.

His eyes glinted down at her; then he smiled slowly, a dangerous smile that alarmed her. "Let's see if you feel the same way in the morning," he drawled, and began moving against her in a compelling caress.

Hours later only the barest graying of the horizon signaled the approach of dawn, the room darker than ever because clouds had moved in to cover the moon. A light rain began to spatter against the window with a metallic rhythm. Cathryn stirred in the warm cocoon created by the sheet and Rule's radiant body heat, aware that he had lifted his head and was listening to the rain. With a sigh he dropped his head back onto the pillow.

"It's morning," he muttered, his dark voice flowing over her. The arm beneath her head tensed and he became a darker shadow against the blackness of the room, leaning over her, drawing her beneath him. His hips pressed against hers, his desire for her obviously aroused, and his powerful legs parted hers to allow the intimate contact.

Her breath caught at this renewed evidence of his virility. "Again?" she whispered into the warm hollow of his throat. They had gotten very little sleep during the night and her body ached from the demands he had made on her, though he had been nothing but tender. Surprisingly, she was more relaxed and physically content than she had thought possible. During the long hours of the night it had been impossible to keep even a mental distance. They had been as one, moved together as one, explored and stroked and experimented with the other's responses, until now she knew his body as well as she knew her own. She gasped helplessly as he took her, and his low chuckle fanned the hair at her temple.

"Yes," he rasped, the words so low she could barely hear them. "Again."

Afterward she fell into a heavy sleep, undisturbed by his departure from the bed. He bent over her to tuck the sheet about her bare shoulders; then he smoothed the tangle of dark red hair away from her face. She didn't stir. He pulled on his jeans, then gathered the rest of his clothing and left to return to his own room to shower and dress for a day of wet, muddy work.

Cathryn slept on, and though Lorna was curious as the hours wore away, she didn't wake Cathryn. At almost noon Monica came down and disappeared without a word, taking the station wagon and leaving in a spray of water. Ricky sulked for a while, then brightened when one of the hands got into the pickup. Ricky dashed across the muddy yard and climbed into the cab of the truck with him. It didn't matter to her where she went.

The steady rain continued, a welcome rain, but one that was still a mess to work in. Rule returned for a late lunch, his weariness evident only in the tautness of the skin over his cheekbones. Lorna saw and understood the faint smile of satisfaction that curved his hard mouth when she casually mentioned that Cathryn was still asleep. He cast a speculative look at the ceiling, then rejected temptation and ate his lunch before returning to his chores.

The rain had the effect of a sedative on Cathryn, soothing her into long, deep sleep. She woke feeling marvelously rested, stretching lazily and becoming aware of the soreness of her body. She lay drowsily for a moment, remembering when Rule had turned her over on her stomach during the night and straddled her legs, firmly massaging her thighs and buttocks, whispering to her teasingly that if she had let him do that from the beginning, she wouldn't have gotten nearly so sore.

Other remembrances drifted over her and a tiny smile of contentment touched her lips as she felt the caress of the sheets on her bare body. Her sensations were heightened, her skin more than usually sensitive. She was still smiling as she sat up cautiously; then her eyes fell on the bedside clock and the smile faded abruptly. Two-thirty? But her flight back to Chicago was at three!

She scrambled out of bed, ignoring the protests of her muscles. Her feet tangled in the nightgown that Rule had finally tossed aside during the night and she kicked it impatiently out of the way. After jerking on her terry robe and tying it about her, she left her room and ran down the stairs, erupting into the kitchen so swiftly that Lorna dropped the spoon she was using. "Lorna! Where's Rule?"

Lorna took a deep breath and retrieved her spoon from the bowl of cake batter. "There's no telling. He could be anywhere."

"But my flight is in half an hour!"

"No way you can make it now," said Lorna calmly. "The best thing you can do is to call the airline and see if you can get on a later flight."

That was so sensible, and her predicament was so unalterable, that Cathryn sighed and relaxed. "Why didn't I think of that instead of running wild?" she asked ruefully, then went to the study to carry out Lorna's suggestion.

The study had once been her father's domain, but Rule had long since taken it over, to the extent that his masculine scent seemed to linger in the room. The papers on the desk were in his handwriting; the letters were addressed to him. Cathryn sat down in the leather chair and had the uneasy sensation of sitting on his lap. She pushed the thought away and reached for the phone.

It was as she had expected. The later flight that day was booked, but there was plenty of space on the red-eye flight. Knowing that she had no choice, she booked a reservation and resigned herself to a sleepless night. At least sleeping as late as she had would help, she thought; then she remembered why she had slept so late and her mouth tightened.

She couldn't place all the blame on Rule. She had responded to him so strongly that she could deny it neither to herself nor to him. She had never been a woman inclined to casual affairs, which was one reason why she had been so upset years ago when he had first made love to her, one reason why she had avoided him for so long. Knowing David, loving him and being his wife, being with him as he slipped into death had given her maturity and inner strength. She had thought that she would be able to keep Rule at a distance now, but last night had proven to her once and for all that she had no resistance to him. If she stayed she would be in his bed—or he in hers—whenever he had the urge. It was a clear-cut situation: If she wanted to maintain her moral standards, she would have to stay away from Rule Jackson. Returning to Chicago was her only option, regardless of her halfhearted promise to stay.

Her stomach was growling hungrily, but she disregarded it in her haste to leave the ranch. She went upstairs to shower, then put on full battle makeup and subdued her dark red hair by pulling it back with a tortoiseshell clasp. She dressed in sensible dark brown linen slacks and a white cotton blouse, slipped her feet into comfortable cork-soled shoes, and swiftly packed her suitcase and tote bag. Taking them downstairs, she entered the kitchen and told Lorna, "I managed to get on the red-eye flight. Now I have to find Rule and talk him into flying me to Houston.''

"If you can't find him," said Lorna placidly, "maybe Lewis can take you. He has a pilot's license, too."

That was the most welcome news Cathryn had heard all day. She donned a too-large slicker and jammed the matching yellow cap over her head, taking them from the assortment that hung in the small utility room just off the kitchen. The rain wasn't heavy, but it was steady, and the ground seemed like one big puddle as she picked her way down to the stables. The ranch hand she found there wasn't full of good news. A group of cattle had broken through the fencing in the far western pasture, and both Rule and Lewis Stovall were there helping to round up the cattle and repair the fencing, which looked like a long job. Cathryn sighed; she wanted to leave now. Specifically, she wanted to leave before she had to face Rule again. He didn't want her to go, and she doubted her ability to resist him if he got the opportunity to argue with her face to face. There was also the possibility that Rule would flatly refuse to take her to Houston. Lewis Stovall might help her, unless Rule ordered him not to, so she wanted to ask him when Rule wasn't around. Now it seemed that she wouldn't have the chance.

She didn't relish the thought of a long drive, but it seemed her only alternative now. She looked at the ranch hand. "I have to get to Houston," she said firmly. "Can you drive me?"

The man looked startled, and he pushed his hat back on his head while he thought. "I'd be glad to," he finally said, "but there's no way right now. Mrs. Donahue is gone in the wagon, and Rule has the keys to his pickup in his pocket. He doesn't leave them in the ignition."

Cathryn knew he was referring to the dark blue pickup that she had noticed before, and she hadn't even considered using it. Her heart sank at the news that Monica had taken the station wagon. "What about the other truck?" she prodded. It was aging and not very comfortable, but it was transportation.

The man shook his head. "Rule sent Foster into town to pick up more fencing. We'll have to wait until he gets back and gets the fencing unloaded."

Cathryn nodded her understanding and left the man to his work, but she wanted to scream in frustration as she made her way back to the house. By the time Monica returned it would probably be too late to make the drive, and the same thing went for the pickup. Not only that, by then Rule would probably be back.

Her last supposition was right on the money. Several hours later, as the last light was falling, helped by the clouds and light rain that lingered on, Rule came in the back door. Cathryn was sitting at the kitchen table with Lorna, feeling safer in company, and she watched as he removed his slicker and hung it up, then brushed the excess water from his dripping hat. His movements as he leaned down to remove his muddy boots were slow with fatigue. An odd pang hit her as she realized that he hadn't had the benefit of sleeping late. For the past two nights he had managed to get very little sleep and the strain was telling on him.

"Give me half an hour," he muttered to Lorna as he passed her in his stockinged feet. He cast a searing look at Cathryn, all the more effective for the fatigue that lined his face. "Come with me," he ordered shortly.

Bracing herself, Cathryn got to her feet and followed him. As they passed her luggage where it sat in the hallway, Rule leaned down and scooped it up, taking it with him on his way up the stairs. Behind him Cathryn said softly, "You're wasting your time. The bags go right back down."

He didn't answer, merely opened the door to her bedroom and tossed the bags inside with fine disregard for their safety. Then he wrapped his long fingers around her delicate wrist and pulled her after him down the hallway to his room. Even when he was tired she was no match for his strength, so she didn't waste any energy in trying to jerk away. He opened the door and ushered her into his bedroom, which was in almost total darkness because the last of the feeble daylight had gone. Without turning on the light he closed the door and reached for her, folding her against him and kissing her with an angry hunger that belied his obvious weariness.

Cathryn put her arms around his waist and kissed him in return, almost weeping with the knowledge that she didn't dare stay with him. Her senses were swamped by him, by the taste of his mouth, the feel of his hard body against her, the damp smell of his skin and hair and clothing. He released her and snapped on the overhead light, moving away as he spoke.

"I'm not taking you to Houston," he said grimly.

"Of course not. You're too tired," she said with outward calm. "But Lewis can—"

"No, Lewis can't. No one will take you to Houston if they want to keep working on the Bar D," he snapped. "I made that clear to all of them. Damn it, Cat, that very first day, when I picked you up, you told me you'd stay!" He began to unbutton his shirt, shrugging it away from his powerful shoulders and tossing it aside.

Cathryn sat down on the bed and clasped her fingers tightly together as she fought for control. At last she said, "I only said maybe I'd stay. And don't bother with threatening me or any of the hands, because you know I can leave tomorrow, if not tonight."

He nodded his head. "Maybe, if Monica comes back tonight. But she's afraid to drive at night, and since she's not here by now I don't expect her back until tomorrow. Then you'll have to get to the station wagon before I put it out of commission."

Control was forgotten and she leaped to her feet, her eyes narrowing with temper. "I won't be kept here like a prisoner!" she shouted.

"I don't want it that way either!" he yelled back, rounding on her. "But I told you that I won't let you run away from me again, and I meant it. Hell, woman, didn't last night tell you anything?"

"It told me it's been a while since you had a woman!" she flared.

"Don't kid yourself!"

Silence fell and Cathryn admitted uneasily that he could have a woman whenever he wanted one—a particularly unpalatable thought. When she said nothing else he unfastened his belt and jeans and pushed them down, stripping off his socks in the same movement and stepping away from the pile of clothing, as unconcerned about his nudity as if she hadn't been in the room. But then, weren't they as familiar with each other as a man and woman could be? Cathryn eyed the tall, vital body with secret hunger, then turned her gaze away before he could read the expression in her eyes.

He gathered up clean clothing and tossed it into her arms. She caught it automatically, holding his clothes to her. After a few moments he muttered, "Give it a chance, Cat. Stay here. Call your boss tomorrow and tell him that you quit."

"I can't do that," she said quietly.

He erupted again. "Damn it, why not? What's stopping you?"

"You are."

He closed his eyes and she could have sworn that he was snarling under his breath. An unwanted smile tried to break over her lips, but she subdued it. How had Wanda described him? Still dangerous but controlled? It was a safe bet that no one knew as well as she did just how volcanic Rule really was. Finally he opened his eyes and glared at her, the dark irises gleaming with angry frustration. "Ricky got to you. You believe her."

"No!" she burst out, unable to control her reaction. He didn't understand and she couldn't tell him, couldn't say that she was afraid to trust him on such an intimate level. He was asking for more than just sex . . . and she didn't feel capable of dealing with either scenario. She was afraid of him, afraid of how he could hurt her if she let her guard down. Rule could destroy her, because he could get closer to her than anyone else ever had or would.

"Then *what?*" he roared. "Tell me! Tell me what I have to do to get you to stay here! You've put it all on my shoulders, so tell me exactly what you want me to do."

Cathryn considered him, standing there furious and naked and so magnetically masculine that she wanted to drop the clothing that she held to her breast and run to him, wrap her arms around him and bury her face in the curly dark hair that decorated his muscular chest. How much she wanted to stay! This was her home, and she wanted to be here. Yet she couldn't handle Rule...unless she had his cooperation. An idea glimmered, and she didn't stop to consider it. She simply blurted out, "No sex."

He looked staggered, as if she had suggested that he had to give up breathing. Then he swore aloud, scowling at her. "Do you really think that's possible?"

"It will have to be," she assured him. "At least until I decide if...if..."

"If?" he prodded.

"If I can stay permanently," she finished, thinking swiftly that there had to be some way she could maneuver him into promising to behave himself. "I'm not looking for an affair. I'm not a casual woman and I never have been."

"We can't be 'just friends,'" he said savagely. "I want you, and I've never been good at self-denial. It was bad enough when you were married, but now it'll be damned near impossible. When are you going to face up to what the real situation is?"

Cathryn ignored him, determined to press her point. She sensed that he was off-balance, and it was such an unusual circumstance that she was loath to let the opportunity pass. "I'm not asking for a vow of celibacy from you," she retorted. "Only that you leave *me* alone until I've decided." Even as she said the words she felt furious at the mere thought that he would go to another woman. Just let him dare!

His jaw was like a chunk of granite. "And if you decide to stay?"

Her dark eyes went wide as she realized what such a decision would mean. If she stayed she would be Rule

Jackson's woman. She wouldn't be able to hold him off forever with the shield that she was "trying to decide." He would want a definite answer before long, and now she fully understood that what she had conceived as a delaying tactic had become a trap. She could stay, or she could go, but if she stayed she would be his. She looked at him, standing there as naked and powerful as some ancient god, and pain twisted her insides. Could she really leave him?

She lifted her chin and answered him evenly, using all her woman's courage in the effort. "If I stay, then I accept your terms."

He didn't relax. "I want you to call tomorrow and quit your job."

"But if I decide to leave—"

"You don't need a job. This ranch can support you."

"I don't want to bleed the ranch."

"Damn it, Cat, I said I'll support you!" he snarled. "Just leave it alone for now. Will you quit the job or not?"

"Be reasonable—" she began to plead, knowing that it was a hopeless request. He cut her short with a slashing movement of his hand.

"Quit . . . the . . . job," he ordered from between clenched teeth. "That's the deal. You'll stay if I keep my hands to myself. All right, I'll go along with that if you'll quit your job. We both have to give in."

She saw his muscles quiver and knew that if she said no, his control would be gone. Rule had compromised his position and he would go no further. Either she quit her job or he would keep her on the ranch by any means at his disposal. It seemed to her that she could be either a willing prisoner or an unwilling one, but she gave in on the job in order to keep her advantage in other areas. "All right. I'll quit the job." Even as she promised, she felt lost, as if she had severed her last tie to Chicago and her life with David, as if she had turned her back on his memory.

He sighed and ran his hand roughly through his dark hair. "Lorna's holding dinner," he muttered, taking his clothes from her. "I'll take a fast shower and be right down."

As he opened the door Cathryn leaped across the room and slammed it shut, jerking it out of his hand. He gave her a startled look, and she hissed at him, "You're naked!"

He gave her a tired half smile. "I know. I usually shower this way."

"But someone will see you!"

"Honey, Monica isn't here, Lorna is downstairs, and Ricky hasn't come in from the stables yet. You're the only one who can see me, and I don't have anything to hide from you, do I?" The smile changed from tired to mocking as he opened the door again and sauntered down the hall. Cathryn followed him, so exasperated that she wanted to punch him, but she wasn't that foolish.

After dinner Rule promptly went to bed and Cathryn found herself alone with Ricky, a far from comfortable companion. First she turned on the television and flipped from one channel to the next; then she turned the set off and flopped down on the couch. Cathryn did her best to continue reading the article she had started, but she was completely unbalanced when Ricky said nastily, "Shouldn't you go tuck him in?"

Cathryn jumped, then looked away as she felt her face heat up. "Who?" she managed to say, but her voice wasn't quite steady.

Ricky smiled and stretched her legs, crossing them at the ankle. "Who?" she mimicked sweetly. "It's hard to believe you're really that dumb. Do you think I don't know where he slept last night? But you've got to give Rule credit. When he wants something, he goes after it. He wants this ranch and he's using you to get it, but he's so great in bed that you can't see beyond that, can you?"

"I see a lot of things, including your jealousy," Cathryn snapped. Anger had leaped to life in her, and she wasn't about to deny that Rule had made love to her, if that was what Ricky was trying to provoke her into saying.

Ricky laughed. "That's right, keep your head in the clouds. You haven't been able to think straight since he gave you your first taste of sex when you were seventeen. Did you think I didn't know? I rode up in time to see him help you put your clothes back on. You've been running scared since then; but now you're old enough that you're not scared, and you've been remembering, haven't you? Lord, Cathryn, he's got a reputation that puts those stud horses of his to shame. Doesn't it bother you to be just one on a long list?"

Eyeing her narrowly, Cathryn said, "I can't decide if you hate him or if you're jealous because he doesn't pay any attention to you."

To Cathryn's surprise, color flooded hotly into Ricky's cheeks, and this time it was the other woman who looked away. After a moment Ricky said thickly, "Don't believe me, I don't care. Let him use you the way he's used Mother all these years. Just remember, nothing and no one is as important to him as this ranch, and he'll do whatever he has to do to keep it. Ask him," she dared, jeering. "See if you can get him to talk about it. Ask him what Vietnam did to him and why he holds on to the ranch with a death grip. Ask him about the nightmares, why he spends some nights just walking around the ranch.''

Cathryn was stunned. She hadn't thought that he was still troubled by memories of the war. Ricky laughed again, regaining her composure. ''You don't know him at all! You've been away for years. You don't know anything about what went on here while you were gone. Be a fool. It doesn't matter to me!'' She got up and left the room, and Cathryn heard her running up the stairs.

She sat there, disturbed by the things Ricky had said. She had thought them herself, in part, wondering what motivated Rule. She thought wearily that she would probably go crazy wondering what went on in Rule's mind. Did he want her for herself or because of the ranch? And even if she asked him straight out, could she believe what he told her? She could only make up her mind for herself, using her instincts. At least she had bought time for herself, time free of the sensual pressure he could so easily bring to bear. All she had to do was not let Ricky goad her into some reckless action.

Cathryn woke before dawn and lay awake, unable to sleep again, and soon rosy fingers began piercing through the purple patches of cloud that still remained from the day before. The house began to resound with the familiar, comforting sounds of Lorna preparing breakfast, and soon she heard Rule's heart-stopping tread as he walked past her door and went down the stairs. She threw the sheet back and hurriedly dressed in jeans and an emerald green knit pullover shirt, then ran barefoot down the stairs. For reasons that she didn't want to examine too closely, she needed to see Rule before he left the house for the day, just to see him . . . to make certain that he didn't look as tired as he had the day before.

He was sprawled at the kitchen table with a steaming cup of coffee before him when she entered, and both he and Lorna looked up in surprise. "I thought I'd have an early breakfast," she said serenely, moving to set herself a place at the table and pour a cup of coffee.

After that initial look of surprise, Lorna returned placidly to her cooking. "Eggs or waffles?" she asked.

"One egg, scrambled," said Cathryn as she checked the big homemade biscuits in the oven. They were a perfect golden brown and she took them out, transferring them deftly to a napkin-lined straw basket and setting the fragrant mount in front of Rule. While Lorna was finishing the scrambled eggs, Cathryn also transferred the plate of bacon and sausages to the table and slipped into a chair beside Rule, taking advantage of Lorna's turned back to lean over and plant a quick kiss under his ear. She couldn't have said why she did that, either, but the effect was pleasing. Rule shuddered wildly and Cathryn grinned, absurdly pleased that he was so ticklish in that particular spot. It made him seem so much more vulnerable . . . and, as he had said, he didn't have anything to hide from her.

The fuming dark glance he turned on her promised retribution, but the look lingered on her smiling face and slowly the threat faded from his expression.

Lorna set their plates before them and took her own place across the table. Conversation was nonexistent for a few minutes as they went through their own ritual of salting and peppering and arranging their food exactly as they preferred. Then Lorna asked a question about the sale, and though Rule's replies were characteristically brief, Cathryn managed to learn that he had scheduled a horse sale in three weeks and that it was turning out to be a large event. Over the years he had developed a solid reputation as a horsebreeder and more people were coming to the sale than he had originally anticipated. Lorna was beaming with pride—a pride that Rule didn't allow himself to show.

"Is there anything I can do to help?" asked Cathryn. "Groom the horses, clean out the stables, whatever?"

"Have you made that phone call yet?" Rule growled.

"No. The switchboard doesn't open until nine." She smiled at him with mock sweetness, intent on fully enjoying her opportunity to have him under control.

Lorna looked confused, and Cathryn explained, "I'm quitting my job and staying here, at least for the time being. I haven't made a permanent decision yet." She tacked that last on for Rule's benefit, just in case he was thinking he had already won the war.

"My, that'll be nice, having you in the house for good," said Lorna.

After breakfast Cathryn realized that Rule hadn't answered her question about helping and she followed him outside, stepping on his heels like a determined little bulldog and almost tripping him. He turned on her and planted his fists on his hips, every inch the dominating male. "Well?" he barked.

"Is there anything I can do to help?" she repeated patiently, planting her own fists on her hips in duplication of his stance and tilting her jaw at him.

For a moment he looked as if he were going to explode with frustration; then the iron control she usually saw on his face returned and he even gave her a crooked smile. "Yes, there is. After you make that phone call, take the truck into town and pick up our order of feed supplements. And we'll need more fencing. Foster didn't get enough yesterday." He told her how much fencing to get and dug into his pocket for the keys to his pickup.

As she took the keys, he cupped her chin in his hand and turned her face up to his. "I'm relying on you to be here when I get back," he said, a hint of warning in his voice.

Irritated that he didn't trust her, Cathryn glared at him. "I know. I will be," she replied stiffly. "I'm not a liar."

He nodded and released her chin. Without another word he walked away, and she watched his tall form for a minute before she returned to the house, vaguely irritated that he hadn't even kissed her. That was what she had wanted; it was silly now to be disappointed that he was following her orders. Taking that as an indication of how deeply she had already fallen under his spell, she firmly pushed aside her disappointment.

Promptly at nine she sat down before the phone and chewed on her lips, uncertain in the face of the step she was taking. In a way Rule was asking her to choose between himself and David—an unfair choice, as David was dead. And he had been a very special person. Cathryn knew that a part of her devotion would always be David's . . . but he was gone, and Rule was very much alive. He was asking her to leave the home that she had shared with her husband, to leave behind everything. Yet she had promised, and if she broke that promise she would have to leave the ranch today, before Rule returned. She couldn't do that. Not now, not after that night spent in his arms. She had to know for certain how she felt—and how he felt—or she would regret it for the rest of her life. Picking up the receiver, she dialed.

Ten minutes later she was unemployed. Now that she had done it she was almost in a panic. It wasn't money; she really had no money worries. While talking to her supervisor she had suddenly had the thought that only people in love made such sacrifices. She didn't want to love Rule Jackson, didn't want to let herself get that vulnerable until she was certain in her own mind that she could trust him. She didn't think that Rule had ever been involved with Monica, despite Ricky's tales to the contrary. There was just no sense of intimacy between Rule and Monica, nothing in their behavior that would indicate even a *past* relationship. That was obviously pure mischief making on Ricky's part, something that she excelled in.

No, what Cathryn wasn't certain about was Rule's motive for pursuing her. She wanted desperately to believe that he wanted her simply for herself, but the fact remained that he was extremely possessive of the ranch. He had taken it over, made it his, and she had no doubt that he would fight with whatever weapons he had to in order to keep the ranch. He controlled the ranch, but she legally owned it, and it might be constantly on his mind that she could sell it at any time and his control would be ended. He had denied being concerned with the ranch at all, but the doubt remained in her mind.

If he was so interested in her, why hadn't he made an effort to contact her at some point since David's death? It hadn't been until she came for a visit, indicating a renewed interest in the ranch, that he had suddenly become so smitten with her.

As she drove his truck into town the issue nagged at her. Her entire decision hinged on that one matter. If she trusted him, if she believed that he wanted her as a man wanted a woman, with no other considerations involved, then she would stay with him in whatever capacity he wanted. On the other hand, she refused to let him manipulate her with sex. He was an extremely dominating, virile man. Sex was one of the weapons he could use against her, clouding her senses with the sensual need he aroused simply by touching her. She knew of no way she could reach her decision except by simply being with him, hoping to learn enough about him despite his iron control to be able to say that she trusted him.

Franklin's Feed Store was the only one in town, so Cathryn had no doubt that she was in the right place as she backed up to the loading dock. She had gone to school with Alva Franklin, the owner's daughter, and she grinned as she remembered the day Alva had pushed her older sister Regina into a mud puddle. Alva had been a little devil. She was still smiling as she went up the back steps into the musty atmosphere of the building.

She didn't recognize the man who came over to take her order, but it had been eight years since she had spent any time at all on the ranch, and he was obviously one of the people who had moved into the region since then.

However, the man eyed her doubtfully when she told him what she wanted. "The Bar D order?" he asked warily. "I don't believe I know you, ma'am. What did you say your name is?"

Cathryn stifled a laugh. "My name is Cathryn Donahue...Ashe," she added as an afterthought, guilt-stricken as she realized that she had almost forgotten her married name. It seemed as if David were being pushed away as if he had never existed, and she didn't want that to happen. She hadn't even protested when Rule had introduced her to Lewis Stovall by her maiden name, letting herself slip back into the identity of

Cathryn Donahue and under the domination of her ranch manager. But not now, she thought grimly.

She finished her explanation, but the man still stood uncertainly.

"I own the Bar D."

"Mr. Jackson—" began the man.

"Is my ranch manager," she finished smoothly for him. "I understand that you don't recognize me, and I'm grateful that you're so careful with the orders. However, Mr. Franklin knows me, if you want to verify my identity with him."

He did, and went in search of the store owner. Cathryn waited patiently, not at all put out by his caution. It would be chaos if just anyone was allowed to sign a load slip and have a load of feed charged to any ranch at random. It was only a few minutes before the man returned with Ormond Franklin close behind him. Mr. Franklin peered at her through his glasses; then his gaze settled on her hair and he said, "Why, hello, Cathryn. I heard you were back in town." He nodded to his employee. "Go ahead and load the order, Todd."

"It's good to see you again, Mr. Franklin," said Cathryn pleasantly. "I arrived on Saturday. I had only intended to stay for the holiday, but now it looks as though I'll be here for a longer time."

He smiled so widely that she wondered why her news should be so pleasing. "Well, now, that's good news. Glad to hear that you're taking the ranch over. Never did like that Rule Jackson. Got rid of him, did you? Fine, fine. He's nothing but trouble. I've always thought your pa made a bad mistake in taking on trouble the way he did with Jackson. He was wild enough before he went to Vietnam, but after he came back he was pure crazy."

Cathryn could feel her mouth fall open as she stared at him, stunned. He had made so many fantastic assumptions that she didn't know where to start. But why should Mr. Franklin hold such a grudge against Rule? Then memory stirred and she had a clear vision of Regina Franklin's pretty, sulky face, remembered also that the girl had had a reputation for chasing men she would have done better to avoid. One of those men had been Rule Jackson, and, being the man he was, he had made no effort to hide it.

She made an effort to be reasonable. Mindful of Mr. Franklin's grudge against Rule—even if his daughter had been equally responsible—she said mildly, "I couldn't begin to run the ranch by myself, Mr. Franklin. Rule has done a fantastic job; the ranch looks better now than it did even when Dad was alive. I have no reason to fire him."

"No reason?" he asked incredulously, his brows gathering over the bridge of his glasses. "His morals are reason enough for a lot of decent people around here. There's a lot of people who haven't forgotten the way he acted when he came back from overseas. Why, in your own house you've got to watch him like a hawk or that stepsister of yours—"

"Mr. Franklin, I can understand why you dislike Rule, given the circumstances," interrupted Cathryn, suddenly and fiercely angry at his persistent attack on Rule and at the way he had linked Rule with Ricky. She refused to listen to any more of that. She went straight to the heart of the matter with her counterattack. "But Rule and your daughter were both very young and confused, and that was all a long time ago. Rule was in no way solely responsible for that scandal."

Mr. Franklin turned a dusky red with fury, and he spat from between clenched teeth, "Not responsible? How can you stand there and say that? He forced himself on my girl, then refused to stand by her. Why, she couldn't hold her head up in this town. She had to leave, and he walks around as if he never did anything wrong in his life!"

She hesitated, wondering if he had twisted his own guilt around to rest on Rule because he couldn't face the possibility that his own rigidity had been responsible for driving his daughter away. She didn't want to hurt him, but there was one thing she couldn't let pass, and she said coldly, "Rule Jackson has never forced a woman in his life. He's never had to. I was young, but I can remember the way girls chased him from the time he could even think of growing a beard. After he got out of the army it was even worse. You can think what you like, but I'd advise you not to say things like that out loud unless you want a charge of slander brought against you!"

Their raised voices had gathered the attention of everyone in the feed store, but that didn't stop Mr. Franklin. His gray hair almost stood on end as he shouted, "If that's the way you feel, Miss Donahue, then I suggest you buy your feed from someone else! Your daddy would never have said something like that to me!"

"The name is Mrs. Ashe, and I think my dad would be proud of me! He believed in Rule when no one else did, and it's a good thing he did, because the ranch would have gone under years ago without Rule Jackson!" She was boiling now, and she stomped down the steps to where Todd was waiting, bug-eyed, with the ticket for her signature. She scribbled her name across the bottom of it and crawled under the steering wheel of the pickup. Her foot was heavy with temper and the vehicle shot away from the loading dock, bucking under the demand she was making of it.

Shaking with temper, Cathryn drove only a block and pulled over to calm herself. Fencing . . . she couldn't forget the fencing, she reminded herself, drawing in a deep breath. Her hands were trembling violently and her heart was pounding, her body wet with perspiration. She felt as if she had been in a physical free-for-all rather than an argument. Catching a glimpse of her hair in the rearview mirror she startled herself by giving a shaky giggle. Did the color of one's hair really have anything to do with temper?

She regretted the scene with Franklin now. It would have been bad enough if there hadn't been any witnesses, but with so many people standing around the argument would be repeated verbatim all over town before dark. But she couldn't let anyone talk about Rule like that!

"God, I'm really getting a bad case of it," she moaned to herself. Rule needed protection about as much as a prowling panther did, but she had leaped to his defense as if he were nothing more than a helpless cub. It was just one more measure of the hold he had on her. He had always seemed larger than life, outsized in both his reputation and his domination of her. As a child she had been frightened and awed by him; as a teenager she had bitterly, wildly resented his authority; but now, as a woman, she was so drawn to his rampant masculinity that she felt as if she were battling for her own existence.

After several minutes she made a U-turn and drove down the street to the building supply store. She had no trouble there. Not only had she known everyone employed there all of her life, but Rule had called in an addition to the order he had given her. When everything was loaded the bed of the pickup was riding low on the springs, so she drove carefully back to the ranch, mindful of the heavy load she was hauling.

It was a beautiful day, with everything fresh and sweet and green after the needed rain of the day before, and Cathryn took her time, trying to calm herself completely before she reached the ranch. She didn't quite succeed. Rule was waiting in the yard for her when she drove up, and she remembered that he hadn't fully trusted her to return. As she thought of the battle she had fought on his behalf, resentment welled up in her and her temper surged back in full force. She got out of the truck, slammed the door and yelled at him, "I told you I'd be back!"

He stalked up to her and took her arm, hauling her with him to the house. "I need those supplies right away," he gritted. "That's why I'm here. Now rein in that temper of yours before I put you over my knee right here in front of the men."

Right then she needed nothing more than a chance to work off the energy her temper had raised, and she welcomed the prospect of a fight. "Any time you feel ready, big man," she challenged between her teeth. "After what I've been through this morning, I could take on five of you!"

He pulled her up the steps and she stumbled, only to be rescued by his hard grip on her arm. "Ouch!" she snapped. "You're jerking my arm out of its socket!"

He began swearing softly under his breath as he opened the kitchen door and ushered her inside. Lorna looked up from her permanent station in front of the window, a flicker of amusement in her serene eyes as she continued without pause in her preparation of a beef casserole that Rule was fond of.

Rule sat Cathryn forcibly in one of the chairs, but she bounded out of it like a rubber ball, her fists clenched. With one big hand on her chest he returned her to the chair and held her there. "What in the *hell* is wrong with you?" he growled softly in the almost crooning tone he used when he was about to lose his own temper.

He would hear about it anyway, so Cathryn thrust her chin out at him belligerently and told him herself. "I got in an argument! We have to buy our feed somewhere else now."

His hand dropped away from her chest and he stared at her in disbelief. "Do you mean," he whispered, "that I've managed to do business with Ormond Franklin all these years without having a flare-up, and in one trip you've wrecked all of that?"

Her lip curled, but she didn't tell him the details of the argument. "So we'll go to Wisdom to buy our feed," she said, naming the nearest town.

"That's twenty miles farther, an additional forty miles round trip. Damn it, Cat!"

"Then we'll drive that extra forty miles!" she shouted. "Let me remind you that this is still my ranch, Rule Jackson, and after what Mr. Franklin said I wouldn't buy another sack of feed from him even if the next feed store was a hundred miles away! Is that clear?"

Pure fire sparked from his dark eyes and he reached for her, stopping just before he actually touched her. Then he whirled on his heel and stalked out of the house, his long legs eating up the distance at such a pace that she would have had to run to keep up with him.

After getting out of the chair, Cathryn went to the window and watched him climb into the truck, then head it across the pastures to the far side of the ranch where the fencing was needed. She said aloud, "The ground is wet after the rain yesterday. I hope he doesn't get stuck in the mud."

"If he does, there are enough hands to get him out," said Lorna. She chuckled quietly. "You know exactly how to get a rise out of him, don't you? There's been more life in his face in the few days you've been here than in all the years I've known him."

"People need to stand up to him more often," Cathryn muttered. "He's run roughshod over me since I was a child, but I won't stand for it now."

"He's going to have a hard time letting anyone else have a say in running the ranch," Lorna advised. "It's all been on his shoulders for so long now that he won't know how to let someone share the responsibility with him."

"Then he's going to have to learn," said Cathryn stubbornly, her eyes still on the far dot of the pickup as it drew out of sight. Suddenly it went into a dip and disappeared from view, and she turned away from the window.

"Do you know what you two remind me of?" Lorna asked suddenly, laughing again.

"Do I want to know?" Cathryn responded wryly.

"I don't think it'll come as any great surprise. You remind me of a sleek little cat in heat, and he's the tomcat circling around you, knowing he's going to have the fight of his life if he tries to get what he wants."

Cathryn burst into laughter at the image and admitted that they did fight like two snarling, spitting cats. "You do have a way with words," she choked, and the two women stood in the kitchen laughing like maniacs at what was, after all, a very apt observation.

To Cathryn's disappointment, Rule didn't return for lunch. Lorna told her that she had already packed a basket of sandwiches and coffee and sent it out to the men, and as Ricky was also with the men, Cathryn ate a silent lunch with Monica, who had returned some time during the morning while Cathryn had been in town. The two women had no common interests. Monica was absorbed in her own thoughts and didn't even ask where Ricky was, though perhaps she already knew.

They had finished lunch when Monica leaned back and lit a cigarette, a sure sign that she was nervous, as she seldom smoked. Cathryn looked at her and Monica said abruptly, flatly, "I'm thinking of leaving."

At first Cathryn was surprised, but when she thought about it she was more surprised that Monica had stayed as long as she had. Ranch life had never suited the older woman. "Why now?" she asked. "And where would you go?"

Monica shrugged. "I'm not really certain. It doesn't matter, so long as it's a city and I never have to smell horses and cows again. It's no secret that I've never liked living on a ranch. As for the timing, why not? You're here now, and it's your ranch, after all, not mine. I stayed on after Ward died because you were a minor, but that's not true anymore. I just let time drift, and now I'm tired of all this."

"Have you told Ricky yet?"

Monica gave her a sharp glance from her slanted cat eyes. "We're not a package deal. Ricky's a grown woman; she can do what she wants."

Cathryn didn't reply right away. At last she murmured, "I haven't made a definite decision about staying."

"That doesn't matter," Monica replied coolly. "The ranch is your responsibility now, not mine. You can do what you want, and I'll do the same. Let's not pretend that we've ever been close. The only thing we've ever had in common was your father, and he's been dead for twelve years. It's time I started to live my life for myself."

Cathryn realized that Monica's presence hadn't been required for years anyway, not since Rule had taken over. Even if she herself didn't stay, the ranch would continue to run as always. If Monica left it wouldn't affect her own situation at all; she still had to make the decision whether to stay or go. The thought of selling the ranch slipped into her mind but was quickly pushed away. This was her home and she never wanted to sell it. She might not feel that she could live here, but it would be impossible for her to turn her back on her heritage.

"You know you're welcome to stay here forever," she told Monica quietly, bringing her thoughts back to the subject at hand.

"Thanks, but it's time I dusted off my dancing shoes and make the most of the time I have left. I've mourned Ward for long enough," she said in an odd tone, looking down at her hands. "I felt closer to him here, so I stayed even when there was no reason to stay. I've never been suited to this kind of life, and we both know it. I haven't seriously looked for an apartment, or even decided what city I'll go to, but I think within a few months I'll have it all settled."

Hesitantly, not certain if Monica would like the idea, Cathryn offered, "There's my apartment in Chicago. The lease is paid up through the end of next year. If I stay here it's available, if you think you'd like Chicago."

Monica smiled wryly. "I was thinking more along the lines of New Orleans, but…Chicago. I'll have to think about that."

"There's no hurry. It isn't going anywhere," said Cathryn.

Having said what was on her mind Monica wasn't inclined to linger and chat; she stubbed out her half-smoked cigarette and excused herself, leaving Cathryn dawdling over her iced tea.

Later that afternoon, after hours of trying to pass the time by cleaning the downstairs—a process that didn't proceed as quickly as it should have because she kept going to the window to see if Rule had returned—Cathryn at last heard the pickup and ran to the window again to see him pulling up beside the supply shed. Her heart was beating so swiftly that she could feel her skin heating, and for a moment she forced herself to take slow, deep breaths before she walked down to where he was. She had forgotten the quarrel they'd had that morning. She only knew that he had been gone for hours and that she was hungry for the sight of him, a secret hunger that had to be fed immediately.

She was still out of earshot of the shed when she stopped abruptly, paling as she watched the two figures who had been unloading the remainder of the fencing. Ricky was helping Rule, and though Cathryn couldn't hear what they were saying, she could see

Ricky's face, see how it glowed as the young woman laughed up at him. Suddenly Ricky dropped the box of tools she was carrying and hugged him, her pretty face turned up to him as she laughed unrestrainedly. She rose on tiptoe and quickly kissed him, then sank back as Rule's hands went to her shoulders and moved her back from him. He must not have scolded her, because Ricky laughed again; then the two returned to their task.

Cathryn turned away, moving at an angle so they wouldn't look up and see her. As she did so she caught sight of another figure and she halted, her head jerking around. Lewis Stovall was leaning against the corral, his hard face expressionless as he watched Rule and Ricky unloading the truck. There was a certain tautness about his stance that puzzled her, but she was too upset to worry about him right then.

Cathryn returned quickly to the house, so shaken that she went to her bedroom and sat on the bed, her eyes wide with shock. Ricky had hugged Rule, had kissed him! He hadn't returned the embrace and it certainly hadn't been what she would call a passionate encounter, yet she felt sick as she remembered how Ricky's slender arms had gone around his waist. Lorna had said that Ricky was in love with Rule, but Cathryn hadn't believed it then and still found it hard to swallow. Yet if it were true...no wonder Ricky was so bitter, trying wildly to hurt Cathryn even if she had to use Rule as her weapon. Had Rule ever made love to her? Had Mr. Franklin's accusation not been so wild, after all?

No, it wasn't true. She couldn't let herself think that it was, because she couldn't bear the thought of it. Moaning softly, she pressed her icy hands over her face. Ricky didn't have any right to touch him! That was the basis of it all. Recognizing her sick jealousy for what it was, Cathryn tried to chide herself out of it. After all, hadn't she herself given him permission to go to other women? He wasn't a monk—far from it. He was a healthy, hotly virile man. But she hadn't meant it! She couldn't stand the thought of any other woman melting under his demands.

It had been an innocent scene. She had to believe that, or she wouldn't be able to bear it. It had been only a quick hug and a kiss, and he hadn't returned either of them. She had no reason to be jealous, no reason at all.

Yet it was more than an hour before she felt sufficiently under control to go downstairs and sit through dinner, carefully keeping her face blank and trying not to look directly at either Rule or Ricky. She wanted to do something violent, and she was afraid that if she saw either of them smirk she would lose her temper. Rule would like that; he had a tendency to use her loss of control against her.

She toyed listlessly with her beef casserole, neatly separating it into four equal portions on her plate and taking a tiny bit from each section in turn. The day had been a total disaster. Like a fool she had let Rule bully her into quitting her job. Now she realized that she had given up one more piece of her personal independence, bringing her that much more firmly under Rule's domination. The fight with Mr. Franklin, the fight with Rule, the shock of seeing Ricky kiss him...all of it was just too much. She began to wish he'd say something nasty so she could throw her plate at him.

But the meal continued silently, until at length Rule excused himself and went into the study, shutting himself inside. Feeling like she could scream, Cathryn got ready for bed. What else was there to do? She vented some of her frustration on the pillow, then tried to read.

At length she succeeded in making herself sleepy and she turned out the light, sliding down between the sheets. Moments after she had closed her eyes she heard a faint sound and her eyes flew open, her heartbeat quickening to double time as she wondered if Rule had decided to break their agreement and come to her anyway. But no one was there, and to her horror tears welled up in her eyes. Quickly she subdued the impulse to sob like a child.

Had he already reduced her to that? After one night of his lovemaking, was she so addicted to him that she craved him like a potent drug?

Damn him, didn't he realize how upsetting the day had been to her?

No, he didn't realize, and she was lucky that he didn't. If he had any inkling that she was feeling so weak and uncertain of herself, he would move in like the hungry panther he reminded her of, ready for the metaphorical kill.

If only David were still alive! He had been a warm, sheltering harbor, a quiet, strong man who had loved her and left her free to be herself, instead of demanding more than she had to give. Rule demanded more. He wanted all of her under his control, and the terrible thing about it was that she would glory in being his completely, if only she could be certain of him, secure in his love. But how could she be? He would take everything she had to give but keep himself guarded, locked away from her searching heart.

She wouldn't be able to stand it, every day spent worrying over the puzzle that was Rule's personality, becoming more and more frantic as she failed to solve it. Why had she agreed to stay? Was she trying to drive herself crazy?

The thought of Chicago was heaven. She could still go back; she still had to close up her apartment, and she definitely needed her clothing. She had been scratching by with the bare minimum that she had brought, since she had thought that she would be staying only a weekend. That would be an ironclad excuse to leave, and once she was in Chicago, out of his reach, she wouldn't come back. There were other jobs.

Clinging to the thought of her quiet apartment, she drifted to sleep. It must have been a sound sleep, because she didn't awaken when her door was opened the next morning. It wasn't until a hard hand slapped her bottom lightly that she shot up in bed, pushing her hair out of her eyes to glare up at the tall man standing beside the bed. "What are you doing in here?" she snarled.

"Waking you up," he replied in the same tone of voice. "Get up. You're going with me today."

"I am? When was this decided?"

"Last night, while I watched you sulk over your dinner."

"I wasn't sulking!"

"Weren't you? I've been watching you sulk on and off for quite a few years now, and I know all the signs. So haul your pretty self out of that bed and get your clothes on, honey, because I'm going to keep you so busy you won't have time to pout."

Cathryn debated giving him a fight, but she quickly realized that she was in a difficult position and gave in with poor grace. "All right. Get out so I can get dressed."

"Why should I? I've seen you naked before."

"Not today you haven't!" she shouted furiously. "Get out! Get ... *out!*"

He leaned down and flipped the cover back, then locked his fingers around her wrist and dragged her off the bed. Standing her before him as if she were a naughty child, he pulled her nightgown over her head with one swift movement and tossed it aside. His dark eyes flashed down her body, finding every detail and touching her with heat. "Now I have," he snapped, and turned aside to pull open dresser drawers until he found her underwear. After throwing a pair of panties and a bra at her, he went to the closet and pulled out a shirt and a pair of soft, faded jeans. Thrusting those into her hands, too, he said, "Are you going to get dressed, or are we going to fight? I think I'd like the fight. I remember what happened the last time you tried nude wrestling."

Temper glowing hotly in her cheeks, Cathryn turned her back on him and hastily donned her underwear. Damn him, no matter what she did, he won. If she dressed, she was doing as she was told. If she didn't get dressed, she knew that they would be in bed in a matter of minutes. Having to admit to herself that she didn't have the willpower to resist him left a bitter taste in her mouth. Any abstinence was due entirely to *his* willpower, and Rule had plenty of that. He had been bending everyone to his will for years.

As she jabbed her arms into the sleeves of the shirt, his hands closed on her shoulders and gently turned her around to face him. Swiftly she looked up at him and wasn't surprised to find that his expression was closed, his face stony. He pushed her hands down and buttoned the shirt himself, his fingers lingering on the soft swells of her breasts. Cathryn drew a deep breath and tried to fight back the longing that surged through her, making her nipples ache and pucker tautly under the lace of her bra.

"Would I be breaking our deal if I kissed you?" he murmured harshly.

With a jolt Cathryn realized that he was fiercely angry at the limitations she had set for him. Rule was a man used to having a woman whenever he needed one, and celibacy was riling him. The knowledge that she was upsetting him made her smile. Looking up at him, she hedged, "Just one kiss?"

For a moment he looked as if he would explode with fury. The glare he gave her was so violent that she took a step backward, prepared to scream at the top of her lungs if he made a move toward her. Then he controlled himself, reining in his temper and visibly forcing himself to relax. "I'm going to have you again," he promised softly, holding her eyes with his. "And when I do, I'm going to make up for this, so prepare yourself."

"Written in stone?" she asked just as softly, her tone mocking.

"Written in stone," he assured her.

"That's odd; I'd never thought you'd be rough on a woman."

A smile suddenly lit his somber features. "I wasn't talking about being rough, honey. I was talking about satisfying a lot of urges."

He was making love to her with words, seducing her with memories. Her body quickened as she thought of the night they had spent together. She swallowed and opened her mouth to grant him his kiss...as many kisses as he wanted...but he forestalled her by turning abruptly away. "Get dressed, Cat. Now. I'll be downstairs."

Shivering, she stood for a moment watching the door that he had left open in the wake of his departure. She ached for him, willing him to return. Then she shook herself out of her sensual fog and pulled on her jeans and boots, her hands trembling from both regret and relief. How unlike Rule to deny himself sexual gratification! He had to have known that she had been trembling on the brink of surrender, but he had pulled her back. Because she had threatened to leave? Did he want her to stay so badly?

After brushing her teeth and combing the tangles from her hair, she ran downstairs and burst into the kitchen, suddenly afraid that he hadn't waited for her. He was sprawled at the table, nursing a cup of coffee. Something flickered briefly in his eyes when she entered, then was quickly veiled before she could read it.

Her stomach jumped unpleasantly when she saw Ricky sitting close beside him. Murmuring a good-morning, she sat down and reached for the cup of coffee that Lorna had promptly placed before her.

Ricky arched an eyebrow at her. "Why are you awake so early?" she asked snidely.

"I woke her up," said Rule curtly. "She's going with me today."

Ricky's pretty face pulled into a scowl. "But *I* was planning on going with you again!"

"You can go where you want," Rule said without looking up from his coffee. "Cat's going with me."

Cathryn stared at him, troubled by the way he casually brushed Ricky aside, when only the day before they had been laughing together as they unloaded the truck. A quick glance at Ricky revealed a quivering bottom lip that had been bitten and conquered.

Lorna slid filled plates before them, drawing everyone's attention to their food, for which Cathryn was grateful. Rule ate with his usual hearty appetite, though Cathryn and Ricky did little more than pick at their food, at least until Rule looked up and frowned when he saw Cathryn's full plate. "You didn't eat last night," he said pointedly. "You'll eat that if I have to feed it to you myself."

Delightful visions of egg dripping down his face danced with wicked temptation in Cathryn's mind, but she reluctantly turned them away. Hurriedly she gulped her breakfast, drained her cup and jumped to her feet. Kicking his ankle, she snapped, "Hurry it up! What's taking you so long?"

Behind her she heard Lorna quickly stifle a chuckle. Rule rose to his feet and clamped his fingers around her wrist, dragging her in his wake. He paused at the back door to jam his battered black hat on his head, then grabbed up another one, which he pushed onto Cathryn's head. She knocked at it and said sulkily, "This isn't my hat."

"Tough," he muttered as he hauled her across the yard to the stable.

Cathryn dug her heels in every inch of the way, pulling back on her wrist and trying to twist her arm out of his grasp. When that failed she tried to trip him, managing once to send him stumbling, but she didn't accomplish much, since he retained his grip on her and she had to stumble after him. The thought came fleetingly that it was becoming commonplace for him to drag her across the yard, and she wondered what the ranch hands thought of it. The mental picture of grinning male faces gave her the strength to liberate her wrist with a violent twist. "Stop dragging me around!" she snapped when he whirled to face her, his expression thunderous. "I'm not a dog to be dragged around on the end of a chain!"

"Right now I think a chain would do you good," he snarled softly. "You damned little redheaded wildcat! You refuse to let me touch you, but everything you do is a dare to me. I never had you pegged for a tease, honey, but you could have changed while you were away."

Aghast, Cathryn stared at him. "I'm not teasing you!"

"Does that mean you're serious when you give me the come-on?"

"I'm not giving you any such thing!" she denied hotly. "Just look at the way you've acted this morning—and yesterday, too! Yet you expect everything to be roses. I'm angry with you...no, make that furious. Enraged. Am I getting through to you?"

He looked astounded. "Just what have I done now?"

Out of the corner of her eye Cathryn saw Lewis Stovall leaning negligently against the stable door and almost grinning, which probably meant that he found it all highly amusing. She sniffed and evaded Rule's question by saying, "It's time we got started," and walking around him to the stable.

Only the presence of Lewis and several of the other hands kept Rule under control, she was certain. She saddled her own horse, choosing the gray gelding she had ridden her first day home. When Rule was mounted on his big chestnut he led the way across the pastures, and looking at the set of his broad shoulders, Cathryn knew that he hadn't forgotten the subject of their earlier conversation. Just let him bring it up! she thought fiercely. She had a few things to tell Mr. Rule Jackson!

_____ *Chapter Six*

He waited only until they were out of the others' hearing before he kneed his horse close beside hers and said with dangerous calm, "You'd better have a good explanation."

Cathryn gave him a fierce, narrow-eyed stare. "The same goes for you," she fired back. "For instance, why were you kissing and hugging with Ricky yesterday afternoon, but this morning you treated her like dirt? Was it an act for my benefit?"

Sudden amusement lit his dark eyes. "Ricky's never done anything for your benefit."

"Stop playing games with me, damn it!" she said furiously. "You know what I mean."

"You're jealous," he drawled, looking so pleased with himself that Cathryn almost exploded with anger.

"I am not!" she yelled. "You can run around with every woman in Texas for all I care! I want to know why you were so friendly with her yesterday but treated her like a stray hound this morning. The rumor in town is that you're sleeping with Ricky." She felt sick even saying the words, and her hand tightened on the reins, making the gray dance and shake his head.

"Oh, you care, all right," he replied. "Why else have you been throwing such a tantrum this morning?"

Cathryn ignored the provocation of that remark, no longer able to avoid asking him straight out. "Have you ever made love to Ricky?" she asked in a harsh voice; then she had to swallow a sudden surge of nausea. What would she do if he admitted it, when the very thought of him touching another woman made her feel sick? She wouldn't be able to bear it.

"No," he said easily, totally unaware that her very sanity hinged on his answer. "But not for lack of opportunity. Does that answer your question? Or do you have something else you want to accuse me of? Surely there's some woman left in the county who you've managed not to suspect me of messing around with."

She almost flinched from his sarcasm. Rule didn't usually argue, but when he did he had a deadly tongue. Her dark eyes were huge and miserable as she stared at him. "Ricky's in love with you," she said. She hadn't wanted to tell him, though on reflection she was certain that he knew it. Ricky wasn't a subtle woman.

He snorted. "Ricky doesn't love anyone but herself. She goes from man to man the way a butterfly tries all the flowers. But why should you care who warms my bed? You don't want to share it. You even told me to take myself elsewhere when I needed sex."

Cathryn's throat closed and she stared at him helplessly. Was he so blind? Couldn't he see that every inch of her ached for him? But thank God that he didn't see, because if he knew how she felt she would never be able to control him . . . or herself. She wanted to be sure of him; she wanted to trust him before she became so deeply involved with him that she had no self-protection left, yet she felt pressured from all sides to throw caution to the winds. If she didn't claim him, Ricky would; if she didn't satisfy him sexually, someone else would.

He reined in his horse and leaned across to grasp her reins, stopping the gray. "Look," he said directly, his dark eyes unreadable in the shadow of his black hat. "I need sex. I'm a normal, healthy man. But I control my needs, they don't control me. I don't want Ricky. I want you. I'll wait . . . for a while."

Sudden fury gave her back her voice and she pushed his hand away from her reins. "And then what?" she spat. "Will you go roaming like a tomcat?"

He moved swiftly, his gloved hand darting out and catching her by the back of the neck. "I won't have to roam," he crooned on a dangerously silky note. "I know exactly where your bedroom is." She opened her mouth to yell at him and he leaned over, catching the hot words with his mouth as he brought her closer to him, the steely hand on her neck holding her just where he wanted her.

Cathryn shuddered with hot, soft reaction, her lips shaping themselves to the movement of his, tasting the coffee flavor of his mouth, as she allowed his tongue entrance. His free hand squeezed gently on her breasts, then began to trace a wandering path down her stomach. She was helpless to stop him, not even thinking of stopping him, her body waiting pliantly for his intimate touch. But his horse took exception to the situation and danced away from the gelding, forcing Rule to release her and secure his seat again. He quieted the stallion with a murmur, but his eyes seared her with dark fire. "Don't take too long making up your mind," he advised softly. "We're wasting a lot of time."

She watched in helpless confusion as he rode away from her, his tall body moving in perfect rhythm with the powerful horse. She didn't know what to do anymore. She thought of going back to the house, but the memory of how lost and miserable she had been the day before sent her riding after Rule. At least when she was with him she was able to look at him, to secretly savor the thrill she got whenever she saw him. The need she felt for him was so strong that it was almost an obsession, an illness. It had kept him constantly in her thoughts even though they were separated by years and hundreds of miles, and now that he was so close she was driven by the compulsion to watch him.

For the remainder of the week she rode by his side, taking every step he took, riding endless miles until she ached in every muscle and every bone. Yet a combination of pride and stubbornness kept her from either complaining or giving up. She was well aware that he knew the discomfort she suffered. Too often she caught a gleam of amusement in his dark eyes. But Cathryn wasn't a complainer, so she bore it all silently and every night took comfort from the bottle of liniment that had become a fixture on her nightstand. She could have remained at the house, but that had no attraction at all for her. Riding with Rule had its rewards, despite the physical punishment she was taking, because she had the delight of secretly feasting her eyes on him all day long.

In any case, she became absorbed in the grinding routine that was part of every day on the ranch. After her one trip to pick up supplies, Rule didn't suggest again that Cathryn run any errands for him. He rolled her out of bed every morning before dawn, and by the time the first gray light had appeared they were in the saddle. If he rode fence, she rode fence; if he moved horses from one pasture to another, so did she. Rule turned his hand to every chore on the ranch, disdaining nothing, and she realized more fully than ever before why he had the respect and uncomplaining obedience of every man who worked there.

She was astounded at his stamina. She did none of the physical work that he did, merely followed in his tracks, and by the end of the day she was so tired that she could scarcely stay in the saddle on the ride back to the house. But Rule's shoulders were as straight at the end of the day as they had been at the beginning, and she often saw the admiring, respectful looks that the men gave him. He wasn't a straw boss. He did every thing he asked the men to do, and in addition he oversaw the completion of everything else. Lewis Stovall was his right-hand man, almost sullenly quiet, but so capable that often Rule had only to nod his head in a certain direction and Lewis knew exactly what he wanted. Remembering her accusing words when she had discovered that Lewis was the foreman, she felt ashamed; even with Lewis's help, Rule still did the work of two men.

The horses were Rule's special concern, though in no way did he neglect any other aspect of the ranch. The horses were treated with intense care. No injury, regardless of how slight, was allowed to go untreated. No illness was ignored, and anything that concerned their comfort was done without question. He often exercised the stallions himself and the spirited animals were better behaved with him than with the other men entrusted with their exercise.

Cathryn would sit on the fence and watch him with the stallions, almost dying with envy because she wanted to ride one of the beautiful animals so much, but Rule adamantly refused to let her near them. Though she sulked, she accepted his edict because she knew how valuable they were, and she admitted that if one of them decided not to obey her, she wasn't strong enough to force her will on him. The stallions were always kept carefully separated from each other and never exercised at the same time, not only to prevent fights but to keep them calm. A rival in the vicinity upset the blooded stallions even if things didn't progress to a fight.

Rule reminded her of his stallions; but he behaved himself scrupulously during those days, not even stealing a kiss, though she sometimes caught his gaze lingering on her lips or the thrust of her breasts against the cotton shirts she wore. Though she knew that he was waiting to hear her decision, she didn't even try to make up her mind during those days; she was having fun, and in addition to that she was so tired at the end of the day that she didn't feel like indulging in any soul searching. She was doing exactly what she had wanted: being with him, learning him. But Rule was far too complicated for only a few days to give her any insight into him.

The breeding pens were also off limits to her, another edict she didn't argue with. Though Ricky was apparently completely at ease there, for once Cathryn wasn't jealous of her. Even if Rule didn't care to protect Ricky, he did extend that care to Cathryn, and she was glad. She was too sensitive, too attuned to Rule's sensuality, to be comfortable with the actual breeding. So one day while Rule was occupied in the pens she returned to the house for a rare hour of relaxation. But after sitting for a few minutes feeling her aching muscles slowly unknot, she began to feel guilty for doing nothing while Rule was still working. Then the happy thought that she could relieve him of some of the paperwork occurred to her and she made herself comfortable in the study. After a rapid look though the stacks of correspondence and bills that littered the desk, she realized that he was surprisingly well organized. All of the bills were current. But then, how else would it be? Rule was efficient in everything he did. Only the past couple of days' worth of mail hadn't been opened, but he had been working late and hadn't had a chance to catch up on the paperwork. Satisfied with her choice of occupations, Cathryn sorted the mail into a stack that was addressed to Rule personally, and another stack of bills, which was gratifyingly small, proof that the ranch was on solid ground.

Swiftly she opened the bills and studied them: bills for grain; bills for fencing; utility bills; bills for the mountain of supplies that were needed to keep the ranch running; veterinary bills that seemed astronomical to her. Apprehensive again, she opened the ledger and pulled it to her, wondering if there would be enough to pay these bills and still have enough for the ranch hands' salaries. Her finger moved to the balance column and ran down it to the last figure.

Stunned, she stared at it for a full minute, unable to believe her eyes. Was the ranch doing that well? She had somehow gotten the impression that the ranch was solid but not rich, able to provide a good living but not a luxurious one. How could she reconcile that idea with the figure that stared her in the face, that figure written in Rule's bold, slashing hand? If all the profits were turned back into the operation, what accounted for this?

A sudden chill raced down her spine and she flipped through the bills again. Why hadn't she noticed the first time? Why hadn't she picked up on the hint that she had received in town? Every one of those bills was in Rule Jackson's name. Knowing what she would find, she

hunted for the checkbook and instead found a ledger of
checks, all of them bearing the name Rule Jackson, and
beneath that the legend: Bar D Ranch.

All of that proved nothing, she told herself sternly. Of
course his name was on the checks. He signed them,
didn't he? Yet she got up and went in search of Monica, who had been trustee until Cathryn reached her
twenty-fifth birthday, and whose name should have
been on those checks.

"Oh, that," said Monica in a bored tone, waving her
hand. "I signed control of the ranch over to Rule years
ago. Why not? As he pointed out, he was just wasting
time by having to come to me for decisions."

"You should have told me!" Cathryn said sharply.

"For what reason?" Monica demanded just as
sharply. "You were going away to college, so you
weren't going to be here anyway. If you were all that
concerned, why did you wait until now to come home?"

Cathryn couldn't tell her that; instead she returned to
the study and sat down heavily, trying to get it straight
in her mind. So Rule had had direct control of the ranch
and her money for all of these years. Why did that
alarm her? She knew he hadn't cheated her. Every cent
would be accounted for. She simply felt betrayed in
some way that she hadn't yet figured out.

If Monica had signed control over to Rule before
Cathryn had gone away to college, it had to have been
during that summer when she was seventeen. She had
decided to attend college at the last minute, torn between the agony of leaving her home and the almost
uncontrollable fear she'd had of Rule. Having always
considered that sexual scene by the river to be her fault,
she had been afraid of her own body and the way it responded to him. But now . . . had he made love to her

deliberately? He had already had control of the ranch, but he would have known that it was only a temporary control and could come to an abrupt halt when she came of age. The next logical move was to bring her under his control, too, to dominate her so completely that she would never try to wrest the ranch away from him.

She didn't want to think that. She felt sick, distrusting him so much when he had worked so hard. But, damn it, it wasn't just the ranch that she was concerned with! She had herself to think of! Was she letting herself fall for a man who saw her only as a means to an end, a way of finally making the ranch really, completely his? He knew her better than any other person on earth knew her. He knew that he could control her with his sensual magic. No wonder her demand that he stay away from her had rattled him so badly! She had really thrown his plans off!

Taking a deep breath, Cathryn tried to halt the wild thoughts that were circling madly in her mind. She couldn't be certain of that. She had to give him the benefit of the doubt, at least for now. If only she knew what went on in his head! If only he would talk to her, tell her if the ranch was more important to him than anything else. She would understand. Rule had gone through hell, and she couldn't blame him if the ranch had become a sanctuary that he wanted to cling to. The idea was incongruous in a way. He was so strong. Why would he need a sanctuary? But he wouldn't talk about what he had experienced, wouldn't let anyone else share that burden with him, so she really had no idea what he felt about the ranch or anything else.

She wasn't prepared to face him when the door opened suddenly, nor was she prepared for the black rage that swept over his face when he saw the ledger open on the desk. "What are you doing?" he snarled softly.

A calmness born out of a numbing certainty that her worst fears had been correct enabled her to stay in her chair and face him, and give her voice its even tone when she said, "I'm looking at the books. Do you have any objections?"

"I might, especially when you act like you've been trying to catch me cheating you. Do you want to hire an accountant to go over things to make certain I'm not finagling? You'll find that every penny is right where it should be, but go ahead." He paced around the side of the desk and stood looking down at her, his dark eyes hard. Glancing sideways, she saw that he was gripping his hat so tightly that his knuckles were white.

Abruptly she slammed the ledger shut and jumped to her feet, pain blooming inside her so acutely that she couldn't sit still any longer. Lifting her chin, she met his gaze head on. "I'm not worried that you've taken any money; I know better than that. I was just . . . surprised to find that everything is in your name. Monica isn't even a figurehead any longer, and hasn't been for years. Why wasn't I told? You'd think I'd be aware of what goes on with *my* ranch, or at least I should be."

"You should have been," he agreed. "But you weren't."

"What about now?" she challenged. "I'm involved now. Shouldn't all of this be changed over into my name? Or have you begun to believe all of the talk in town about 'Rule Jackson's spread'?"

"So change it!" he said violently, and a sudden sweep of his hand sent the ledger crashing to the floor. "It's your damned ranch and your damned money; do whatever you want with it! Just don't whine to me because I kept the place running while you never bothered to even ask how it was doing!''

"I'm not whining!" Cathryn yelled, shoving at the stack of bills and sending them fluttering to the floor. "I want to know why you never told me that Monica had signed control of the ranch over to you!"

"Maybe I don't have a reason! Maybe I just never thought of it! I've been working like a slave for years. I haven't had time to chase you down every time some little something came up. Do I have your permission to pay the hands, Mrs. Ashe? Will it be all right if I write a check to pay for the fencing, Mrs. Ashe?"

"Oh, go to hell! But before you do, tell me why there's so much money in the balance column when you've gone out of your way to make me think that there was no extra, that all the profits had been turned back into the ranch?"

One of his hands shot out, and he clamped it on her upper arm, holding her in a grip that would leave the imprint of his hand on her flesh. "Do you have any idea how much money it takes to run a stud?" he ground out. "Do you know what a good stallion costs? We've been breeding quarter horses, but we're branching out into Thoroughbreds and we need two more stallions, more brood mares. You can't charge them on your credit card, baby! It takes a hell of a lot of money on hand to— Hell!" he suddenly snarled. "Why should I explain anything to you? You're the boss, so you can do what you damned well please with it!''

"Maybe I will!" she yelled, wrenching her arm away from his punishing fingers. Despite her best efforts, tears glistened in the darkness of her eyes as she stared up at him for a moment; then she whirled and ran from the room before she could disgrace herself by really crying.

"Cat!" she heard him call as she closed the door, but she didn't return. She went upstairs to her room and carefully locked the door, then settled in the rocking chair with a spy thriller that she held in her hands but didn't—couldn't—read. She refused to give way to tears, though occasionally a lump formed in her throat and she had to struggle with herself. It was a waste of time to cry. She just had to accept things as they were.

Rule's violent reaction at finding her going through the books meant only one thing to her: He didn't want her to know how the ranch operated because he didn't want her to take over any of his authority. Despite his accusation she knew that he was bone-deep honest and she sensed that he didn't really think she suspected otherwise. No, he had attacked her because Rule was a good warrior and he knew the most important rule of combat: Be the first to strike.

So he was something of a fanatic about the ranch, she tried to reason with herself. At least she could depend on him to do the best thing, rather than look for a way to line his own pockets. It was just that she wanted him to think as much of her as he did of the ranch.... Not more, she wouldn't ask that, but simply to care for her and the ranch equally.

She had thought that they had grown closer during these last days; even when they had snapped at each other she had been aware of a bond between them and had known that he felt it too. It had been more than a sexual bond, at least for her. Though she never looked at him without remembering in some small corner of her brain the intensity of his lovemaking, she had felt close to him in other ways. So much for daydreams, she thought, letting the book drop to her lap. Hadn't she learned yet that Rule was a difficult man to read?

Though she was awake early the next morning, she didn't go downstairs to have breakfast with him and spend the day by his side. Instead she remained in bed until she knew that he had gone, then spent the day giving the upstairs a good cleaning, more to keep herself busy than because the house was in dire need of it. She avoided Rule at lunch, too, though she heard Ricky's laughter wafting upward and knew that her stepsister was keeping him company. So what if she was?

After Cathryn's own hurried lunch, eaten while standing in the kitchen after Rule had returned to the range, she returned to her cleaning. She had left Rule's room for last, and she was stunned when she entered it to find herself so moved by his lingering presence. His warm male scent seemed to fill the room. The pillow was still dented where his head had rested. His bed looked like a war had been fought on it. The clothing he had worn the day before had been dropped to the floor and probably kicked out of the way. Nothing else could have produced such a tangle of shirt, shorts, jeans and socks.

She had restored the room to order and was polishing the oak furniture when Ricky came in and draped herself across the bed. "The housewifely bit won't impress him," she drawled.

Cathryn shrugged, holding on to her temper with difficulty. Everything about Ricky rubbed her the wrong way lately. "I'm not trying to impress him. I'm cleaning house."

"Oh, come on. You've spent every day with him, showing him how interested you are in the ranch. It won't make any difference. He'll take whatever you offer him and use it for as long as he wants it, but he doesn't offer anything of himself in return. That's the voice of experience speaking," she added dryly.

Cathryn dropped the polishing cloth, her fingers clenching into fists. Whirling on Ricky, she said heatedly, "I'm getting tired of that line. I think you're plain poison jealous. He's never been your lover and you can't convince me that he has. I think you've tried your best to get him to go to bed with you and he's always turned you down flat, but now you've finally faced the fact that he never will be your lover and you can't stand the truth."

Ricky sat up, her face turning pale. Cathryn tensed herself for an assault, knowing that Ricky always flared up at the least hint of opposition; but instead the other woman looked at Cathryn for a long time, her entire body taut. Then slow tears welled in her eyes. "I've loved him for so long," she whispered. "Do you have any idea how I feel? I've waited for years, certain that he'd decide one day that it's me he really wants; then you show up to claim your own and it's just like he's slammed a door in my face. Damn you, you were gone for years! You wouldn't give him the time of day, but because you own this godforsaken ranch he's dropped me flat so he can chase after you."

"Make up your mind," Cathryn snapped. "Is he using me, or am I using him?"

"He's using you!" Ricky spat. "You're not my rival; you never have been, not even when he was making love to you on riverbanks. It's this ranch, this piece of land, that he loves! You're nothing to him, none of us are. I've tried to get you to ask him about it, but you're too much of a coward, aren't you? You're afraid of what he might tell you!"

Cathryn's lip curled. "I don't ask for statements of commitment unless the relationship is serious."

"And you're using him to let off steam?" Ricky sniped. "Does he know that?"

"I haven't used him for anything," denied Cathryn, looking around for something to throw, a holdover from childhood that she stifled with difficulty.

"I'll just bet you haven't!"

Only Ricky's departure, as abrupt as her entrance had been, saved Cathryn from a temper tantrum in the end. She stood in the middle of the floor, her breasts heaving as she tried to control her temper. She shouldn't let Ricky upset her like that, but she had a hair-trigger temper and Ricky had always known just how to set it off. She had obtained some measure of serenity while married to David, but since returning to Texas it seemed that it had all fled. These days she was reacting simply to the signals that she received from her brain, whether to love or to fight; all her control seemed to be gone.

She still didn't want to see Rule, so the phone call she had that afternoon from Wanda Wallace was very welcome, especially when Wanda cheerfully reminded her of the long-standing Saturday night dances. It was Saturday, and suddenly Cathryn wanted to go. "I've told everyone that you're coming," Wanda laughed, indulging in a bit of gentle blackmail. "All the old gang will be there, in dancing shape or not, so you can't let us down. It'll be fun. It's still informal, nothing fancier than a sundress at the most. We older ones tend to stay away from jeans now that our fannies are so much wider," she said wryly.

"It seems forever since I've been in a dress," sighed Cathryn. "You've talked me into it. I'll see you there."

"We'll save a seat for you," Wanda promised.

The thought of seeing her old classmates filled Cathryn with anticipation as she showered and applied her makeup, then brushed her dark-fire hair into a loose cloud that swirled around her shoulders. The sundress she chose was simple, with wide straps that were comfortable on her shoulders, and the flaring skirt emphasized the slenderness of her waist. She clasped a gold serpentine belt around her waist and slid graceful matching bracelets onto each wrist. Dainty sandals with only a small heel completed the outfit. She made a face at herself in the mirror. In that innocent white dress she looked like a teenager again.

She popped into the kitchen to inform Lorna of her destination and the cook nodded. "Do you good to socialize some. Why don't you pick one of those gardenia blossoms off the bush in front and put it behind your ear? I'm partial to gardenias," she said dreamily.

Wondering what past romance had been associated with gardenias, Cathryn obediently plucked one of the creamy white blossoms and held it to her nose for a moment to inhale the incredibly sweet scent. She anchored it behind her ear and returned to the kitchen to show Lorna the result, and the older woman indicated her approval. With Lorna's admonition to drive carefully following her, she went out to the station wagon and slid behind the wheel, glad that she had avoided catching even a glimpse of Rule all day long.

The dance had been held at the community center for as long as she could remember. It was a fairly large building, able to accommodate a crowd of dancers, enough tables and chairs for those who wished to sit, a live band on a raised stage, and a small refreshment center that sold soft drinks to the younger dancers and beer to the older ones. The teenagers had little chance of getting a beer because everyone knew everyone else, so they had no hope of lying about their ages. There already was a respectable crowd when Cathryn arrived and she had to park the station wagon at the far end of the lot, but even before she was able to reach the building she was being hailed by former classmates, and she finally entered at the center of a noisy, laughing group.

"Over here!" she heard Wanda call, and looked around until she saw her friend stretched on tiptoe and waving frantically. Cathryn waved back and made her way through the milling crowd until she reached Wanda's table, where she dropped thankfully into the chair that had been saved for her.

"Whew!" she laughed. "I must be older than I thought! Just getting through the crowd has tired me out."

"You don't look tired," a dark-haired man said admiringly, leaning across the table to her. "You still look like the charmer who broke my heart back in junior high."

Cathryn looked at him with intense concentration, trying to place him among her classmates and utterly failing. Then his lopsided smile fell into place in her memory and she said warmly, "Glenn Lacey! When did you come back to Texas?" His family had left Texas when she was still in junior high, so she had never thought to see him again.

"When I finished law school. I decided that Texas needed the benefit of my wisdom," he teased.

"Don't pay any attention to him," advised Rick Wallace, Wanda's husband. "All that education has addled his wits. Do you recognize everyone else?'' he asked Cathryn.

"I think so," she said, looking around the table. Her special friend Kyle Vernon was there with his wife, Hilary, and she hugged both of them. She remembered again that it had been the fond prediction of both Ward Donahue and Paul Vernon that their children would get married to each other when they grew up, but the childhood friendship had remained friendship and neither of them had ever been romantically interested in the other. Pamela Bowing, a tall brunette who concealed a genius for mischief behind a languorous demeanor, had been Cathryn's best friend in high school, and they had an enthusiastic reunion. Pamela was with a man Cathryn didn't recognize, and he was introduced as Stuart McLendon, from Australia. He was visiting the area while he studied Texas ranching. That left Glenn Lacey as the only unattached male, which automatically paired him with Cathryn. She was happy enough with that arrangement, because she had liked him when they were younger and saw no reason now to change her opinion.

They tried to catch up on old gossip for a time, but the band was in full swing and they gave up the effort. Wanda grimaced at the whirling crowd. "Since the Texas swing has become popular it's gotten harder and harder to get the band to play nice, slow, dreamy numbers," she complained. "And before that, it was disco!"

"You're showing your age," Rick teased her. "We didn't dance nice, slow, dreamy numbers when we were in school."

"I wasn't the mother of two monsters when we were in school, either!" she retorted. But regardless of what she thought of the current style of dancing, she took his hand and led him onto the dance floor. Within minutes the table was empty, and Cathryn was naturally still paired with Glenn Lacey. He was tall enough that she felt comfortable dancing with him. His technique was smooth and easy to follow and he didn't bother with any fancy steps. He simply held her firmly, but not so closely that she would have protested, and they moved in time with the music.

"Are you back to stay?" he asked.

She looked up into his friendly blue eyes and smiled. "I don't know yet," she said, not wanting to go into the whole story.

"Any reason why you shouldn't stay? The ranch is yours, isn't it?"

He seemed to be the only one who realized that, and the smile she flashed him reflected her appreciation. "It's just that I've been away for such a long time. I have a life and friends in Chicago now."

"I was away for a long time, too, but Texas was always home."

She shrugged. "I haven't decided yet. But I don't have any immediate plans to return to Chicago."

"That's good," he said easily. "I'd like to give you a chance to break my heart again, if you don't mind."

She threw back her head and laughed up at him. "That's a good line! When did I break your heart, anyway? You moved away before I was old enough to begin dating."

He considered that and finally said, "I think it began when I was twelve and you were about ten. You were a shy little thing with huge dark eyes, and you aroused my protective instincts. By the time you were twelve I was hooked for good. I never was able to get away from those big eyes of yours.''

His eyes were twinkling as he told her of his youthful infatuation and they were able to laugh together, remembering the painful and awkward loves that everyone developed in adolescence.

''Wanda told me that you're a widow,'' he said gently a moment later.

She never failed to feel a twinge of grief at the thought of David, and her dark lashes swept down to cover the sadness in her eyes. ''Yes. My husband died over two years ago. Have you married?''

''Yes, while I was still in college. It didn't last through law school. Nothing very traumatic,'' he said with his charmingly crooked smile. ''It couldn't have been a lasting love because we just drifted apart and divorced without any of the bitter fights that seem almost mandatory. We had no children or property to fight over, so we just signed the papers, collected our clothing, and that was it.''

''And no special friends since then?''

''A couple,'' he admitted. ''Again, nothing lasting. I'm in no hurry. I'd like to get my practice established before I begin seriously looking for a wife, so it'll be another few years.''

''But you definitely want a wife?'' she asked, a little amazed at such an attitude. Most single men she knew, especially those who had been through a divorce, had definite ideas about avoiding marriage again and living life in the fast lane instead.

''Sure. I want a wife, kids, the whole bit. I'm domesticated,'' he admitted. ''I'd probably take the plunge now if I met the woman who gave me that special zing, but so far I haven't found her.''

Cathryn was relieved to find out that he hadn't felt that special zing with her, and the knowledge left her totally relaxed in his presence. He looked on her as a friend, not a romantic interest, which was exactly what she wanted. Because of that she danced several dances with him and returned to the table in desperate need of something cold to drink.

"I'll do the honors," said Kyle Vernon. "Any of you ladies want a beer?"

None of the women did, opting instead for soft drinks, and he pushed his way into the crowd. Despite the number of people there he returned in five minutes with a tray on which were crowded long-necked bottles of beer and the requested cans of cola. The time passed pleasantly as they talked and occasionally traded dance partners. Glenn asked Cathryn out to dinner for the following weekend and she accepted, certain that by then she would go crazy without the prospect of some time away from Rule's territory.

It was growing late and she was dancing with Glenn again, the crowd having thinned out because some people had started to leave, when she found herself staring straight across the room into Rule's dark eyes. He was standing well back, not talking with anyone, and she felt the heat of his gaze on her. Startled, she got the feeling that he had been standing there for some time, watching her as she danced with Glenn. His face wore that hard, expressionless mask. Casually she looked away from him and continued dancing. So he was here. So what? She had done nothing to feel guilty about.

Within fifteen minutes everyone was making preparations to call it a night. As she was saying good night to her friends, she felt long fingers wrap themselves around her arm and she knew that touch, knew who held her arm before she turned to look at him.

"I need to beg a ride back to the ranch," he said softly. "One of the men came with me and he's borrowed my truck."

"Certainly," Cathryn agreed. What else could she do? She didn't doubt that he had loaned his pickup out, though she did wonder how long he'd had to hunt to find someone to loan it to. None of that really mattered, though. Within seconds she was walking down the long expanse of the parking lot with him by her side, his hand still warm on her elbow.

"I'll drive," he said, taking the keys from her hand as she started to unlock the door. Without protest she got in and slid over to the passenger side of the car.

He drove in silence, his hard-planed features revealing nothing in the dim lights glowing from the dash. Cathryn looked up at the thin sliver of moon in its last quarter now, and she remembered the full silvery light that had bathed the bed when he had made love to her. The memory ignited a slow-burning flame in her body and she moved in involuntary response. If only she wasn't so aware of him sitting beside her! She could smell the warm, excitingly delicious male scent of him, and she recalled in frustrating detail just how it felt to be clasped against him in the timeless movements of lovemaking.

"Stay away from Glenn Lacey."

The low, raspy growl startled her, tore her from her sensual dreams, and she stared at him. "What?" she demanded, though she knew that she had understood him perfectly.

"I said I don't want you going out with Glenn Lacey," he obliged her by explaining more fully. "Or any other man, for that matter. Don't think that just because I agreed to stay out of your bed I'll stand by and watch you let someone else into it."

"If I want to go out with him, I will!" she said defiantly. "Who do you think you are, talking to me as if I'm in the habit of jumping into bed with any man who asks me? We're not engaged, Rule Jackson, and you have no right to tell me who I can see."

She saw his jaw tighten, and he snapped, "You may not have my ring on your finger, but you're a fool if you think I'll pretend there's nothing between us. You're mine, Cathryn Donahue, and I don't let anyone trespass on what's mine."

Cathryn was almost paralyzed by a confusing surge of mingled pleasure and rage. She was delighted that he might be jealous, but then her inevitable response to his arrogant manner overwhelmed her sense of pleasure and she lashed back at him. "You don't own me, and you never will!"

"Do you feel secure in that little dream world you've built?" he asked with silky menace, and the tone of his voice was a warning. She fell silent, and nothing more was said during the drive to the ranch.

Despite, or perhaps because of, the silence, the atmosphere between them became heavy with hostility and a growing sensual awareness. Just that afternoon she had thought herself so angry and disillusioned with him that he couldn't tempt her any longer but already she was discovering how deeply in error that assumption had been. She couldn't even glance at him now without being reminded of the moonlight on his face as he had made love to her, without tasting his mouth in memory or reliving the strong rhythm of his movements.

When he pulled the car up by the steps to the house, she was out of the vehicle before the tires had stopped rolling. She hurried up the steps and through the kitchen almost at a run, hearing the thudding of his bootheels echoing behind her as he followed. The house was dark, but she knew her home and moved swiftly through the darkness, wanting to reach the safety of her room and shut him out. But it was his home, too, and she was only halfway up the stairs when the force of his body knocked her off-balance and she was swept entirely off her feet by a hard arm that passed around her waist and lifted her like a child.

"Put me down!" she whispered, kicking backward in an effort to trip him as she disregarded their precarious position on the stairs. He grunted as she made painful contact with his shin, just above his boot top. Shifting his hold on her, he slid his other arm under her knees and lifted her up against his chest. She could see only the shadowy form of his face as it came closer and she demanded once more, "Rule! Put me down!" There was no answer, and when she tried to protest again he cut her off by clamping his mouth on hers in a hot, rough kiss that bruised her lips and set drums to thundering in her veins.

The darkness and his movements confused her, left her feeling disoriented as he removed his arm from beneath her knees and let her body slide downward against his, all the while keeping his hungry, bruising mouth fused to hers. Cathryn shivered as she felt the burgeoning proof of his virility brush against her; then his hand cupped her bottom and pulled her firmly in to him, branding her through the layers of their clothing with the heat and power of his desire.

It took a supreme effort of will, but she pulled her mouth away from his and protested in a fierce whisper, "Stop it! You promised! Monica—"

"Damn Monica," he growled, the sound rumbling up from deep in his chest. His hard hand cupped her chin and lifted it. "Damn Ricky, and damn everyone else. I'm not some tame gelding you can prance in front of without expecting to be taken up on what you're offering, and I'll be damned if I'll watch you waltz off with some other man."

"There's nothing like that between Glenn and me!" she almost yelled at him.

"And I'm going to make damned sure there never is," he said roughly.

Abruptly he reached out and snapped on the light, and Cathryn saw with astonishment that she was in her own bedroom. She had been so confused by the darkness that she had thought they were still in the hallway. Swiftly she stepped back from him, wondering uneasily if she could talk him out of his dangerous mood. He looked more than dangerous; with his eyes narrowed, his nostrils flared, he reminded her for all the world of one of those blooded stallions in the paddocks. He began unbuttoning his shirt with silent intent and she rushed into speech. "All right," she gave in shakily. "I won't see Glenn if that's what you want—"

"It's too late for that," he cut in with that soft, almost soundless tone that told her he meant business.

She had never seen a man undress so fast. He shed his clothing with a few economical movements and tossed the garments aside. If anything, he was even more menacing naked than he was clothed, and the sight of his hard, muscle-corded body stifled any further arguments in her throat. She put out a slim, useless hand to hold him off and he caught it, turning it palm up and bringing it to his mouth. His lips seared her skin; his tongue danced an ancient message against her sensitive palm. Then he pressed her hand to his hair-roughened chest. Cathryn moaned at the heady sensations aroused by touching him, unaware that she had even made the sound. Already the rising heat of desire was making her forget that she hadn't wanted this to happen again. He was so beautiful, so dangerous. She wanted to stroke the panther just one more time, feel his sleek muscles flex under her fingertips. She moved closer and put her other hand on his chest, spreading her fingers out and flexing them against his hard, warm flesh. His chest was rising and falling with increasing speed as his breath began to race out of his lungs, and his heart was thudding wildly against her palm, slamming against the strong rib cage that protected it.

"Yes," he moaned. "Yes. Touch me."

It was a sensually loaded invitation that she would never be able to resist. She sought out his small, flat male nipples with her sensitive fingertips and teased the tiny points of flesh into rigidity. He made a sound deep in his throat that was half purr, half snarl, and reached behind her to find the zipper of her dress. In half a minute she stood before him wearing only the bracelets on her wrists and the blossom in her hair. The sight of her soft, womanly body broke his control and he snatched her hard against him, crushing the soft fullness of her breasts to the hard planes of his body. His lips were on hers and his tongue penetrated her mouth and conquered a foe that didn't resist. The panther was no longer lying down to be stroked.

"Gardenias are my favorite," he muttered, releasing her long enough to pluck the flower from her hair. Her breasts were still pressed against him by the hard circle of his right arm around her, and he tucked the creamy flower into her cleavage, trapping it between their bodies. Then he was moving her backward and the bed touched the back of her knees; she fell onto it and he fell with her, never letting their bodies separate.

"I want you so much," he said on a groan, sliding down to bury his face in the sweet valley of her breasts, laden with the rich perfume of the crushed gardenia. His lips and tongue roamed over the rich mounds, sucking the pink nipples into taut buds; and wild shivers began to race through her body. Why did it have to be like this with him? Not even David had been able to persuade her to make love with him before their marriage, but with Rule it seemed that she had no will, no morals. She was his for the taking, whenever he wanted. The bitter self-knowledge in no way diluted the strength of her response to him. Heavy need was throbbing in her loins, making her entire body ache with an intimate pain that only he could assuage. She arched against him and he left her breasts to come fully over her, his hairy legs rough and heavy on the graceful length of hers. "Say you want me," he demanded harshly.

There was no use in denying it when her own body would make her a liar. Cathryn ran her palms down his muscled sides and felt his entire body tense with desire. "I want you," she said freely. "But this doesn't solve anything!"

"On the contrary, it solves a major problem of mine," he said, nudging her thighs apart. He fit himself solidly against her and Cathryn closed her eyes on a spiral of delight. Instantly he was shaking her, making her open her eyes again. "Look at me," he directed from between clenched teeth. "Don't close your eyes when I'm making love to you! Look at me; watch my face while I enter you."

It was so erotic that she couldn't bear it. She slowly took him inside her while she watched his face mirror the same sensations that were swamping her. His eyes were dilated; waves almost of pain washed again and again over his features as he initiated the rhythm of lovemaking. Tears flooded her eyes as she felt herself arching helplessly closer to fulfillment. "Stop it!" she wept, begging, digging her nails into his side. "Rule, please!"

"I'm trying to please you. Cat—oh, *Cat!*"

She heard the cry that was wrenched out of him, then it was all too much. Dying had to be like that, the utter loss of self, the gathering intensity, then the explosion of senses, followed by a drifting, a growing weaker, a falling away from reality. It was the most frightening experience of her life, yet she embraced it completely and let herself be conquered by it. She was aware, on the fringes of perception, of the demands his powerful body was making on hers as he also reached completion, and for a moment that physical perception was her only link with consciousness. Her full range of senses returned gradually and she opened her eyes to find him above her, stroking her hair away from her face while he softly crooned to her and enticed her back to him. His entire body was glistening with perspiration, his dark hair plastered to his skull, his dark eyes gleaming. He was the quintessential male, primal and triumphant in his renewed victory over the mystery of woman.

But his first words were tenderly concerned. "Are you all right?" he asked, disentangling their bodies and cradling her close to his side.

She wanted to shout that she couldn't possibly be all right, but instead she nodded and turned her face into the damp hollow of his shoulder, still too stricken to attempt speech. What could she tell him, anyway? That she needed him with a need that went beyond rational thought, beyond the control of a will that had held her proudly upright even during her husband's death? She couldn't understand it herself, so how could she explain it to him?

His palm gently cupped her chin and tilted it up. She didn't open her eyes, but she felt the kiss that he placed on her soft, bruised lips with a touch as delicate as a whisper. Then he wrapped his arms around her and settled her more closely against him, his breath stirring the hair at her temple. ''Go to sleep,'' he ordered in a soft growl.

She did, exhausted by the night of dancing, the late hour, and his steamy, demanding lovemaking. It felt so perfect to sleep in his arms, as if she belonged there.

Yet she woke with the certain knowledge that something was wrong. She was no longer in his arms, though her hand was lying on his chest, the fingers buried in the curly hair that decorated it. The room was dark, the moon no longer lending its meager light. There were no unusual sounds, nothing was stirring, yet something had awakened her. What?

Then, as she came more fully awake, Cathryn became aware of the unnatural rigidity of Rule's body beneath her hand, the fast and shallow breathing that made his chest rise and fall. She could feel the perspiration forming on his skin.

Alarmed, she started to shake him, wanting to make certain that he was all right, but before she could move he bolted upright in the bed, silently, not a sound coming from him. His right hand was clenched around the sheet. With obvious effort, every movement as slow as death, he opened his hand and released the sheet. A curiously soft sigh eased from his lungs; then he swung his long legs off the bed and got up, moving to the window, where he stood staring out at the night-darkened land.

Cathryn sat up in the bed. "Rule?" she asked in a puzzled voice.

He didn't answer, though she thought she saw the outline of his body stiffen at the sound of her voice. She remembered what Ricky had said, that he sometimes had nightmares and would spend the night walking around the ranch. Had this been a nightmare? What sort of dream was it, that he suffered it in such taut silence?

"Rule," she said again, getting out of bed and going to him. He was stiff and silent as she put her arms around him and rested her cheek on his broad back. "Did you have a dream?"

"Yes." His voice was guttural, wrenched out of him.

"What happened?" He didn't answer, and she prodded, "Was it about Vietnam?"

For a long moment he didn't answer; then another "Yes" was forced past his stiff lips.

She wanted him to tell her about it, but as the silence lengthened she realized that he wouldn't. He had never talked about Vietnam, never told anyone what had happened that had sent him back to Texas as wild and dangerous as a wounded animal. Suddenly it was important to her that he tell her what had haunted him in his dreams; she wanted to be important to *him*, wanted him to trust her and let her share the burden that still rode his shoulders.

She moved around to face him, sliding her body between him and the window. Her hands moved in a soft caress on his hard form, giving him the comfort of her touch. "Tell me," she demanded in a whisper.

If anything, he went even stiffer. "No," he said harshly.

"Yes!" she insisted. "Rule, listen to me! You've never talked about it, never tried to put it in perspective. You've kept it all locked inside, and it can't be that way, don't you see? You're letting it eat you alive—"

"I don't need an amateur psychiatrist," he snapped, thrusting her away from him.

"Don't you? Look at how hostile—"

"God damn you," he snarled thickly. "What do you know about hostility? What do you know about perspective? I learned one thing pretty damned fast: there's no perspective about death. The dead don't care one way or the other. It's the ones who are left alive who have to worry about it. They want it clean. They don't want to be blown into a thousand bloody little pieces in somebody else's face. They don't want to be burned alive. They don't want to be tortured until they're not even human anymore. But do you know something, honey? You're just as dead from one neat bullet as you are if you're scattered over a solid acre. That's perspective."

His raw anger, the bitterness in his voice, slammed into her like a body blow. Involuntarily she reached out for him again, but he stepped back, evading her touch as if he couldn't bear the closeness of another human being. Her hands fell uselessly to her sides. "If you would talk about it . . ." she began.

"No. Never. Listen to me," he growled. "What I saw, what I heard, what I went though will never go any further. It stops with me. I'm handling it; maybe not the way the textbook reads, but I'm handling it my way. It took years before I could sleep an entire night without waking up with my guts in knots, my throat tight with other people's screams. I can do it now, the dreams only come every so often, but I'm not about to lay this on someone else."

"There are organizations of veterans—"

"I know, but I've always been a lone wolf, and I'm already over the worst. I can look at a tree now; I can let someone walk up to my back. It's finished, Cat. I don't wallow in it."

"It's not finished if it still bothers you," she said quietly.

He drew a ragged breath. "I got out of it alive. Don't ask for anything else." A soundless laugh moved his chest as he walked even farther away. "And I didn't even ask for that. At first...God, at first I prayed every night, every morning. Just get me out alive, let me get through this alive, don't let me be blown into obscene little red pieces of meat. Then, after about six months, the prayer changed. Every morning I prayed that I wouldn't make it out alive. I didn't want to come back. No human being should have to live through that and still face the sunrise every morning. I wanted to die. I tried to. I took chances that no sane person would take, but I made it anyway. One day I was in the jungle, and the next I was in Honolulu, and those damned fools were walking under trees, letting people walk up to them, smiling and laughing and staring at me, some of them, like I was some kind of freak. Oh, hell..." he finished, his voice sliding away.

Cathryn felt something on her face and brushed the back of her hand over her cheek, surprised to feel dampness. Tears? She had been too young to understand the horror of Vietnam while it was happening; but she had read about it since, had seen pictures, and she could remember Rule's face the day her father had brought him to the ranch. Rule's battered, bitter face, the silence of him, was her picture of Vietnam.

But while she had only a picture, he had the reality of his memories and his dreams.

A low cry came from her as she rushed across the floor to him, wrapping her arms about him so tightly that he couldn't shove her away again. He didn't try to; he enclosed her in the tempered steel of his embrace, bending his head down to rest it on hers. He felt the liquid grief on her face as it touched his chest, and he dried her cheeks with the palm of his hand. "Don't cry for me," he muttered, kissing her hard, almost brutally. "Give me comfort, not pity."

"What do you want?" she whimpered.

"This." He lifted her high, kissing her again and again, stealing her breath until she was dizzy and clung to him with her arms and legs, afraid that she would fall if he relaxed his hold. But he didn't let her fall. He lowered her slowly, slithering her body along his torso, and she cried out as she felt his entry.

"I want this," he said harshly, his breath rasping in and out of his lungs. "I want to bury myself in you. I want you to go wild beneath me when I'm making love to you, and you do, don't you? Tell me, Cat. Tell me you go wild."

She buried her face in his neck, sobbing with the fire he had ignited with his powerful, driving loins. "Yes," she moaned, giving in to any demand he made.

The hot rush of delirium swept over them simultaneously. He went down with her to the floor and she didn't even notice the hardness or her discomfort as he surged against her. At last the sweet, hot pulsing of his body had stopped and he lifted her onto the bed, once again cradling her soft body to him until she slept.

When she awoke again it was a sunny morning and Rule still lay beside her, a faint smile gentling the hard contours of his face as he watched her as she stretched and realized that she wasn't alone. She looked at him and gave him a sleepy smile. Then he drew her to him with one hand on her waist and without a word made love to her again.

When it was over he lifted his head and dared her in a velvet rasp, "Marry me."

Cathryn was so stunned that she could only gape at him.

A rueful smile curved his hard, chiseled lips, but he repeated the words. "Marry me. Why do you look so surprised? I've planned to marry you since you were . . . oh, fifteen or so. Since the day you slapped my face and got your little fanny tanned for your effort, as a matter of fact."

Suddenly terrified of this new demand he was making on her, Cathryn sat up away from his arms and said in a shaking voice, "I can't even decide if I should stay here or not, and now you want me to marry you. How can I decide about that?"

"That part's simple," he assured her, drawing her down beside him again. "Don't think about it; don't worry about it. Just do it. We may fight every inch of the way to bed every night, but once we get there it will be worth every bruise and scratch. I can promise you that you'll never crawl into a cold bed at night."

Cathryn was shaken to the core. Oh, God, she wanted him so much! But despite the drugging intensity of his lovemaking, he would share nothing of himself with her except for the physical part of a relationship. She had all but begged him to trust her and he had shoved her away.

Shudders of reaction began racing through her. "No!" she cried wildly, afraid most of all of the powerful temptation to blindly do as he said and marry him despite everything. She wanted him so much that it was terrifying, but he hadn't said that he loved her, only that he had planned to marry her. He had planned everything. He made no secret of his devotion to the ranch. He was obsessed with it, perhaps to the point that he would marry simply to keep it under his domination. Last night she had seen part of what Vietnam had done to him and she understood more fully why he clung so fiercely to this ranch. Hot tears suddenly scalded her face and she almost screamed, "I can't! I can't even think when you're around! You promised you wouldn't touch me, but you broke your word! I'm going back to Chicago. I'm leaving today. I can't stand being pressured like this!"

She had never been more miserable, and she was made more so by his tight-lipped silence as he dressed and left her room. Cathryn lay rigidly, occasionally wiping at the tears that managed to escape despite her desperate efforts at control. She ached in both body and mind, battered by the fierce, untamed need for him that she could neither control not understand. She had wanted him to leave her alone, but now she lay feeling as if part of her had been torn away. She had to grind her teeth together in concentration to prevent herself from creeping down the hall to his room and crawling into the strength of his embrace. She *had* to leave. If she didn't get away from his influence, he would use her weakness for him as a means of binding her to him permanently, and she would never know if he wanted her for herself or for the ranch.

It was obvious that Rule desired her physically. Why not? She wasn't a raving beauty, but she was passable in most areas and many people found her leggy grace and exotic coloring attractive. Rule was a normal male with all the normal male needs and responses, so there was no reason why he shouldn't want her. It was when she delved below the surface that she became overwhelmed by doubts and possibilities, none of them pleasant.

As well as she knew Rule, as intimate as she was with every line of his body and nuance of his expression and voice, she was violently aware that he kept a great deal of himself locked away. He was a man who had lived through hell and emerged from the fires with nothing of value left, no illusions or dreams to buffer him from the stark reality of what he had experienced; and he had returned "home" to find that in fact he had no home, that emotionally he had been cast adrift. The hand that Ward Donahue had extended to him had literally saved his life, and from that moment he had poured his devotion into the ranch that had sheltered him and allowed him to rebuild the blasted ruin of his life.

She could marry him, yes, but she would never know if he had married her for love of herself or for love of the ranch that came with her. She was a package deal, and for the first time in her life she wished that the ranch weren't hers. Leaving wouldn't solve the problem for her, but it would give her the opportunity to decide in a rational way whether she could marry Rule and live with him in any sort of serenity, able to accept that she would never know for certain. She couldn't be rational around Rule; he reduced her to the most basic responses.

It was an old problem, one that heiresses were traditionally troubled with: Did he want her or her possessions? In this case it wasn't a question of money but of security and dark emotions buried so deep in Rule's subconscious that perhaps even he wasn't aware of his motivation.

Cathryn finally got out of bed and listlessly began packing. She had barely begun when the door opened and Rule stood there.

He was dressed in fresh clothing, his expression blank, but lines of weariness scored his face. He said evenly, "Come riding with me."

She looked away. "I have to pack—"

"Please," he interrupted, and she quivered at hearing that unaccustomed word from him. "Come riding with me this one last time," he coaxed. "If I can't convince you to stay, then I'll take you to wherever you want to go to catch a flight out of Texas."

She sighed, rubbing her forehead in an agitated gesture. Why couldn't she just make a clean break? She had to be the world's biggest glutton for punishment. "All right," she gave in. "Let me get dressed."

For a moment he looked disinclined to leave, his dark eyes telling her that that was a silly thing to say to a man who had made love to her as he had the night before. But then he nodded and closed the door. With her senses acutely aware of him, she felt his presence and knew that he was leaning against the wall outside her room. Quickly she dressed and brushed the worst of the tangles from her hair. When she opened the door, he straightened and extended his hand to her, then let it drop before she could decide whether to take it or not.

They walked in silence to the stables, where they saddled the horses. The early morning was pleasantly cool and the horses were full of energy, impatient with the slow walk that the firm hands on the reins held them to. After several minutes of silence Cathryn kneed her horse closer to Rule's and said abruptly, "What did you want to talk about?"

His eyes were shadowed by the battered black hat that he habitually wore low as protection against the fierce Texas sun, and she could read nothing in the portion of his face that was exposed to her gaze. "Not now," he refused. "Let's just ride and look at the land."

She was content enough to do that, loving the well-tended look of the pastures, and aching inside at the thought of leaving all of this again. The fencing was sturdy and in good repair; all of the outbuildings were clean and freshly painted. Rule's stewardship had been nothing short of outstanding. Even when her resentment had been at its hottest she had never doubted his feelings for the land. She had acknowledged that even in the depths of adolescent confusion.

They were away from the paddocks and barns now, and crossing a pasture. Rule reined in his horse and nodded in the direction of the ranch buildings. "I've been holding this place for you," he said harshly. "Waiting for you to come back to it. I can't believe you don't want it."

She swallowed a flash of anger and cried indignantly, "Not want it! How can you think that? I love this place; it's my home."

"Then live here; make it your home."

"I've always wanted to do that," she said, bitterness lacing her tone. "It's just that...oh, damn you, Rule, you must know that you're the reason I've stayed away!''

His mouth twisted as her bitterness was reflected back at her. "Why? Do you believe everything that was said about me when I came back from Nam?"

"Of course not!" she denied hotly. "Nobody does!"

"Some did. I have a vivid recollection of several people trying their level best to make me pay in blood for everything they thought I'd done." His face was stony, cold, as he brought one of his black memories up into the fresh and sunny morning.

Cathryn shuddered and reached out to grasp his muscular forearm, bared by the rolled-up sleeve of his denim work shirt. "It was never anything like that, believe me! I . . . at the time, I resented you so much that I couldn't think straight."

"Do you still resent me?" he demanded.

"No." The confession was made in a low voice; she looked at him with troubled, doubtful eyes. Somehow she couldn't just tell him that she was afraid that he wanted the ranch more than he wanted her. She knew that if she exposed her doubts to him, he would be able to talk her out of them using her weakness for him to railroad her into doing whatever he wanted. She didn't just want him physically. She wanted his emotional commitment, too.

"Will you reconsider?" he rasped. "Will you think about staying?"

She had to force herself to look away, to keep him from seeing the longing in her eyes. If only she *could* stay! If only she could be content with what he was offering her, what she suspected was all he was capable of offering to any woman. But she wanted so much more than that, and she was afraid that she would destroy herself if she tried to compromise on that. "No," she whispered.

He danced Redman around to face her and closed his gloved hand over her reins. His dark face was taut with frustration, his jaw set in a grim line. "Okay, so you leave. What if you're pregnant? What then? Are you going to insist on handling that on your own? Will you even tell me if I'm going to be a father, or will you just get rid of my baby and pretend that it never existed? When will you know?" he said fiercely

The words, the idea, stunned her almost as deeply as his unexpected proposal of marriage had done a few hours before. Helplessly she stared at him.

One corner of his mouth curled upward in a smile that was a travesty of amusement. "Don't look so surprised," he taunted. "You're old enough to know how it happens, and neither of us did anything to prevent it."

Cathryn closed her eyes, shaken by the sweetness she felt at the thought of having his child. Against all common sense, for a moment she prayed with wild longing that it was so, that she was already harboring his child. A tiny, otherworldly smile touched her lips and he cursed between clenched teeth, his gloved hand moving up to grip the nape of her neck.

"Get that look off your face!" he growled. "Unless you want to be on the ground with me, because right now I want you—"

He broke off and Cathryn opened her eyes, devouring the sight of him, unable to control her expression. A muscle flexed in his cheek as he repeated, "When? When will you know?"

Silently she counted, then said, "In a week or so."

"And if you are? What will you do?"

Cathryn swallowed, facing the inevitable. She really had no option. She wasn't a woman who could force illegitimacy on a child when the father was more than willing to marry her. A pregnancy would settle everything except her own doubts. She whispered, "I won't keep it from you if...if I am."

He took his hat off and ran his hand through his thick dark hair. Jamming the hat back on his head, he said harshly, "I've sweated it out before, wondering if I had made you pregnant. I guess I can do it again. At least this time you're not just a kid yourself."

She swallowed again, inexplicably moved to learn that he hadn't been so unaffected by that day so long ago. She started to speak, though she had no idea what she was going to say, but Rule kneed his horse away from her. "I have work to do," he muttered. "Let me know when you decide what time you're leaving. I'll have the plane ready to go."

She watched as he rode away from her; then she turned her horse's head and walked it slowly back to the stables. Their talk had accomplished exactly nothing, except to make her aware of the possible consequences of their nights together.

After returning to the house and picking at her breakfast, she called the airline in Houston and made reservations for the following day, then made a stab at packing. She hadn't much to pack, really. Most of her clothing was still in Chicago. She had been making do with the old clothes that she had left at the ranch.

The hours dragged; she could scarcely wait until lunch, when she would be able to see Rule again, even if she had forbidden herself the joy of having him. She went downstairs and puttered around, helping Lorna put the meal together, looking constantly out the window.

A horse was galloped into the yard and the rider flung himself off. Cathryn could hear muffled shouts and sensed his urgency, but she couldn't hear what he was saying. She and Lorna exchanged worried glances and both stepped to the back door. "What is it?" Cathryn called as Lewis's tall, lean form ran from the stables to the pickup. "What's wrong?"

He turned, his hard face drawn. "Rule's horse went down with him," he called tersely. "He's hurt."

The words punched her in the stomach and she reeled backward, then forced herself upright. On shaking legs she ran to the pickup, where a man had placed one of the mattresses from the bunkhouse in the bed of the truck, and she clambered into the cab beside Lewis. He shot a look at her utterly white face and said nothing, instead slamming the gearshift through its pattern as he raced the truck across the pastures. It seemed that they spent an eternity bouncing in the dust before they reached a small knot of men grouped anxiously around the prone figure on the ground.

Cathryn was out of the truck before it had stopped, sliding to her knees beside him and kicking a fine spray of dust over him. A sickening panic seized her as she saw his closed eyes and pale face. "Rule!" she cried, touching his cheek and not getting a response.

Lewis knelt beside her as her shaking fingers tore at the buttons of Rule's shirt. It wasn't until she slid her hand inside and felt the reassuring thud of his heartbeat that she let out the breath she had been holding and raised frantic eyes to Lewis. Lewis was running his hands over Rule's body, pausing when he reached a point about halfway between knee and ankle on his left leg. "His leg's broken," he muttered.

Rule drew in a shuddering breath and his dark lashes fluttered open. Quickly Cathryn bent over him. "Rule . . . darling, do you understand me?" she asked, seeing the unfocused look in his eyes.

"Yes," he muttered. "Redman?"

She swiveled her head around to look at the horse. He was standing on all four legs and she couldn't see any serious swelling. "I think he's okay. He's definitely in better shape than you are. Your left leg is broken."

"I know. I felt it snap." He gave her a weak smile. "I took quite a knock on the head, too."

Once again Cathryn raised her worried eyes to meet Lewis's. A knock on the head meant a possible concussion, and coupling that knowledge with the length of time Rule had been unconscious, the possibility became a probability. Despite his rational answers, the quicker he was taken to a hospital, the better. There was also the horrifying thought of neck or back injuries. She would have given anything to be able to take the pain herself if he would be spared, and in that moment she admitted beyond doubt that she loved him. It wasn't just desire that she felt for him; she loved him. Why else would she have been so upset that he might have made love to someone else? Why else be so jealous of his kisses? Why else feel so hopeful that he had made her pregnant? She had loved him for a long time, long before she had been mature enough to recognize it for what it was.

The men were moving quickly, efficiently, and she was gently crowded away from Rule. They lifted him gently onto a blanket that had been spread on the ground beside him. She heard a stifled cry of pain and bit down hard on her lower lip, bringing tiny dots of blood to the surface. Lewis said, "You must be getting clumsy, boss, falling off a horse like that," which brought a tight grin to Rule's face. The grin faded abruptly when he was lifted, the blanket serving as a stretcher. From between clenched teeth he spat words that Cathryn had heard separately, but never together and with such inventiveness as Rule was using. Sweat was beaded on his face by the time he was placed on the mattress in the back of the truck. Cathryn and Lewis climbed in back with him and Cathryn automatically wiped his face.

"Take it easy on the ride back," Lewis instructed the man who was doing the driving now, and the man nodded his understanding.

Even when taken at a slow pace, every bump in the ground made Rule's hands clench into fists, and his face took on a grayish tinge. He brought his hands up and clenched them around his head as if he could buffer it from the swaying of the pickup. Cathryn hovered over him anxiously, suffering for him with every lurch of the truck, but there was nothing she could do.

Lewis met her eyes across Rule's prone form. "San Antonc is closer than Houston," he said quietly. "We'll take him there."

When they reached the ranch two seats were quickly removed from the plane and Rule was placed, mattress and all, in the vacated space. His eyelids were drooping and Cathryn cupped his face in her hands. "Darling, you can't go to sleep," she said softly. "Open your eyes and look at me. You can't go to sleep."

Obediently he looked at her, his eyes dazed as he concentrated on what she said with heart-wrenching intensity. A half smile touched his pale lips. "Look at me," he whispered, and she remembered his lovemaking. Was he remembering, too?

"I'll be all right," he assured her drowsily. "It's not that bad. I had a lot worse than this in Nam."

The doctor at the hospital in San Antonio agreed. Though Rule did have a concussion and would be kept under observation at least overnight, his condition was in no way severe enough to indicate a need for surgery. Except for the lump on his head and his broken leg, they could find no other injuries but various bruises. After the strain of crouching beside him during the flight and trying to keep him awake, finding out that he would be all right had the same effect on Cathryn that bad news would have had: she turned her head into Lewis's chest and burst into tears.

Instantly his arms went around her and he hugged her tightly. "Why cry now?" he sputtered with relieved laughter.

"Because I can't help it," she sniffled.

The doctor laughed and patted her shoulder. "Cry all you want," he said kindly. "He'll be fine, I promise. You can take him home in a day or so, and the headache from that concussion should keep him in bed long enough for that leg to get a good start on healing."

"May we see him now?" asked Cathryn, wiping her eyes. She wanted to see him for herself, to touch him and let him know that she and Lewis were still close by.

"Not yet. We've taken him downstairs to have his leg X-rayed and set. I'll let you know when we have him settled in a room."

She and Lewis waited in the visitors' lounge with cups of bitter coffee obtained from the vending machine in the corner. She was grateful for the presence of the man, stranger though he was. He had never once acted upset or out of control, though he had moved swiftly. If he had revealed any fear, Cathryn knew that she would have fallen apart.

Lewis sprawled back in the uncomfortable plastic chair, his long, booted legs outstretched and reminding her of Rule. Her stomach rumbled and she said, "Rule must be starving. He didn't have any breakfast this morning."

"No, he won't be hungry until after his system is over the shock," said Lewis. "But we're another matter. Let's find the cafeteria. We could both use a meal and a decent cup of coffee."

"But Rule—"

"Won't be going anywhere," insisted Lewis, taking her hand and urging her out of the chair. "We'll be back long before they're finished with him, anyway. I've had my share of broken bones, just like he has; I know how long it will take."

His prediction was correct. Though they lingered in the cafeteria it was almost an hour after they returned to the waiting room that a nurse approached them and gave them the welcome information that Rule was now in a room. They went to the proper floor and met the doctor in the corridor.

"It was a clean break. He'll be as good as new," he assured them. "I'm certain we don't have anything to worry about. He's too ill-tempered to be injured very badly." He looked at Lewis and shook his head in awe. "He's the toughest son of a—" With a quick glance at Cathryn he cut himself off short. "He refused any sort of anesthetic, even a local. Said he didn't like them."

"No," said Lewis blandly. "He doesn't."

Cathryn moved impatiently and the doctor smiled at her. "Do you want to see him now?" he asked in amusement.

"Yes, of course," said Cathryn quickly. She needed to get to Rule, to touch him and satisfy herself that he was really all right.

She wasn't certain what to expect. She was braced for bruises and bandages—something she didn't know if she could bear when Rule was the patient concerned. What she found when they opened the door was tousled dark hair, a face that managed to be both sleepy and annoyed, and a leg encased in a pristine cast that was supported by a sling rigged from a contraption stationed at the foot of the bed.

They had put him in a regulation hospital gown, but that state of affairs hadn't lasted long. The garment was in a tangled heap on the floor, and she knew that beneath the thin sheet there was only Rule. Despite herself, she began to laugh.

He began to turn his head with the utmost care, and behind her, Cathryn heard Lewis's stifled chuckle. Rule gave up trying to turn his head and instead only moved his eyes, which still caused him to wince noticeably. "Well, don't just stand there gloating," he growled at Cathryn. "Come hold my hand. I could use some sympathy."

Obediently she crossed to his bedside, and though she was still laughing she felt the hot sting of tears in her eyes. She took his hand in hers and lifted it to her lips for a quick kiss on the lean, powerful fingers. "You scared me half to death," she accused him, her voice both teasing and tearful. "And now you don't even look hurt, except for your leg. You just look grouchy!"

"It hasn't been a picnic," he told her feelingly. His hand tightened on hers, and he drew her even closer to the bed; but his glance shifted to Lewis. "Lew, how badly is Redman hurt?"

"Nothing serious," Lewis assured him. "He was walking okay. I'll keep an eye on him, watch for swelling."

Rule forgot himself and nodded, a lapse that he paid for immediately. He groaned aloud and put his hand on his head. "Damn," he swore weakly, "I've got a hell of a headache. Didn't they leave an ice pack or something?"

Cathryn looked around and found the ice pack on the floor where it had evidently been flung along with the hospital gown. She picked it up and placed it on his forehead. He sighed with relief, then returned to Lewis.

"Go on back to the ranch," he instructed the foreman. "There's too much to be done before the sale for both of us to be gone, even for a day. The dun mare should come in tomorrow or the next day. Put her with Irish Gale."

Lewis listened attentively as Rule outlined what had to be done during the next two days. He asked a few brief questions; then he was gone before Cathryn could quite comprehend that she had been left behind. Rule hadn't released his grip on her hand in all that time. Now he turned his sleepy attention to her.

"You don't mind staying with me, do you?"

It hadn't occurred to her to leave, but asking her permission after she had already been stranded made her give him a wry look. "Would it have mattered if I did?"

His dark eyes grew even darker; then his jaw hardened. "No," he said flatly. "I need you here." He shifted on the bed and muttered a curse when his head throbbed. "This changes things. You can't leave the ranch now, Cat. With the sale coming up I need your help. There's too much for Lewis to handle on his own, and when it comes down to basics, it's your responsibility because it's your ranch. Besides, if you'll ever be safe from me, that time is now. I couldn't fight a kitten, let alone a full-grown Cat."

She couldn't even smile at his pun. He looked so unnaturally helpless that she wished she had never said anything. All thoughts of leaving the ranch had disappeared from her mind the minute she'd heard that Rule was hurt, but she didn't tell him that. She merely smoothed a damp strand of dark hair back from his forehead and said quietly, "Of course I'll stay. Did you really think I'd leave now?"

"I didn't know," he muttered. "I couldn't stop you if you wanted to go, but I hoped the ranch meant more to you than that."

It wasn't the ranch that held her, it was Rule; but his accident hadn't deprived her of her common sense, and she didn't tell him that, either. Instead she plucked the sheet a little higher on his torso and teased, "I have to stay, if only to protect your modesty."

He gave her a roguish look despite the pallor of his face and the not-quite-focused expression in his eyes. "You're too late to save my modesty. But if you'd like to protect my virtue, I could use some help in fighting off these fresh nurses."

"Does your virtue need protecting?" She felt almost giddy with the unusual pleasure of teasing him, of actually flirting. It was odd that he had to be flat on his back and unable to move before she felt easy enough with him to tease him, but then, she had always been wary of him. It just wasn't good sense to turn your back on a panther.

"Not at the moment," he admitted, his voice fading away. "Even the spirit isn't willing right now."

He slipped easily and swiftly into sleep and Cathryn tucked his hand under the sheet. The air-conditioner was on full blast and it felt cold in the room to her, so she lifted the sheet over his naked shoulders, then sat down in the chair by his bedside and drew her legs up under her.

"What now?" she wondered aloud, her eyes never leaving the hard profile, softened somewhat as he relaxed deeply into sleep. In one morning everything had changed. Instead of fleeing to safety she was sitting by his side, and she knew that nothing could induce her to leave. He was weak and injured and he hadn't been lying when he had said that he would need her at the ranch during the coming weeks. The horse sale alone involved a great deal of work, and regardless of how competent Lewis was, he wasn't a superman. He couldn't be everywhere at once. That took care of any logical arguments she had. On an emotional level she admitted that she wouldn't leave Rule now even if there were no need for her to stay at all.

Rather than suddenly falling in love with him, she had awakened to the realization that she had loved him for a long time. She had loved David, too, with a very real love, but it had been a shallow emotion compared to the intensity of her feelings for Rule. It was so intense that when she was younger it had frightened her and she had fled from it. It had destroyed her control and her self-confidence, prevented her from accepting its existence. She was still frightened of the furious strength of her emotions. She had been running yet again because she wasn't certain that he returned even a fraction of that emotion. Watching him now, Cathryn made a painful decision, wondering wryly if she had reached a new level of maturity or if she were merely being foolhardy. At whatever risk, she was going to stay at the ranch. She loved him. It didn't make sense. It was against all the rules of human behavior that she should have loved him so young and so fiercely; but she had, and the feeling had endured.

Her glance swept blindly around the small, dim room and settled on a black object so familiar that it took her breath. How had his hat gotten here? She couldn't remember its being on the plane, but it must have been, because here it was. Had Lewis brought it? Or had Rule unconsciously clutched it in his hand? It didn't really matter, though she gave a wobbly smile at the thought.

Rule's hats were disaster areas. He was rougher on his headgear than any man she had ever seen. She had no idea what he did to his hats to get them in such shape, though she had sometimes suspected him of stomping on them. Whenever he was forced to buy a new one— something he did only reluctantly—within a week the new hat had taken on a battered, defeated shape, as if it had been run over by a herd of stampeding cattle. Tears blurred her eyes as she reached out for the dusty, shabby hat and hugged it to her breast.

She could be risking her entire future if she were wrong in staying, but today she had been forced to realize that Rule was as human and as vulnerable as any other man. An accident could easily take him from her at any time, and she would be left with nothing but the bitter thought, what if? He had asked her to marry him. She didn't know about that. She was far too upset and confused to plan anything concrete, but she was finished with running. It hadn't solved anything before. She had been haunted by thoughts of him, memories that had continually surfaced until his face had been a mental veil through which she had viewed all other men. She loved him. She had to face it squarely and accept whatever that love brought her, whether pain or pleasure. If she had learned nothing else from the eight years she had spent away from him, she had learned that she could never forget him.

Rule was an angel. He was a perfect patient—obedient, uncomplaining, as docile as a lamb...as long as Cathryn was by his side. She had had no idea what she was letting herself in for when she had promised to stay with him, until the first time a nurse came in to wake him up and check his pulse rate and blood pressure. Rule's eyes flared open wildly and he tried to sit up before the pain in his head made him sink back with a groan. "Cathryn?" he demanded hoarsely.

"I'm here," she reassured him quickly, jumping up from her chair to take his hand and twine her fingers through his.

He glared at her with dazed intensity. "Don't leave me."

"I won't leave you. I promised, remember?"

He sighed and relaxed, closing his eyes again. The nurse frowned and leaned closer, asking, "Mr. Jackson, do you know where you are?"

"I'm in a damned hospital," he snarled without opening his eyes.

The nurse, a chubby brunette with sharp brown eyes, smiled up at Cathryn in sympathy. "We'll be waking him every hour to make certain it's a normal sleep and that he hasn't gone into a coma. It's just a precaution, but it's always better to be safe."

"Don't talk about me like I'm not here," he grumbled.

Again the nurse's eyes met Cathryn's and she rolled them expressively. Cathryn squeezed Rule's fingers and admonished, "Behave yourself. Being grouchy won't help."

Still without opening his eyes, Rule carried her hand to his face and cuddled it against his cheek. "For you," he sighed. "But it's hard to smile when your head is exploding."

He was as good as his word; for Cathryn, he was so docile that it was ludicrous. The nurses, however, quickly learned that if they asked Cathryn to step aside, he refused to cooperate with anything they wanted to do. He demanded her constant presence, and after a few abortive attempts to manage him, so did the nurses. Cathryn knew that he was shamelessly using his injuries to keep her by his side, but rather than being exasperated, she was filled with an aching tenderness for him and she fetched for him and waited on him tirelessly.

It was late afternoon before her rumbling stomach reminded her that she was stranded without benefit of money, makeup, a change of clothes, or so much as a comb. Lewis had paid for the sandwich she'd left half-eaten that morning, and now she was in danger of starving to death, or so her stomach warned her. She carefully spoon-fed Rule the few bites of gelatin that he would eat, but he refused the split pea soup and when she tasted it she understood why. Even as hungry as she was, she couldn't eat it. Split pea soup had never been on her personal menu, and Rule shared the same lack of interest in it.

He wasn't so ill that he didn't notice what went on around him. After watching through slitted eyes as she tasted the soup and grimaced, he said gently, "Go on to the cafeteria and get something to eat. You must be hungry by now. I'll be good while you're gone."

"I'm starving," she admitted, but added wryly, "However, I don't think they'll feed me on the basis of my looks. I don't even have a comb with me, let alone money or fresh clothes. I never thought to get my purse. We just loaded you up and took off."

"Call Lewis and tell him what you need. He can bring it down tonight," he instructed.

"I couldn't ask him—"

"You *can* ask him. It's your ranch, isn't it?" he demanded testily. "No, I'll call him myself. In the meantime, get my wallet out of the upper drawer in the nightstand and go feed yourself."

She hesitated. Then, as he tried to push himself into an upright position, his face blanching even whiter when he moved, she snapped, "Okay, okay!" as she quickly eased him back onto the pillows. When she opened the drawer the wallet was right on top and she lifted it out, then stood for a moment looking at it regretfully. She hated to spend his money, though why it should bother her, she couldn't say.

"Go on," he ordered, and because she was so hungry she did.

While she was sitting in the cafeteria, slowly chewing on stale crackers and eating potato soup, she succumbed to the temptation to go through his wallet. Looking around guiltily as she did so, she first examined the few snapshots he carried. One was obviously of his mother, whom Cathryn couldn't remember at all, because she had died when Rule was a small boy. The faint resemblance in the shape of the brows and mouth was all that proclaimed their family ties. Another was of Rule's father, tall and lean, with a thin ten-year-old boy standing stiffly beside him, scowling at the camera. Cathryn smiled mistily, having seen that scowl many times on the adult man's face.

When she flipped the plastic holders again her mouth dropped open. While she had half hoped to find a snapshot of herself, the one that she found wasn't what she had expected. She had thought that perhaps he would carry the class portrait made in her senior year in high school, or even one of her college snapshots, but the picture that Rule carried with him was the one that had been made when she started first grade. She had been the youngest in her class, still in possession of all of her teeth, and those little teeth had been clamped down on her lower lip in painful intensity as she stared at the camera with huge, somber dark eyes. How had he gotten that snapshot? She had been at least twelve, perhaps thirteen, when he came to the ranch. She couldn't remember exactly. He could only have gotten this particular picture by going through the family album.

There was one other picture... of Ward Donahue. Cathryn stared at her father with blurred eyes, then returned to her prying. Rule carried only the basic means of identification: his driver's license, pilot's license and social security card. Except for that and forty-three dollars, his wallet was empty.

Tears stung her eyes. Four pictures and three cards were the extent of his personal papers. There was nothing tucked in any of the slots, no notes, nothing to indicate the nature of the man who kept himself so tightly locked inside. She suddenly knew that in his whole lifetime Rule Jackson had said "I need you" to only one person, and she had almost walked out on him anyway.

She drew a deep, shaky breath. She had nearly made the worst mistake of her life, and she was almost grateful for Rule's accident, because it had kept her from leaving and perhaps causing an irreparable rift between them. She loved him, and she would fight for his love.

She had decided not to say anything to him, but late that night the words tumbled out anyway. "How did you get that picture of me that you have in your wallet?"

A wry smile tugged at one corner of his mouth. "I wondered if you'd be able to resist the temptation. Obviously you weren't."

Though she flushed, Cathryn ignored his teasing. "Where did you get it?" she persisted.

"Out of a shoebox crammed full of old snapshots. There are several stored in the attic. Why?"

"I don't understand. Why that particular picture?"

"It reminds me of something," he finally said reluctantly.

"Such as?"

He carefully turned his head to look at her, his eyes as dark as midnight. "Are you sure you want to know?"

"Yes. It seems such an unlikely choice."

"Not really. It was the eyes that got me," he muttered. "You had that same serious, frightened expression in your eyes when you opened them and looked up at me after we had made love that first time, by the river."

The memory was like a lightning bolt, stunning her, as vivid in her mind as if it had just happened. He had lifted himself to his elbows, taking his weight from her young, delicate breasts, and he had said, "Cat," in a quietly demanding voice. Until that moment she had been wrapped in unreality, but at the sound of his voice she had become aware of many things: the searing heat of the sun overhead; the prickle of the grass beneath her bare body; the lazy drone of a bee as it searched for a tempting little wildflower; the musical calls of the birds in the tree nearby. She had also become aware of the enormity of the thing she had just done and whom she had done it with, the identity of the man who still held her in intimate possession. She had become aware of the unfamiliar aches in her body, while the echoes of pleasure still lingered. Terrified as she was of the tumult that had shaken her emotionally and physically, the budding desire to do it all over again had almost been more than she could bear. Her frightened eyes had flown open to stare at him, reflecting in their soft dark depths the uncertainty she had felt at having taken the first and most important step into womanhood.

She was unable to say anything now, and after a moment he sighed wearily and closed his eyes. Anxiously her eyes wandered over his pale face. She had stood vigil beside David's bed for the long weeks before he died, and she was painfully reminded of those endless days. Not that there was any real comparison—Rule would assuredly recover—but the surface resemblance was enough to twist her heart. It had been awful to lose David. If anything happened to Rule, she would never be able to bear it.

* * *

It was a bad night. Cathryn never even bothered to put on the nightgown Lewis had brought her. Though she rented one of the cots that were available to people who stayed the night with the patients, she might as well have sat in the chair for all the sleep either she or Rule had that night. Between the discomfort of his leg and the nauseating headache he was suffering, Rule was restless, and it seemed that every time he managed to settle down and drift off to sleep, a nurse came in to wake him. By dawn his stated opinion of that practice had long since passed out of the realm of politeness and Cathryn would have been in a nervous fit if she hadn't been so weary.

Perhaps it was the pain he was enduring that caused him to dream of Vietnam, but over and over again he would awake from light, fretful sleep with his hands clenched and sweat pouring from his body. Cathryn didn't ask him any questions, merely soothed him with her presence, talking gently to him until he relaxed. She was exhausted, but she was by his side every time his eyes flared open, her love evident in every tender touch of her fingers. He might not have been able to put a name to it, but he responded to her touch, calming down whenever she was near. He was a sick man that night, and all the next day he ran a low fever. Though the nurses assured her that it wasn't unusual, she hovered over him anyway, keeping an ice pack on his forehead and continually cooling his torso with a damp cloth.

He slept the entire night through the second night, which was fortunate, because Cathryn had collapsed onto the cot and didn't stir all night long. It was doubtful that she would have heard him if he had called her.

On Tuesday morning she was both relieved and alarmed when the doctor released him to go home. They would be more comfortable at the ranch, but she wasn't at all certain that Rule was well enough to do without constant medical supervision. The doctor assured her kindly that he was doing well, but gave her careful instructions to keep Rule quiet for at least the remainder of the week. He was to stay strictly in bed until his headache and dizziness were completely gone, as it would be too risky for him to attempt walking with crutches while his balance wasn't what it should be.

The flight back to the ranch left him exhausted, and his face was alarmingly pale when, not without some difficulty, several of the ranch hands carried him upstairs and placed him on the bed. Despite their careful handling he was clutching his head in pain, and Lorna, who had met them with expressions of relief and anxiety warring on her face, left the room with tears in her eyes. The men filed out and left Cathryn to get him settled.

Gently she removed his shirt and jeans, the left leg of which had been cut off to enable him to get them on over the cast. After propping his leg on pillows and bracing it on either side with rolled-up blankets, she tucked the sheet around him. "Are you hungry?" she asked, worried that his appetite was still almost nonexistent. "Thirsty? Anything?"

He opened his eyes and looked around the room. Without answering her questions he muttered, "This isn't my room."

Cathryn had done a great deal of thinking about the situation at the house and had instructed Lorna to have Rule's things moved into the front guest room. His own bedroom was at the back corner of the house, overlooking the stables, and Cathryn didn't think he would be able to rest with all the activity in the yard. Not only that, the guest room was next to her own bedroom, making it more convenient for her if he called her; and it had a connecting bath, the only bedroom in the house with that luxury. Considering Rule's relative immobility, the location of the bathroom was a major factor. She only hoped he would cooperate.

Calmly she said, "No, it's the room next to mine. I wanted you close to me during the night. It also has a bathroom," she added.

He considered that, his eyelashes drooping to shield his eyes. "All right," he finally conceded. "I'm not hungry, but ask Lorna for some soup, or something like that. It'll make her feel better."

So he had noticed that Lorna was upset, despite his own condition. Cathryn didn't question Lorna's devotion to him. Who knew what secrets were hidden behind the cook's stoic face? And she was glad that he cared for other people, because for too long she had thought him incapable of caring.

"Where's Lew?" Rule was fretting. "I need to talk to him."

Cathryn looked at him sternly. "Now you listen to me, Rule Jackson. You're under strict orders to stay quiet, and if you give me any trouble I'll have you loaded up and taken back to that hospital so fast that your head will spin even worse than it already is. No working, no worrying, no trying to get up by yourself. Agreed?"

He glared at her. "Damn it, I've got a sale coming up and—"

"And we'll handle it," she interrupted. "I'm not saying that you can't talk to Lewis at all, but I'm going to make certain that you do a lot more resting than you do talking.''

He sighed. "You're mighty big for your britches now that I'm as helpless as a turtle on its back," he said with deceptive mildness. "But this cast won't be on forever, and you'd better remember that."

"You're frightening me to death," she teased, leaning down to kiss him swiftly on the mouth and straightening before his dulled reflexes could react. His sleepy dark eyes drifted down her form with a lazy threat; then his lashes refused to open again and just like that he dozed off.

Cathryn quietly raised the window to let in some fresh air, then tiptoed out and closed the door behind her.

Ricky was leaning against the wall outside the room, her slanted hazel eyes narrowed in fury. "You told Lewis not to take me to the hospital so I could see Rule, didn't you?" she charged. "You didn't want me to be with him. You wanted him all to yourself."

Afraid that the woman's angry voice would wake him, Cathryn grabbed Ricky's arm roughly and pulled her away from the door. "Be quiet!" she whispered angrily. "He's sleeping, and he needs all the rest he can get."

"I'll just bet he does!" Ricky sneered.

Cathryn had spent a horrible two days and her temper was frayed. She snapped. "Think what you like, but stay away from him. I've never meant anything as much as I mean that. I'm warning you, I'll do whatever I have to do to keep you from upsetting him while he's still so ill. This is my ranch, and if you want to stay here you'd better pay attention to what I'm saying!"

"Oh, God, you make me sick! *Your* ranch! *Your* house! You've always thought this stupid little ranch made you better than everyone else."

Cathryn's fist doubled. *She* was sick. Sick and tired of Ricky's jealousy and pure nastiness, even though she understood them. Perhaps Ricky saw the last bit of control vanish from Cathryn's expression, because she moved quickly away and went downstairs, leaving Cathryn standing in the hallway trying to control the rage that burned through her.

After several minutes she went down to the kitchen and passed along Rule's request for soup, knowing from previous experience that his nap would be a short one, and wanting to have something ready for him to eat when he awoke. Lorna's damp eyes lit up at the information that Rule wanted her to do something for him and she began rushing about the kitchen. Within half an hour the tray was prepared with a bowl brimming with the rich, thick vegetable soup that she made, and a glass of iced tea. As Cathryn carried the tray upstairs she reflected that if Rule were still asleep she could eat the soup herself, because suddenly she was starving.

But Rule stirred when she opened the door, moving restlessly on the bed. He tried to struggle into a sitting position and she hurriedly set the tray on the night table and rushed to help him, putting an arm behind his neck to provide support while she punched the pillows into position to brace him. Then she had to get his leg settled comfortably, a process that had him clenching his jaw before it was finished.

He ate the soup with more appetite than he had shown for anything in the hospital, but the bowl was still half-full when he pushed it away and said irritably, "It's hot in here."

Cathryn sighed, but he had a point. The windows faced southwest, and the room took the full blast of the hot afternoon sun. It wasn't so noticeable to someone who didn't have to spend the entire day in the room, but already perspiration was glistening on his face and torso. Central heating and air-conditioning had never been installed in the old house, so the only solution she could think of was to buy a window unit. In the meantime she remembered that they had an electric fan and searched it out. At least that would keep the air moving until she could buy an air-conditioner.

She plugged the fan into the outlet and turned the switch on, directing the flow of air onto his body. He sighed and threw his right arm up to cover his eyes. "I remember one day in Saigon," he murmured. "It was so ungodly hot that the air was almost syrupy. My boots were sticking to the pavement when I walked across the helicopter pad. *That* was hot, Cat—so miserably hot that if Nam wasn't hell, it came in second. For years the feel of sweat crawling down my back was as bad as a snake crawling on me, because it reminded me of that day in Saigon."

Cathryn stood as if she had been turned to stone, afraid to say anything. It was the first time he had shared any of his memories of the war, and she wasn't certain if he was slowly becoming accustomed to talking about it or if he wasn't quite rational. He resolved that question when he moved his arm and looked at her, his dark eyes steady. "Until one day in July, eight years ago," he whispered. "It was hot that day, blistering hot, and when I saw you swimming naked in the river I envied you, and I thought about jumping in with you. Then I thought that some other man could have seen you as easily as I had, and I wanted to shake you until your teeth rattled. You know what happened," he continued softly. "And while I was making love to you the sun was burning down on my back and sweat was running off me, but I didn't think of Vietnam that day. All I could think of was the way you had turned so sweet and wild in my arms, lying under me and burning me with a different kind of heat. I never minded being hot and sweaty after that day, because all I had to do was look up at that Texas sun and I thought of making love with you."

Cathryn swallowed, unable to speak or move. He held out his hand to her. "Come here."

She found herself on her knees beside the bed, his hand clenched in her hair as he pulled her forward. He didn't make the mistake of trying to meet her halfway; he forced her all the way to him, stretching her half across the bed. Their mouths met wildly and his tongue sent her a virile message that left her senses spinning. "I want you now," he murmured into her mouth, taking her hand and sliding it down his body. Cathryn moaned as her fingers confirmed his need.

"We can't," she protested, pulling her lips free, though she mindlessly continued to caress him gently, her hand straying upward to stroke his lean hard belly. "*You* can't. You shouldn't be moving...."

"I won't," he promised, cajoling in a husky murmur. "I'll be perfectly still."

"Liar." Her voice was vibrantly tender. "No, Rule. Not now."

"You're supposed to keep me satisfied."

"That's not what the doctor said," she sputtered. "I'm supposed to keep you quiet."

"I'll be quiet—if you keep me satisfied."

"Please be reasonable."

"Horny men have never been reasonable."

Despite herself she had to laugh, burying her face against the curly hair of his chest until she had her giggles under control. "You poor baby," she crooned.

He smiled and abandoned his attempt to talk her into bed, though she doubted that she could have resisted his sensual pleas if he had persisted for much longer.

He drew his fingers through her hair, watching the dark red strands sift downward. "Are you thinking of leaving, now that I can't do anything to stop you?" he asked, his manner deceptively casual.

Cathryn raised her head swiftly, pulling her hair as she did so. She winced and he dropped the strands that he still held. "Of course not!" she denied indignantly.

"You haven't thought about it at all?"

"Not at all." She smiled down at him and traced a finger around the tiny male nipple that she had found in the curls of hair. "I think I'll stay around after all. I couldn't possibly miss my chance to boss you around. I may never have another."

"So you're staying for revenge?" He was smiling, too, a crooked little smile that barely lifted the corners of his mouth, but for Rule that was something. Laughter didn't come easily to him.

"I certainly am," she assured him, teasing the little point of flesh into tautness. "I'm going to pay you back for every kiss and enjoy watching you squirm. I still owe you for that spanking you gave me, too. I may not be able to pay you back in kind, but I'm certain I'll think of something."

A shuddering breath lifted his chest. "I can hardly wait."

"I know," she said gleefully. "That's my revenge. Making you wait...and wait...and wait."

"You've made me wait for eight years. What do you do for an encore? Turn me into a monk?"

"You were far from that, Rule Jackson, so don't try to tell me different! Wanda told me about your reputation in town. 'Wild as a mink' was the way she described you, and we both know what that means."

"Gossiping women," he grumbled.

Despite his better mood he was tiring rapidly, and when she moved to help him lie down he didn't protest.

The air-conditioner was first on her list of things to get, but Lewis, having taken the time to fetch Rule home from the hospital, was far too busy now for her to ask him to fly back to San Antonio, which would probably be the nearest city where she could purchase a small air-conditioner that wouldn't require additional electrical work on the house. That meant she would have to drive, a trip that took almost two hours one way. And the weather report called for more of the same: hot, hot and hot. Rule needed that air-conditioner.

But she was exhausted now, and the thought of that long drive was more than she could face. She would get up early in the morning and be at the appliance store in San Antonio when it opened. That way she could be back on the ranch before midday and would miss the worst of the heat.

After a long shower she checked in on Rule again and found him still asleep. That was the longest he had slept at any one stretch and she was reassured that he was mending. Gazing pensively at the white cast that covered his leg from knee to toes, she wished that it was gone and Rule was once more where he belonged, out on the range. As much as she relished the thought of having him at her mercy for at least a few days, it still hurt her to see him weak and helpless.

Taking advantage of the quiet, she stretched out across her own bed and instantly fell asleep, only to be awakened by a deep, irritable voice calling her name. She sat up and pushed her hair out of her face, glancing at the clock as she did so. She had slept for almost two hours. No wonder Rule was calling her! He must have been awake for some time, wondering if he had been abandoned.

Hurrying to his room, she found that that wasn't the case at all. His flushed face and tousled hair testified that he had just woken up himself and had called for her in instant demand. After two days of having her constantly with him, he was used to having her at his beck and call.

"Where've you been?" he snapped fretfully.

"Asleep," she said, and yawned. "What did you want?"

For a moment he lay there looking grumpy; then he said, "I'm thirsty."

There was a pitcher of water and a glass on the table beside his bed, but Cathryn didn't protest as she poured the water for him. The doctor had told her that Rule's headaches would give him the very devil for several days, and that the least movement would be painful. She slipped her arm under his pillow to gently raise his head as she held the glass for him. He gulped the water. "It's so damned hot in here," he sighed when the glass was empty.

She had to agree with him on that point. "I'm driving into San Antone in the morning to buy a window air-conditioner," she said. "Stick it out for the rest of the day, and tomorrow you'll be comfortable."

"That's a lot of unnecessary expense—" he began, frowning.

"It's not unnecessary. You won't regain your strength as fast if you lie here sweating yourself half to death every day."

"I still don't like—"

"It's not up to you to like it," she informed him. "I said I'm buying an air-conditioner, and that's that."

His dark eyes settled on her sternly. "Enjoy yourself, because when I'm up and around again, you're in trouble."

"I'm not afraid of you," she laughed, though it was a little bit of a lie. He was so tough and hard and held such sensual power over her that she was, if not actually afraid of him, more than a little cautious.

After a long moment the expression in his eyes softened fractionally. "You still look like you're dead on your feet. Instead of running back and forth, why don't you sleep in here with me? We'd both probably sleep better."

His suggestion was so provocative that she almost climbed in beside him right then, but she remembered his half-serious attempt at seduction only a few hours before and she reluctantly decided against such a move. "No way. You'd never get any rest if you had a woman in bed with you."

"How about next week?" he murmured, stroking her bare arm with one finger.

Cathryn was torn between laughter and tears. Did he sense how drastically her feelings had changed? It was as if he knew that the only thing keeping her out of his bed was her concern for his injuries. He was acting as if everything were settled between them, as if there were no more doubts clouding her mind. Perhaps there weren't. She hadn't really had time to decide exactly what she would do in regard to his marriage proposal, but she knew that no matter what happened now she couldn't run from him again. Maybe her decision was already made and she had only to face it. So many maybes...

But she would be foolish to commit herself to anything right now. She was tired, exhausted from the trauma of the past two days. And she had a ranch to run, a horse sale to prepare for, Ricky's malice to contend with, Rule's demands on her time. She had too much on her mind right now to make such a serious decision. One of her basic rules was not to make any irrevocable decisions when she was under stress. Later, when Rule was back on his feet, there would be plenty of time for that.

She smiled at him and stroked his hair back from his forehead. "We'll talk about that next week," she said.

"Cat!"

"Mrs. Ashe, what do you think about—"

"Cathryn, we need—"

"Cat, I need a shave—"

"For God's sake, Cathryn, can't you do something about—"

"Cathryn, I'm sorry, but Rule won't let me do anything for him—"

Never before had Cathryn had so many people calling her name and demanding her time and attention. It seemed that everywhere she turned, someone had a problem that needed her immediate attention. There were a thousand and one things to be done every day on the ranch and Lewis Stovall was indispensable, but there were decisions that he couldn't make and that Rule wasn't in any shape to be handling. Monica always seemed to want something, and Ricky had her share of complaints. Lorna tried to take some of the burden of nursing Rule from Cathryn's shoulders, but she was thwarted in that by Rule himself. No one but Cathryn could shave him, feed him, bathe him, see to his personal needs. No one but Cathryn could keep him entertained.

Of all the voices calling her every day, Rule's sounded by far the most often. She ran up and down the stairs countless times every day to answer his demands. It wasn't that he was a difficult patient, simply that he wanted her—and only her—to take care of him.

She had bought an air-conditioner the day after bringing him home from the hospital, and he rested better when the room was a more comfortable temperature. The quiet hum of the motor also masked the noises that might have disturbed him otherwise. He slept a great deal, but when he was awake he wasn't very patient if Cathryn didn't come immediately.

She couldn't get angry with him, not when she could see for herself how pale he became if he tried to move very much at all. His leg still hurt him, and was beginning to itch under the cast, as well, and he couldn't do anything to ease either condition. She wasn't surprised that he was short-tempered; anyone would have been under the circumstances. For a man of his temperament, he was doing much better than she had expected.

However, understanding didn't stop her legs from aching after a hundred trips up the stairs. She wasn't getting enough sleep, or enough to eat, and the only time she was sitting down was when she was either on a horse or feeding Rule. After only two days she was ready to drop in her tracks.

That night she actually did fall asleep beside Rule. She could remember feeding him, and when he was finished she had set the plate back on the tray and leaned down for a moment to rest her head on his shoulder. The next thing she knew it was morning, and Rule was groaning from the cramp in his arm. He had held her all night long and spent the night propped up on his pillows, his right arm wrapped around her. He kissed her and smiled, but discomfort shadowed his face and she knew that he had slept badly, if at all.

The entire morning was hectic, with one problem after another cropping up. She had just ridden into the stables, having returned to feed Rule his lunch, when a pickup truck rolled into the yard and a familiar figure emerged.

"Mr. Vernon," Cathryn called warmly, going up to greet her old friend. Another man got out of the vehicle and she glanced at him curiously before she recognized him. He was the man who had been with Paul Vernon the day she had met him in front of the drugstore, but she couldn't recall his name.

Paul Vernon solved that problem by indicating the man with a sweep of his big hand and saying, "You remember Ira Morris, don't you? Met him a week or so back."

"Yes, of course," said Cathryn, extending her hand to the man.

He shook hands, but he wasn't looking at her. His eyes were sliding over the stables and barns, resting finally on the horses that were grazing peacefully in the pastures.

"I've heard a lot about this place," he said, "and none of it was bad. Good, solid, well-mannered horses, the best quarter horses to be found in the state. But you're breeding for speed now, too, I hear. Branching out into Thoroughbreds, aren't you? They doing well?"

A few days before Cathryn wouldn't have known if they were or not, but she had absorbed a lot of the business by necessity. "We sold a colt last year who's been winning big in California this season."

"I've heard of him," said Ira Morris. "Irish Venture, by Irish Gale, out of Wanderer. Word is out that the mare's dropped another foal by Irish Gale; I'd like to get in ahead of the sale."

"None of the horses listed in the catalog will be sold until the day of the sale," said Cathryn firmly.

"All right, I can understand that," he readily agreed. "Would it be all right if I saw the colt?"

She shrugged and smiled. "I don't mind, but the foal is a filly, not a colt. Her name is Little Irish, but Rule calls her Hooligan."

"She's headstrong?" Paul Vernon asked.

Cathryn's smile grew broader and she lifted her hand to point out a dainty filly prancing around in the pasture. "Hooligan is just different," she said. They watched the graceful movements in silence as the young horse danced lightly over the green grass. It was only when the filly came alongside another horse that you could get an idea of her size. Because she was so graceful, it wasn't at first apparent that she was a tall, strong horse. Her sleek hide effectively masked the strength of her muscles; an observer first noticed her burnished beauty, the spirited arch of her neck and the delicacy with which she placed each hoof as she ran. Later, like a slow dawn, would come the realization that the filly had speed to burn, that those slender legs were as strong as steel.

"She's not for sale," said Cathryn. "At least not this year. Rule wants to keep her."

"If you don't mind, I'd like to speak to him."

"I'm sorry," said Cathryn, stretching the truth a bit. She didn't quite like Ira Morris. He seemed to be a cold, calculating man. "Rule had an accident earlier this week and he's restricted to bed; he can't be disturbed."

"I'm sorry to hear that," Mr. Vernon said instantly. "What happened?"

"His horse stumbled and went down with him, then rolled on Rule's leg."

"Broken?"

"I'm afraid so. He also has a concussion, and we have to keep him quiet."

"That's a damned shame, with this sale coming up."

"Oh, he won't miss the sale," Cathryn assured him. "If I know Rule Jackson, he'll be hobbling around before then. I just hope I'll be able to keep him down for the rest of this week."

"Headstrong, ain't he?" Mr. Vernon laughed.

"As a mule," agreed Cathryn fervently.

Ira Morris shifted impatiently and she realized that he wasn't interested in Rule's health. He was interested only in the horses, and as far as she was concerned they had no horses to sell until the day of the sale. Rule would know instantly which horses he had listed in the catalog, but as the catalogs hadn't arrived yet from the printers, Cathryn had no way of knowing without running to ask him, which she refused to do.

Mr. Morris cast another look over the ranch. "Just one thing, Mrs. Ashe," he said brusquely. "I came here to talk business, but now I'm not sure who I should be talking to. Who runs this outfit, you or Jackson?"

Cathryn paused, considering that. "I own the ranch," she finally said in a neutral tone. "But Mr. Jackson runs it for me, and he knows more about the horses than I do."

"So his decisions are final?"

She was beginning to feel annoyed. "Just what are you asking, Mr. Morris? If you want to buy horses now, then my answer is, I'm sorry, but not until the sale. Or is there something else on your mind?"

He smiled a hard, wintry smile, his cold eyes flashing at her. "What if I want to buy it all? Everything—horses, land, buildings."

That shook her. Pushing a wayward strand of hair away from her eyes, she looked around. Sell the Bar D? That old house was where she had been born. She knew every inch of this land, every rise and dip, every scent and sound of it. This was where she had first begun to love Rule, where she had come to know herself as a woman. It would be impossible to sell it.... She opened her mouth to tell him so, but then came the unbidden thought that if she didn't own the Bar D she wouldn't have to worry whether Rule wanted her land more than he wanted her. She would know for certain....

If she wanted to know. A sharp pain went through her at the thought that the answer might be more painful than the question. Rule would never forgive her if she sold the ranch.

To Mr. Morris, she gave a forced smile. "That's a big 'if,' " she said. "And it's one that I haven't considered before. I couldn't make a snap decision on that."

"But you will think about it?" he pressed.

"Oh, yes," she assured him wryly. "I'll think about it." It would be hard for her to think about anything else. In a twisted way Mr. Morris had just reversed the roles for her and Rule. Which did she want more, the ranch or Rule Jackson? If she kept the ranch she might never know how he really felt about her; on the other hand, if she sold it she might lose him forever, but she would know exactly where she stood.

It was an offer that she knew would have to be discussed with Rule, though she also knew in advance what his reaction would be. He would be violently opposed to selling the ranch. But he was the manager and he was entitled to know what was going on, even though she dreaded the idea of upsetting him.

She was later than usual in taking his lunch up. First she had been detained by Paul Vernon and Ira Morris; then she was so dusty that she took a quick shower before she did anything else. While Lorna prepared Rule's lunch tray, Cathryn leaned against the cabinets and wolfed down a sandwich, wondering why Rule wasn't already calling her. Perhaps he was napping. . . .

He wasn't asleep. When she opened the door he carefully turned his head to look at her and she was struck by the flinty expression in his eyes. His gaze went slowly over her, taking in her freshly scrubbed appearance from the top of her head, where she had subdued her hair into one long braid, down over her cool sleeveless cotton blouse, faded jeans, and finally her bare feet. Carefully placing the tray on the nightstand, she asked, "What's wrong? Is your head hurting—"

"I hear you're considering selling the ranch," he said harshly, trying to lever himself up on his elbow. The abrupt movement dislodged his broken leg from the cushions where it was propped and he fell back against his pillows with a sharp cry, followed by some lurid cursing. Cathryn leaped around the end of the bed and gently lifted his leg back onto the pillows, bracing it more securely. Her mind was racing. How had he heard about that so fast? Who had told him? The yard and stables had been busy. Any one of twenty men could have overheard the offer to buy the ranch, but she didn't think that any of them had made a special trip to the house to tell Rule about it. Lewis was in the house a lot, but she knew that at the moment he was in the far south pastures.

"Ricky told me," Rule snapped, accurately reading her thoughts.

"She made the trip for nothing," Cathryn replied evenly, sitting down beside him and reaching for the tray. "I was going to tell you myself."

"When? After the papers were signed?"

"No, I was going to tell you about it while you were eating."

He angrily waved away the spoon that she lifted to his mouth. "Damn it, don't try to poke that in my mouth like I'm a baby. This would solve all your problems, wouldn't it? Get rid of the ranch, get rid of me, make a lot of money to live it up on in Chicago."

With difficulty Cathryn restrained her impulse to lash back at him. She set her jaw and replaced the tray on the nightstand. "Evidently Ricky also took it upon herself to add a few little details to the original conversation. First, I didn't agree to sell the ranch. Second, you will be involved in any decision I make concerning the ranch. And third, I'm damned tired of you jumping down my throat, and as far as I'm concerned you can feed yourself!" She got up and stomped out, closing the door sharply on his furious order that she come back.

Ricky stood at the head of the stairs, an openly delighted smile on her face, and Cathryn realized that the other woman had been listening to every word. Her eyes narrowing, she stopped in front of her stepsister and said from between clenched teeth, "If I see you in Rule's room again, or hear of you being in there, I'll throw you off this ranch so fast you'll have windburn."

Ricky arched a mocking brow. "You will, little sister? You and who else?"

"I think I can handle it, but if I can't, there are a lot of ranch hands to help me."

"And what makes you think they'll side with you? You're a stranger to them. I've ridden beside them, worked with them, been close...friends...with some of them."

"I'm sure you have," said Cathryn cuttingly. "Fidelity has never been one of your characteristics."

"And has it been yours? Do you think it's such a well-kept secret that you've been Rule's little plaything since you were only a kid?"

Horrified, Cathryn realized that Ricky had probably been spreading her malicious gossip for years. The Lord only knew what the woman had said about her. Then she straightened her shoulders and even smiled, thinking that she wasn't ashamed of loving Rule. He wasn't the easiest man in the world to love, but he was hers, and she didn't care if the whole world knew it.

"That's right, I have been," she admitted freely. "I love him, and I'll keep on loving him."

"You loved him so much that you ran away and married another man?"

"Yes, that's right. I don't have to explain myself to you, Ricky. Just make certain you stay away from Rule, because that was your last chance."

"Well, Ricky, you can't say you weren't warned," Monica drawled from behind them, her voice amused. "And unless you're prepared to find a job and start supporting yourself, I suggest that you listen to her."

Ricky tossed her head. "I've helped the ranch hands for years, but I've never seen you do anything more than make your own bed. What about you? You live off of this ranch, too."

"Not for long," said Monica breezily. "I'll never find another husband while I'm stuck out here in the sticks."

Oddly, Ricky turned pale. "You're leaving the Bar D?" she whispered.

"Well, surely you knew that I wouldn't stay here forever," said Monica, mildly puzzled. "The ranch belongs to Cathryn, and it looks as if she's come home to stay. It's time I made a home for myself, and I've never wanted it to be on a ranch. I tolerated ranch life, but only for Ward Donahue." She gave a graceful shrug. "Men like him don't come along too often. I'd have lived in an igloo if that was what he wanted."

"But...Mother...what about me?" Ricky sounded so distressed that suddenly Cathryn felt sorry for her, even if she was a spiteful witch.

Monica smiled. "Why, darling, you can find your own husband. You're a little too old to be living with Mommy, anyway, aren't you? Cathryn has offered me the use of her apartment in Chicago and I just might take her up on it. Who knows? I may find a Yankee who just loves my accent."

Magnificently unconcerned, Monica continued down the stairs, then stopped and turned back to look at her daughter. "My suggestion to you, Ricky, is to stop playing games with that cowboy you've been teasing. You could do a lot worse than to take him up on what he'd like to offer you." She continued on her way, leaving a thick silence behind her.

Cathryn looked at Ricky, who was slumped against the railing as if she had been hit over the head. Perhaps she had, because Monica could never be accused of subtlety. "What was she talking about?" Cathryn asked. "Which cowboy?"

"Nobody important," Ricky mumbled, and walked slowly down the hall to her room.

Feeling both battered and confused, Cathryn sought refuge in the kitchen with Lorna. She collapsed into a chair and propped her elbows on the table.

"Ricky told Rule that I was going to sell the ranch," she said baldly. "Rule jumped to the conclusion that the tale was true. We had an argument and I told him to feed himself; he's probably thrown the tray against the wall. Then I had an argument with Ricky over Rule, and right in the middle of it all Monica told Ricky that she's planning to leave the Bar D, and Ricky looked like someone had slapped her. I don't know what's going on anymore!" she wailed.

Lorna laughed. "Mostly what's going on is that you're so tired you're functioning on willpower alone and nothing's making a lot of sense to you right now. Monica and Ricky have argued all their lives; it's nothing unusual. And Monica has always said that if you came back she was leaving. Ricky... well, what Ricky needs is a good, strong man who loves her and makes her feel like she's worth something."

"I feel sorry for her," said Cathryn slowly. "Even when I want to choke her, I feel sorry for her."

"Sorry enough for her to let her have Rule?" Lorna put in slyly.

"No!" Cathryn's response was immediate and explosive, and Lorna laughed.

"I didn't think so." She wiped her hands on her apron. "I suppose I'd better go upstairs and see to Rule, though if he hasn't thrown the tray at the wall he'll be sure to throw it at me when he sees I'm not you. Are you going to see him at all?"

"I suppose I'll have to," Cathryn sighed. "But not right now. Let him cool down, and maybe then we can talk without yelling at each other."

After Lorna had gone upstairs, Cathryn sat at the table for a long while, staring at the homey, comfortable kitchen. It wasn't only Rule who needed to cool down; her temper was at least as hot as his, and if she were being truthful with herself, she had to admit that he usually controlled his far better than she did hers.

The back door opened and Lewis Stovall leaned his tall frame against the doorway. "Come on, Cathryn," he cajoled. He'd dropped the "Mrs. Ashe" during the last few days and started calling her by her given name, which was only the logical thing to do considering how closely they had been working together. "There's work to be done."

"Did Rule tell you to keep me so busy that I wouldn't have the energy to do anything but work and sleep and look after him?" she asked suspiciously.

His hard eyes crinkled at the corners as a tiny smile touched his face. "Tired, aren't you?"

"Punch-drunk," she agreed.

"It won't be for much longer. Rule should be up and around next week, and he'll probably be back in the saddle the week after that. I've seen him do it before."

"With a cast on his leg?" she asked doubtfully.

"Or his arm, or with his ribs taped up, or his collarbone broken. Nothing's kept him down for long. This concussion has put him on his back longer than anything else."

She got up and went over to the door, sighing as she pulled on clean socks and stamped her feet into her boots. Lewis stood watching her with an odd expression in his eyes, and she looked up in time to catch a fleeting glimpse of it. "Lewis?" she asked uncertainly.

"I was just thinking that underneath the big-city glamour you're really nothing but a country girl."

"Glamour?" she laughed, tickled by the idea. "Me?"

"You'd know what I'm talking about if you were a man," he drawled.

"If I were a man you wouldn't even be thinking it!"

His laughter acknowledged the truth of that. As they walked across the yard, Cathryn worked up enough nerve to ask him a question that had been in the back of her mind since she'd first met Lewis. "Were you in Vietnam with Rule?" she asked casually.

He looked down at her. "I was in Vietnam, but not with Rule. I didn't meet him until almost seven years ago."

She didn't say anything else, and when they were almost at the stables he asked, "Why?"

"You seem so much alike," she replied slowly, not certain why they seemed to be cut out of the same mold. They were both dangerous men, hard men who had seen too much death and pain.

"He's never mentioned Vietnam to me." A harsh note crept into Lewis's voice. "And I don't talk about it, either—not anymore. The only people who would know what I was talking about were there too, and they have their own troubles. My marriage broke up because my wife couldn't handle it, couldn't handle *me* when I first came back."

The look she gave him was painful with sympathy, and he grinned—actually grinned. "Don't drag out the violins," he teased. "I'm doing okay. Some day I'll probably even get married again. Most men moan and groan about marriage, but there's something about women that keeps them coming back for more."

Cathryn had to laugh. "I wonder what that is!"

Her new sense of closeness to Lewis carried her through the remainder of the day, which was as hectic and troubled as the morning had been. One of the stallions was colicky, and two mares showed signs that they would be foaling before the night was over. When she finally trudged back to the house it was after seven, and Lorna reported that she had already carried Rule's tray up to him.

"He's in an awful mood," she reported.

"Then he'll have to stay in one," Cathryn said tiredly, "I don't feel up to soothing him down tonight. I'm going to take a shower and fall into bed."

"You're not going to eat?"

She shook her head. "I'm too tired. I'll make up for it in the morning, I promise."

After showering she fell across her bed, too tired even to crawl under the sheet. She fell asleep immediately, which was fortunate, because in what seemed like only a few minutes she was being shaken awake.

"Cathryn, wake up." It was Ricky's voice, and Cathryn forced her eyes open.

"What's wrong?" she asked groggily, noticing that Ricky was still dressed. "What time is it?"

"It's eleven-thirty. Come on. Both mares are in labor, and Lewis needs help." Ricky's voice was totally lacking in hostility, but then she had always been interested in ranch work. It didn't seem strange that Lewis had sent for the two women instead of waking some ranch hands to help him; they had both aided foaling mares before, though it had been years since Cathryn had done so. But the ranch was hers, and it was her responsibility.

Quickly she dressed and they hurried to the foaling barn, where only a few dim lights burned in the stalls with the mares. They had to be quiet to keep from up-setting the expectant mothers, so they didn't talk ex-cept in low tones. Lewis and the foaling man, Floyd Stoddard, were waiting in an empty stall.

Lewis looked up as the two women entered the stall. "Shouldn't be too much longer with Sable," he said. "Andalusia will take a while more, I think."

But though they waited, Sable still didn't foal, and Floyd began to get worried. It was almost two in the morning when he checked on her again and came back to the stall where they had remained, his face strained. "Sable's down," he reported. "But the foal's turned sideways. We're going to have to help it. Everybody wash up."

The two men stripped to the waist and washed in warm soapy water, then ran to Sable's stall. Ricky and Cathryn rolled their sleeves up as far as they would go and washed too, though they wouldn't actually be helping to turn the foal. The lovely dark brown mare was lying down, her swollen sides bulging grotesquely. "Hold her head," Floyd directed Ricky, then knelt be-hind the mare.

At a loud, distressed whinny from the other stall, they jerked their heads around. Lewis swore. "Cathryn, see about Andalusia!"

Andalusia was down, too, but she wasn't in any un-due stress. Cathryn reported back, then considered the situation. Ricky was using all her energy holding Sa-ble's head down; Lewis was applying external pressure to help Floyd turn the foal.

"Andalusia's fine, but she's ready now, too. I'll stay with her."

Sweat was pouring down Lewis's face. "Do you know what to do?" he grunted.

"Yes, don't worry. I'll call if there's any trouble."

Andalusia raised her pearl gray head and gave a soft whinny when Cathryn entered her stall, then dropped her head into the hay again. Cathryn knelt beside her, her gentle touch telling the mare that she wasn't alone. The animal's large, dark eyes rested on Cathryn with touching, almost human serenity.

The mare's sides heaved with another contraction, and the sharp, tiny hooves appeared. Andalusia didn't need any help. Within minutes the foal was squirming on the hay, still encased in the shimmering sac. Quickly Cathryn slit the sac and freed the little animal, then took a soft, dry cloth and began rubbing it with long, rhythmic strokes. She crouched on the hay as the mare struggled to her feet and stood with her head down, her sides heaving. Cathryn tensed, ready to grab the foal and run if the mare didn't accept the baby. But Andalusia blew softly through her muzzle and came over to investigate the little creature trembling on the hay. Her loving, motherly licking took the place of Cathryn's cloth.

The little chestnut colt struggled to place his front legs, but as soon as he had them braced and tried to make his back legs obey, the front ones would betray him and he'd collapse. After several abortive tries he managed to stand, then looked around in infant confusion, not certain what he was supposed to do next. Andalusia, fortunately, was an old hand at this; she gently nudged the foal in the proper direction and instinct took over. Within seconds he was greedily nursing, his thin little legs braced wide apart as he balanced precariously on them.

When Cathryn returned to the other stall, Ricky was kneeling beside an unusually small foal, rubbing it and crooning to it. Lewis and Floyd were still working with the mare and Cathryn saw at once that this was a double birth. Her heart twisted a little, because so often with twin foals one or both of them failed to survive. From the looks of the frail little creature with Ricky, the odds were all against it.

Soon the other foal was on the hay and it was larger than the other one, though the markings were almost identical. It was an active little filly, who struggled to her feet almost immediately and raised her proud little head to survey the strange new world she was living in.

Floyd was taking care of Sable, so Lewis came over to examine the other foal. "I don't think she'll be strong enough to nurse," he said doubtfully, taking in the limp way the foal was lying. But no one on the Bar D just left a horse to die. They worked all night with the foal, keeping her warm, rubbing her to keep her circulation stimulated, dribbling a few drops of milk from her mother down her throat. But she was very weak, and soon after sunrise she died without ever having been on her feet.

Tears burned Cathryn's eyes, though she had known from the beginning what the outcome was likely to be. There was nothing to say. Everyone in the barn was silent, looking at the still little creature. But when they looked in the other direction they saw not death but glorious, beautiful life as the other two newborns pushed their delicate muzzles into every nook of their expanded territories.

Lewis shrugged his shoulders, shaking the kinks out of them. "It's been a long night," he sighed. "And we've got a long day in front of us. Let's go clean up and eat."

Cathryn had almost reached the house when she realized that Ricky wasn't with her. Looking around, she saw that Ricky was standing with Lewis. She opened her mouth to call out, when suddenly Lewis's hand shot out to grab Ricky's arm. Evidently they were quarreling, though they hadn't been just a moment earlier. Then Lewis slid his arm around Ricky's waist and forced her along as he strode to the small house that was his private quarters. Not that Ricky needed to be forced, thought Cathryn wryly, watching the door shut behind them.

Well, well. So Lewis was the cowboy Monica had mentioned. She hadn't even suspected, though if she'd been less preoccupied with Rule she might have noticed the way that Lewis looked at Ricky. He had been watching Ricky that day when Cathryn had seen her hug Rule. Maybe Ricky didn't know it yet, but Lewis Stoval was a man who knew what he wanted and how to get it. Ricky had better enjoy her last days of freedom, thought Cathryn, smiling. That should certainly take care of Ricky's chasing after Rule.

"How did things go?" Lorna asked as Cathryn moved slowly into the kitchen, groaning with every step.

"Sable had twins, but one died just a few minutes ago. But Andalusia's foal is a big colt, as red as fire, so that should please Rule. He likes red horses."

"Speaking of Rule..." said Lorna meaningfully.

Cathryn flinched. "Oh, Lord. Lorna, I can't. Not just yet. I'm dead on my feet and he'll make mincemeat out of me."

"Well, I'll try to explain." But Lorna looked doubtful, and Cathryn almost gave in. If her body hadn't been throbbing with weariness she might have surrendered to the urge to see him, but she was just too tired to face him now.

"Tell him about the foals," she directed, yawning. "And tell him that I've gone straight to bed for a few hours of sleep, and I'll see him when I get up."

"He won't like that. He wants to see you *now*."

Suddenly Cathryn chuckled. "Tell you what. Tell him that I've forgiven him. That'll make him so mad that if you're lucky he won't even speak."

"But you won't see him now?"

"No, not now. I'm really too tired."

Later, lying drowsily in her bed, she wished that she had gone to talk to him. She could have told him about the foals and he would have understood if she had cried a little on his shoulder. She was teaching him a lesson, but she wished that she didn't have to learn it with him. She wanted to be with him, to touch him and take care of him. It was a good thing that she had promised to see him later, because a day without being with him was almost more than she could bear.

Lorna woke her that afternoon to take a phone call. Groggily she staggered to the phone. "Hi," said Glenn Lacey cheerfully. "I just wanted to remind you of our date tonight. Guess where we're going."

Cathryn was dumbfounded. She had forgotten all about having made a date with Glenn for that night. "Where?" she asked weakly.

"I've got tickets to the Astros' game in Houston tonight. I'll pick you up at four and we'll fly in to the city for an early dinner before the game. How does that sound?"

"That sounds great," Cathryn gulped, thinking bleakly of the man lying upstairs.

If it hadn't been for Rule, Cathryn would have had fun. On the surface she was happy, smiling and talking, but underneath she was miserable. It was as if he were on the date with her, invisible to everyone but her. If she laughed at something, she thought of Rule lying in bed waiting for her to come to him because he was unable to get up and go to her, and she felt guilty for laughing. She felt guilty anyway, because Glenn was an amusing, undemanding companion and she just couldn't give him her complete attention.

Once they were at the ball game she was able to concentrate on what was happening and push thoughts of Rule aside. She had never been a great baseball fan, but she liked watching the crowd. There were people of every shape, size and description wearing every type of outfit imaginable. One couple, obviously in a mellow mood, paid no attention at all to the ball game and proceeded to conduct a romance in the midst of thousands of witnesses. A man sitting just below them, wearing only sneakers, cutoffs, and a tee shirt tied around his head, cheered loudly and equally for both teams. Glenn was of the opinion that he didn't know which team was which.

But even crowd watching had its painful moments. A man with thick dark hair caught her eye and her breath squeezed to a halt for a painful moment. What was Rule doing now? Had he eaten anything? Was he in pain?

She had upset him, and the doctor had told her to keep him quiet. What if he tried to get up by himself and fell?

She was aware, as if of a deep chill in her bones, that if he hadn't been furious before, he would be now. Yet she couldn't have backed out of the date with Glenn at the last minute; Glenn was too nice to be treated so shabbily. Perhaps he would have understood and been a good sport about it, but Cathryn felt that it would have been tacky to stand him up after he had already gotten the tickets to the ball game.

Sudden, bitter tears burned her eyes and she had to turn her head away from Glenn, pretending to look over the crowd. She ached to be home, just to be under the same roof with Rule, so she could look in on him and make certain he was all right, even if he were angry enough to eat nails. Love! Who ever said that love made the world go round? Love was a killing pain, an addiction that had to be fed; yet even in her pain she knew that she wouldn't have it any other way. Rule was a part of her, so much so that she would be only half-alive without him. Hadn't she already learned that?

She loved Rule and she loved the ranch, but between them they were driving her crazy. She didn't know which was more demanding, and the way she felt about both only complicated matters.

Glancing at Glenn, she realized that she couldn't imagine Rule sitting hunched over in a stadium, absently chewing on an already mangled hot dog and drinking warm, watery beer. She had never seen Rule relaxing at anything. He pushed himself until he was so tired that he had to sleep, then began the cycle again the next morning. He read a great deal, but she couldn't say that it was recreational reading. He read thick technical books on breeding and genetics; he studied lineages, kept abreast of new medicines and veterinary practices. His life was built around the ranch. He had gone to the dance, but he hadn't participated. He had gone merely to make sure that she didn't get involved with any other man. Did anything exist for him except that ranch?

Suddenly a wave of resentment washed over her. The ranch! Always the ranch! She would be better off if she *did* sell it. She might lose Rule, but at least then she would know one way or the other how he felt about her. She realized bitterly that she was far more jealous of the ranch than she had ever been of any woman. Ricky's attempts to attract Rule's attentions had been infuriating, but rather pitiable, because Cathryn had known that her stepsister had no chance of succeeding. Ricky didn't have what it took; she didn't have the ranch.

If she had any guts at all she'd ask Rule right out what he wanted from her. That was the hard part of loving someone, she thought bitterly; it left you so insecure and vulnerable. Love turned sane people into maniacs, bravery into cowardice, morals into quivering need.

When Glenn stood and stretched, yawning, Cathryn realized with a start that the ball game was over, and she had to look quickly at the scoreboard to figure out who had won. The Astros had, but only by one run. It had been a low-scoring game, a duel of pitchers rather than hitters.

"Let's stop for some coffee before we start back," Glenn suggested. "I only had one beer, but I'd like to feel a little more alert before I get in a plane and start flying.''

At least *he* was still sane, thought Cathryn. Aloud she agreed that coffee sounded like a good idea and they spent a leisurely hour in the coffee shop at the airport. She was aware of the minutes ticking by, aware that if Rule was still awake he would be shaking with fury by now. The thought made her both eager and loath to return, wanting to put it off for as long as possible.

When they were strapped into their seats in the plane, it seemed that she would get her wish. Glenn abruptly killed the engine. ''Fuel pressure isn't coming up,'' he muttered, crawling out of his seat.

The fuel pump had gone bad. The time it took to obtain and install a new one made it past midnight before they were finally in the air. Rather than wake everyone at the ranch by landing, Glenn took the plane back to its hangar and drove her home. After he had kissed her casually on the cheek and left her at the door, she took off her shoes like a kid sneaking in late from a date and tiptoed through the dark house, avoiding the places in the old floor that she knew would creak.

As she tiptoed past Rule's door she noticed the thin line of light beneath it and hesitated. He couldn't reach the lamp to turn it off. If everyone had gone to bed without turning the lamp off for him it would burn all night. Not that there was much left of the night, she thought in wry amusement. Why not just admit that she wanted to look at him? It had been roughly thirty-six hours since she had seen him, and suddenly that was far too long. Like any drug addict, she needed her fix.

Moving slowly, cautiously, she opened his door and peeped in. At least he was lying down, so someone had remembered to help him from his propped-up position. His eyes were closed and his broad, heavily muscled chest rose and fell evenly.

A hot little quiver ran through her and rattled her composure. God, he looked so good! His silky dark hair was tousled, his jaw darkened with stubble; one powerful arm was thrown up beside his head, his long-fingered hand relaxed. Her gaze wandered down the sheen of his bronzed shoulders, stopped at the virile growth of dark hair that covered his chest and ran down his abdomen, then fought free to linger on the naked expanse of muscled thigh that was visible. He had the sheet pulled up to just below his navel, but his left leg was completely uncovered, the heavy cast propped on the pile of pillows for support.

Trembling in appreciation of his male beauty, she walked silently to the bed and leaned down to feel for the switch on the lamp. She made no noise at all, she was certain of it, yet abruptly his right arm snapped out and his fingers clamped around her wrist. His dark eyes flared open and he stared at her for several seconds before the feral gleam in the dark depths faded. "Cat," he muttered.

He had been sound asleep. She would have sworn to it. But his instincts were still honed to battle pitch, aware of any change in his surroundings, any other presence, and his body had acted even before he was awake. She watched him as the jungle faded from his mind and he recalled his present location. His look of hard savagery changed to one of narrow-eyed anger. The pressure of his fingers lessened, but not enough to allow her to pull away. Instead he drew her to him, bending her over the bed in an awkward position, holding her by the strength of his arm.

"I told you to stay away from Glenn Lacey," he snarled softly, holding her so closely that his breath heated her cheek.

Who had told him? she wondered bleakly. Anyone could have. The entire ranch must have seen Glenn arrive to pick her up. "I'd forgotten that I'd made a date with him," she confessed, keeping her voice low. "When he called, he already had tickets to the ball game in Houston and I just couldn't turn him down after he'd gone to so much trouble. He's a nice man."

"I don't care if he's the next American saint," Rule replied, still in the same tone of soft, silky menace. "I told you that I won't have you going out with other men and I meant it."

"It was just this once, and besides, you don't own me!"

"You think so? You're mine, and I'll do whatever it takes to keep you."

She gave him a guarded, painful look. "Would you?" she murmured, afraid that she knew all too well what his reaction would be if she sold the ranch. He would hate her. He'd drop her so fast that she'd never recover from the devastation of it.

"Push me and find out," he invited. "That's what you've been doing anyway. Pushing me, trying to find the limits of the invisible chain that's around your pretty little neck. Well, honey, you've reached it!"

The pressure on her arm resumed and he pulled her closer. Cathryn braced her left arm on the bed and tried to pull away, but even flat on his back he was still far stronger than she was. She gave a soft cry as her arm gave way and she sprawled across him, trying frantically to keep from jarring him or knocking against his broken leg.

He released her arm and thrust his hand into her hair, tangling his fingers in the long silky length of it and forcing her head down. "Rule! Stop it!" she wailed, an instant before his mouth clung to hers.

She tried to refuse his kiss, tried to keep her teeth clenched and her lips firmly together. She failed in both. Without hurting her, he caught her jaw and applied just enough pressure to open her mouth to him, and his tongue moved past the barrier of her teeth, licking little fires into life everywhere it touched. Dazed, she felt the strength leave her body and she sank limply against him.

He kissed her so long and so hard that she knew her lips would be swollen and bruised the next day, but at the time all she was aware of was the intoxicating taste of him, the sensual thrust of his tongue, the stinging little bites that he used as both punishment and reward, stringing them from her mouth down her throat and over her sensitive collarbone to the soft curve of her shoulder. It was only then that she realized he had unbuttoned the front of her dress and pulled it open, and she moaned in her throat. "Rule...stop it! You can't...."

Carefully he let his head fall back on the pillow but he didn't release her. His hand shoved under the cup of her bra and he nestled her breast in his hot palm. "No, I can't, but you can," he murmured.

"No...your head...your leg," she protested incoherently, closing her eyes against the heated delight that coursed through her veins as he continued to fondle her.

"My head and my leg aren't bothering me right now." He pulled her closer and began kissing her again, insisting on the response that he knew she was capable of. The thrusting depth of his kisses made her head spin, and she sank against him once more.

He tugged at the straps of the bra until they came free; then he reached behind her and deftly unsnapped the back strap, freeing her breasts completely. Cathryn whispered a choked, "Please," not even knowing herself if she was begging him to stop or continue. She shuddered wildly when his hand swept up under her skirt and caressed her with bold aggression, and though she kept mindlessly whispering her mingled protests and pleas, she was clinging to him with all the strength in her arms.

He groaned harshly and tugged her leg over his hips, pulling her into position. Sudden tears dampened her cheeks, though she hadn't been aware that she was crying. "I don't want to hurt you," she sobbed.

"You won't," he crooned. "Please, honey, make love to me. I need you so much! Can't you feel how I ache for you?"

At some point during those bold, intimate caresses he had removed her panties, impatiently tossing away the silken barrier that kept him from the secrets of her body. His hands guided her slowly, easing her down until they were fully joined.

It was so sweet and wild that she almost cried out, stifling the sound in her throat at the last moment. With every fiber of her body she was aware of the particular sexiness of a man who lay back and let a woman enjoy his body, let her set the tempo of their loving. It was all the more enticing because Rule was so compellingly masculine, his power undiminished by his injuries. She loved him, loved him with her heart and soul and the undulating magic of her body. With exquisite tenderness she took what he offered and returned it to him tenfold, presenting him with the gift of her soaring pleasure and returning to earth to savor his writhing response as he too was pleasured.

She was lying on his chest in drowsy completion, her half-closed eyes moving idly over the room, when she saw the open door and stiffened. "Rule," she moaned in mortification. "I didn't close the door!"

"Then close it now," he instructed softly. "From the inside. I'm not finished with you, honey."

"You need to sleep...."

"It's almost dawn," he pointed out. "We seem to do all our loving in the early morning hours. And I've done nothing but sleep for a week. We need to talk, and now's as good a time as any."

That was true, and she was loath to leave him anyway. She eased out of the bed, careful not to jostle him any more than she already had, and closed the door, locking it for good measure. It would be just like Ricky to come bursting in in the morning, knowing that Cathryn was with him. Then she slipped out of her dress, poor covering that it was, considering that he had dropped the top of it to her waist and lifted the skirt to the same level. Naked, she climbed under the sheet with him and pressed against his side, almost drunk with the pleasure of lying beside him once more. She nuzzled her face into the hollow of his shoulder and inhaled the heady male scent of him. She was so relaxed, so replete...

"Cat," he murmured into her hair, feeling the way she lay against him. She didn't answer. A sigh of raw frustration escaped him as he realized that she was asleep; then he curved her slender body more tightly against him and pressed a kiss into the tumble of dark red hair that streamed across his shoulder.

When Cathryn woke several hours later, roused by a pain in her arm caused by the fact that she had been resting all her weight on it, Rule was asleep. Cautiously she raised her head and studied him, seeing how pale and tired he looked, even in sleep. Their lovemaking had been sweet and urgent, but he hadn't really been well enough. She eased away from him and stood up, massaging her arm to restore circulation to it. A thousand tiny pins pricked her skin and she hugged the arm to her until the worst of it had passed; then she silently pulled on her dress and picked up the remainder of her clothing, slipping out before he woke.

She was tired. Those few hours of sleep hadn't been nearly enough, but she showered and dressed for the day's chores. Lorna smiled at her when she entered the kitchen. "I thought you'd give it a rest today," she clucked.

"Did Rule ever give it a rest?" asked Cathryn wryly.

"Rule's a lot stronger than you are. We'll get by; the ranch is too well run to fall apart in a couple of weeks. How about waffles for breakfast? I've already got the batter mixed."

"That'll be fine," Cathryn replied, pouring a cup of coffee for herself. She leaned against the cabinet and sipped it, feeling the weariness weighing her limbs down like lead weights.

"Mr. Morris has called twice already," Lorna said casually, and Cathryn's head jerked up. She had almost spilled her coffee and she set the cup down.

"I don't like that man!" she said fretfully. "Why doesn't he leave me alone?"

"Does that mean you're not going to sell the ranch to him?"

Nothing was private, Cathryn realized, rubbing her forehead absently. No doubt everyone on the ranch knew that Mr. Morris had offered to buy the ranch. And no doubt everyone also knew whose bed she had woken up in that morning! It was like living in a fishbowl.

"In a way I'm tempted," she sighed. "But then again..."

Lorna deftly poured the batter into the waffle iron. "I don't know what Rule would do if you sold the ranch. He couldn't work for Mr. Morris, I don't think. So much of his life is tied up with this place."

Cathryn felt every muscle in her body tense at Lorna's words. She knew that. She had always known it. She might own the Bar D, but she was only a figurehead. It belonged to Rule, and he belonged to it, and that was far more important than what was recorded on any deed. He had paid for it in his own way, with his time and sweat and blood. If she sold it he would hate her.

"I can't think," she said tensely. "There are so many things pulling me in different directions."

"Then don't do anything," Lorna advised. "At least until things have settled down some. You're under a lot of pressure right now. Just wait a while; in three weeks your outlook could be completely different."

Lorna's common sense advice was only what Cathryn had told herself many times, and she realized all over again that it really was sensible. She sat down and ate her waffle, and surprisingly the few minutes of quiet made her feel better.

"Cat!"

The low, compelling call wafted down from upstairs and immediately she was tense again. Lord, she was almost terrified at the thought of talking to him! It doesn't make sense, she told herself sternly. She had just slept in his arms; why should she dread talking to him so much?

Because she was afraid that she wouldn't be able to prevent herself from throwing herself in his arms and promising to do anything he asked, that was why! If he asked her to marry him again she'd probably melt against him like an idiot and agree without thinking, completely disregarding the fact that he had never said anything about *love,* only about his plans.

"Cat!" This time she thought she could discern a tautness in his voice and she found herself on her feet, automatically responding to it.

When she opened his door he was lying with his eyes closed, his lips pale. "I knew it was too soon!" she cried softly, placing a cool hand on his forehead. His dark eyes opened and he gave her a tight smile.

"It seems you're right," he grunted. "God, my head feels like it's going to explode! Fill up the icepack, okay?"

"I'll bring it right up," she promised, smoothing his hair with her fingertips. "Do you feel like eating anything?"

"Not just yet. Something cool to drink will do fine, and turn on the air-conditioner." As she turned away to do his bidding, he said evenly, "Cat..."

She turned back to him and raised her eyebrows inquiringly. He said, "About Glenn Lacey..."

She flushed. "I told you, he's just a friend. There's nothing between us, and I won't be going out with him again."

"I know. I realized that last night when I saw that you were wearing a bra."

He was looking at her from beneath half-closed lids, stripping her, and the flush on her cheeks grew hotter. She didn't need him to finish the thought, but he did anyway. "If you had been with me, you wouldn't have been wearing a bra, would you?" he asked huskily.

Her voice was weak as she admitted huskily, "No."

Again the corners of his mouth moved in a little smile. "I didn't think so. Go get that drink for me, honey. I'm not in any shape for provocative conversation right now."

She couldn't stop the chuckle that escaped her lips as she left the room. How like him to put her on the defensive, then reveal that he had attacked with nothing more dangerous in his armory than a smile and a sensual remark. He was more than she could handle, and abruptly she realized that she didn't *want* to handle him. He was his own man, not something to be controlled. Nor did he really try to handle her. Sometimes she felt, oddly, that he was a little wary of her, but he didn't usually tell her if she could or couldn't do something. Except in the case of Glenn Lacey, she thought, smiling. And even then she had done as she had wanted. In her case, her red hair was a signal of stubbornness as well as temper.

Rule didn't feel well enough to start any deep conversations, for which she was grateful. She tended to him and got him settled after he had downed a glass of iced tea; with an icepack easing his headache, he lay quietly and watched her as she straightened the room. "Lewis told me about the other night," he murmured. "He said that you helped Andalusia by yourself. Did you have any trouble?"

"No, the mare knew just what to do."

"She's a good little mother," he said sleepily. "It was too bad about the other foal. We had a set of twins survive a few years ago, but it was a chancy thing. The smaller foal never did catch up to its twin in size or strength, but she was a sweet little horse. She was so small that I was afraid it would kill her if I tried breeding her to any of the other horses, so I sold her to a family who wanted a gentle horse for their kids."

Cathryn felt guilty for not checking on the other mare's well-being, and she said hesitantly, "Did . . . has Lewis said anything about Sable? How she's doing?"

"She's fine. Have you seen the foal?"

"Not since she was born. She's a strong little thing, tall and frisky. She was on her feet almost right away."

"Her sire is Irish Gale. Looks like he's turning out fast fillies instead of colts. Too bad about that; most fillies can't run with the boys, even when they're fast."

"What about Ruffian?" demanded Cathryn, indignant on behalf of the fillies. "And a filly won the Derby not so many years ago, smarty."

"Sweetheart, even in the Olympics the women don't run with the men, and the same goes for horses...except in special, isolated cases," he conceded. His eyes slowly closed, and he muttered, "I need to get up. There's a lot to be done."

She started to assure him that everything was under control but realized that he had slipped into a light doze, and she didn't want to disturb him. She had noticed that sleep was the best remedy for his headaches. Let him rest while he still would. Soon, probably too soon, he would be forcing his body to do his bidding. That was the first time in days that he had mentioned getting up, but she knew it wouldn't be the last.

When she stepped outside, the heat slammed into her like a blow to the body. It probably wasn't any hotter than it had been before, but in her fatigue she felt it more intensely. It wasn't just the scorching rays of the sun. It was the heat that rose in shimmering waves from the earth and slapped her in the face. It had been this hot that July when Rule had— Forget about that, she told herself sternly. She had work to do. She had shirked her duty yesterday, and today she was determined to make up for it.

She stopped in at the foaling barn to check on the two new mothers and their foals. Floyd assured her that Sable was in good condition after her ordeal, then invited her to help him any time he had a mare in foal. Cathryn looked at him doubtfully and he laughed.

"You did just fine with Andalusia, Miss Cathryn," he assured her.

"Andalusia did just fine," she corrected, laughing. "By the way, do you know what direction Lewis went in this morning?"

Floyd frowned, thinking. "I'm not sure, but I think it was Lewis I saw with Ricky this morning, tearing across the pasture in the truck." He pointed due east to where she knew the small herd of cattle was grazing.

If Ricky was in the truck, it probably was Lewis in there with her, Cathryn thought shrewdly with her new knowledge of their relationship. She was torn between relief that Ricky had evidently transferred her attentions away from Rule and sympathy for Lewis. Didn't he realize that Ricky was nothing but trouble?

Suddenly she was riveted by a shout that curdled the blood in her veins. She stood frozen, staring at Floyd, and on his face she saw mirrored the same horror.

"Fire! In the stables!"

"Oh, God," she moaned, suddenly released from her spell, whirling on the spot and starting for the door at a dead run. Floyd was right beside her, his face pale. Fire in the stables! It was one of the worst things that could happen on a ranch. The animals panicked and often resisted any efforts to rescue them, resulting in tragedy. And as she ran the agonized thought surfaced that if Rule heard the commotion he would force himself out of bed and do any amount of damage to his health by trying to assist them.

"Fire!"

"Oh, God, be quiet!" she yelled. The ranch hand looked startled; then he saw her glance at the house and he appeared to understand. Heavy black smoke was drifting almost lazily out the open doors, and she could hear the frightened whinnies of the horses, but she couldn't see any flames.

"Here!" Someone slapped a wet towel across her face and she dashed into the murky interior, coughing even through the towel as the acrid smoke sifted into her lungs. She couldn't feel any heat, though, but now wasn't the time to look for any flames; the horses came first.

The frightened animals were rearing in their stalls and kicking at the wood that held them. Cathryn fumbled for a door and opened it, squinting through the smoke at the horse and recognizing it as Redman, Rule's favorite. "Easy, easy," she crooned, taking a deep breath and whipping the towel away from her face to drape it over the horse's eyes. He calmed down enough to let her lead him swiftly out of the stable into the fresh air. Behind her, other horses were being led out in a quick, remarkably quiet operation. Willing hands helped settle the animals down.

The fire was caught while it was still smoldering. Luckily it hadn't gotten into the hay or the entire stable would have gone up in minutes. A young man whom Rule had hired only two months before discovered the source of the smoke in the tack room, where a fire had started in a trash can and spread to the saddle blankets and leather. The tack was ruined, the room blackened and scorched, but everyone breathed a sigh of relief that it hadn't been any worse than it was.

Astonishingly, Rule seemed to have been undisturbed by the commotion. Probably the whirr of the air-conditioner had masked the noise. Cathryn sighed, knowing that she would have to tell him, and knowing that he would be enraged. A fire in the stables was something that wouldn't have happened if he had been in charge. Knowing that the boss was out of commission, someone had gotten careless with a match or a cigarette, and only luck had prevented things from being much worse. As it was, a great deal of tack would have to be replaced. She had tried so hard to take up the slack, and then something like this had to happen.

Lorna's comforting arm slipped around her drooping shoulders. "Come on back to the house, Cathryn. You could use a good hot bath. You're black from head to foot."

Looking down, Cathryn saw that her crisp clothing, donned only a short time earlier, was now grimy with soot. She could feel the ash on her face and in her hair.

The feeling that she had let Rule down grew stronger as she stood under the shower. She couldn't even begin to imagine what he would say when she told him.

He had turned on the small radio by his bed, and that had kept him from being disturbed. He looked at her when she opened the door and his eyes narrowed at the strained expression on her face. He took in her wet hair and different clothing and set his jaw.

"What happened?" he ground out.

"There was a . . . a fire in the tack room," she stammered, coming a hesitant step closer. "It didn't spread," she assured him quickly, seeing the black horror that spread across his face. "The horses are all fine. It's just the . . . the tack room. We lost just about everything in there."

"Why wasn't I told?" he asked through clenched teeth.

"I—it was my decision. There was nothing you could do. We got the horses out first and—"

"You went into the stable?" he barked, heaving himself up on his elbow and wincing at the pain the movement caused him. Red fires were beginning to burn in the dark depths of his eyes, and suddenly she felt chills running down her back. He was more than angry; he was maddened, his fists clenching.

"Yes," she admitted, feeling tears form in her eyes. Hastily she blinked them away. She wasn't a child to burst into tears whenever she was yelled at. "The flames hadn't spread beyond the tack room, thank God, but the horses were frightened and—"

"My God, woman, are you stupid?" he roared. "Of all the reckless, half-witted things to do . . . !"

She *was* stupid, because the tears rolled down her cheeks anyway. "I'm sorry," she choked. "I didn't mean to let it happen!"

"Then what did you mean? Can't I let you out of my sight for a minute?"

"I said I'm sorry!" she gasped at him, and suddenly she couldn't stand there and listen to the rest of it. "I'll be back later," she sobbed. "I have to send someone to town for more tack."

"Damn it, come back here!" he was roaring, but she scooted out the door and slammed it behind her. She slapped at the wetness on her cheeks, then went into the bathroom and splashed cold water on her face until most of the redness had faded. She wanted nothing more than to hide in her room, but pride stiffened her back. There was work to be done, and she wasn't about to let someone else shoulder the burden for her.

Someone had notified Lewis, and the pickup came tearing across the pasture and slid to a stop in the yard. Lewis was out of it in a flash, taking Cathryn's arm in a hold that was painfully tight. "What happened?" he asked, tight-lipped.

"The tack room caught on fire," she said wearily. "We got it before it spread, but the tack is ruined. All the horses are okay."

"Hell," he swore. "Rule will be fit to be tied."

"He already is." She tried to smile. "I told him a little while ago. Fit to be tied is putting it mildly."

He swore again. "Have you found out how it started?"

"The trash can caught on fire somehow; it looks as if the fire started there."

"Who's been in the tack room this morning? More importantly, who was in there last?"

She looked at him blankly. "I don't know. I hadn't thought to ask."

"When I find out who's responsible he can start looking for another job. No one, but no one, is supposed to smoke around a stable."

It seemed to Cathryn that no one would ever admit to smoking and causing the fire, but from the determined expression on Lewis's face, someone had better confess or everyone was in trouble. She found that she couldn't summon enough energy to care. She looked around vaguely, noticing that Ricky hadn't cared, either; she was walking to the house, twisting her hair up and pinning it carelessly on top of her head.

The stench of smoke still lingered on the hot, breeze-less air, keeping the horses restless. Dull thuds reverberated through the stable as the nervy animals kicked at the stalls that held them. Everyone was kept busy trying to calm them and keep them from injuring themselves. Cathryn gave up trying to keep Redman settled down and led the big horse out of his stall, walking him around and around the yard. Part of his trouble was that he wasn't used to being cooped up, but with Rule out of commission no one had been giving him the exercise he thought was rightfully his.

Suddenly a ride seemed like just the thing. Cathryn was on the point of calling for a saddle when she remembered that there were no saddles left. She leaned her face into the horse's muscular neck and sighed. A day that had begun so delightfully had turned into a nightmare, and it seemed that there would be no escape from it.

Lewis was systematically questioning everyone who worked on the ranch, but Cathryn realized that the fire in the trash can could have smoldered for some time before actually blazing, and there were a lot of hands who were still out on the range, having left early that morning and not planning to return until dusk. She beckoned Lewis over to her. "Please, let it wait until later," she requested, then explained her reasoning to him. "We've got a lot of work to do right now. We have to notify the insurance company and I'm sure they'll want to do an on-site inspection."

Lewis was too sharp-eyed for anything to be hidden from him for long. He took a long, hard look at her and his stony expression softened slightly. "You've been crying, haven't you? Don't let it get to you. The fact that there was a fire at all is serious, but the damage could have been a lot worse."

"I know," she said tightly. "But I should have checked everything and I didn't. It was my fault that it got as out of hand as it did."

Lewis took Redman's lead rope from her hand. "Your fault, hell! You can't be expected to poke your nose into every corner—"

"Rule would have spotted it."

He opened his mouth to say something, then shut it because she was right. Rule *would* have spotted it. Nothing about the ranch escaped his notice. Lewis scowled as a thought struck him. "What did Rule say?"

"He had quite a lot to say," Cathryn replied cryptically, giving him a painful smile.

"Such as?"

In spite of herself those stupid tears began burning in her eyes again. "Do you want to start with the insults, or go on to the central theme?"

"He was just mad," said Lewis uncomfortably.

"I'll say!"

"He didn't mean it. It's just that a stable fire is so serious...."

"I know. I don't blame him." She really didn't. His reaction was understandable. He could have seen a lot of what he had worked so hard for over the years go up in smoke, and his beloved horses would have died a horrible death.

"He'll cool down and apologize to you. You'll see," Lewis promised.

Cathryn turned her eyes up to him in a doubtful gaze and he began to look sheepish. The idea of Rule Jackson apologizing was almost more than she could imagine, and evidently Lewis realized that, too.

"If it's anyone's fault, it's mine," Lewis sighed. "I should have been here, but instead I was—" He stopped abruptly.

"I know." Cathryn studied the tips of her boots, not certain if she should say anything else, but the words bubbled out. "Don't hurt her, Lewis. Ricky's stubbed her toes on a lot of rocks, and she's just not able to handle any more hurts right now."

He narrowed his eyes. "I could only hurt her if she was serious; she's not. She's playing with me, using me as entertainment. I know that, and I'm playing along with her. *If* I decide to put my foot down, she'll be the first to know. But for now I'm just not ready."

"Are men ever ready?" she asked a little bitterly.

"Sometimes. Like I told you before, women are a habit that's hard to break. It's the little things that get in a man's blood, like the smell of a hot meal when he comes dragging in, or the back rub, the laughter, even the fights. It's really special when you can have a roaring argument with someone and know that they still love you."

Yes, that would be special. And what was really painful was to have a roaring argument with a man you loved but whom you suspected of not loving you in return. Every angry word from Rule tore into her like a knife.

"Take Ricky," Lewis drawled. "She's been married twice, but all she's ever been is a decoration. Nobody has ever needed her; she's never felt useful. Why do you think she hangs around and works with the horses? It's the only time she's actually doing something productive. What that woman needs is a man who'll let her take care of him.''

''Are you that man?''

He shrugged his big shoulders. ''I've been taking care of myself for a long time now, and that's another habit that's hard to break. Who knows? Would you mind if I was?''

Cathryn looked up at him, startled. ''Why should I mind?''

''I've got a lot of rough edges, and I've seen a lot of trouble.''

She had to smile. ''And started your share of it, too, I'll bet.''

He started to smile too; then the sound of a car caught their attention and they turned to look at the vehicle coming up the road. ''Who's that?'' she asked, raising her hand to shade her eyes as she stared at it.

After a moment Lewis growled, ''I think it's that Morris fellow.''

She muttered an uncomplimentary word under her breath. ''He's certainly pushy enough, isn't he? He doesn't like to take no for an answer.''

''I wasn't sure that no was going to be the answer,'' said Lewis laconically, looking down at her.

''Well, it is,'' she said forcefully. She couldn't say just when she had decided. Perhaps she had always known that she wouldn't be able to sell the ranch. Too much of herself was bound up there to contemplate selling it to some stranger. She was tied by both the past and the future to this piece of Texas.

''Redman's settled down,'' Lewis observed as Ira Morris got out of his car. ''I'll take him back to his stall.''

She stood waiting for her unwelcome visitor, keeping her expression carefully blank. "Mr. Morris," she said in a neutral tone.

"Mrs. Ashe. I heard in town that you'd had some trouble out here this morning." His cold eyes darted over the stable, and Cathryn was amazed at how quickly the news had spread.

"Did you come out to see if you might want to withdraw your offer?" she asked sweetly. "As you can see, the damage is minor and none of the horses were hurt; however, I'll save you any additional time and trouble by telling you straight out that I won't be selling the ranch."

He didn't look surprised; he merely looked determined. "Don't be so hasty with that decision. You haven't heard my offer yet. When people start talking actual dollars and cents, a lot of them change their minds."

"I won't. I was born in that house, and I plan on dying there."

Totally ignoring her, he named a sum of money that would have staggered her if she had been wavering in her decision. As it was, she wasn't even tempted. She shook her head. "Not interested, Mr. Morris."

"You could live in comfort for the rest of your life with that much money."

"I live in comfort now. I'm where I want to be, doing what I want to do. Why should I throw that away for money?"

He sighed and thrust his hands into his pockets. "Think about it. A house is just a house. A piece of land is just a piece of land. There are other houses, more land. This kind of life isn't really suited to you. Look at you. You've got big city written all over you."

"What I have all over me, Mr. Morris, is dust. Texas dust. *My* dust. I lived in Chicago for several years, yes, but there wasn't a day that I didn't think about this ranch and wish that I was here."

Without a single change in his expression he raised his offer.

Cathryn was beginning to feel harried. "No. No. I'm not interested—at any price," she said firmly.

"You could travel all over the world—"

"No!"

"Buy jewelry and furs—"

Goaded almost beyond control, Cathryn clenched her jaw. "I don't intend to sell," she said stonily. "Why can't you believe that?"

"Mrs. Ashe," he warned, "if you're trying to force me to raise my offer again, it just won't work. I've talked with your Mr. Jackson and he gave me a fair idea of what this stud is worth. I'm in the market for horses and I like the idea of owning my own stud; not only that, but I was given to understand that you'll be returning to Chicago soon."

Cathryn was so stunned that she almost lost her breath. She grasped his arm. "What?" she gasped.

"I said I talked to your manager. You told me yourself that he knows more about the horses here than anyone else, so he was the logical person to ask. He also told me that you'd probably be leaving."

"Just when did you talk to him?"

"Last night. On the telephone."

The guest room had a telephone jack in it, so she could only suppose that someone had carried the phone into the room for Rule to use. But why would Rule tell this man anything? He was dead set against selling the ranch . . . or was he? What was going on?

"Just what did Mr. Jackson tell you?" she demanded.

"We didn't talk long. He merely indicated to me that he thought you were returning to Chicago and would sell if the price was right, and we discussed what that price should be. Going on the information he gave me, I think my last offer is more than fair."

Cathryn drew a shaking breath. "Well, he was wrong in his thinking, and so are you!" She was so upset that she was trembling, and she wavered between fury and tears. Just what was going on? She didn't know what game Rule Jackson was playing, but she was going to find out before another minute had passed. "The answer is no, Mr. Morris, and that's my final answer. I'm sorry you've wasted your time."

"So am I," he said tightly. "So am I."

She didn't wait to see him leave. She turned away and almost ran to the house, her entire being concentrated on reaching Rule and finding out what he had meant by telling Mr. Morris that she would sell. Was he trying to make her leave? No, he couldn't be! Only last night he had made love to her as if he couldn't get enough of her. But...*why?*

She brushed past Lorna, not even seeing her, and flew up the stairs, her feet barely touching the steps. Without warning she threw open the door to Rule's bedroom.

At first the tangled bodies on the bed didn't make any sense to her and she stared at them blankly; then realization sank in and she had to lean against the doorframe to keep from collapsing to the floor. Of all the shocks she had sustained that day, this one was the worst. This one hit her in the stomach and drove all the breath from her body. This one tore at her insides, draining the blood from her face. Ricky was on the bed with Rule, her arm under his neck, her mouth glued to his while she writhed on top of him and her hands stroked his hard-muscled body. Her blouse was open, hanging half out of her jeans. Rule's hand was tangled in her hair.

Then the horror faded from Cathryn's mind and she saw the scene clearly. Rule wasn't holding Ricky's head to him; he was pulling back on her hair in an effort to free his mouth from her determined assault. Finally he managed to force her away, and he muttered, "Damn it, Ricky, would you stop? Leave me alone!"

Rage exploded through Cathryn's veins. She wasn't aware of crossing to the bed. A red mist swam before her eyes, blurring her vision as she grabbed the collar of Ricky's shirt and hauled her bodily off Rule. Fury gave her strength that she had never before known she possessed. "This is it," she ground out, the words rough as sand as she tore them from her constricted throat. "This finishes it."

"Hey!" Ricky squealed as Cathryn slung her around to the door. "What do you think you're doing? Have you gone crazy?"

Without a word, so angry that she couldn't say anything else, Cathryn dragged the other woman through the door and slammed it shut behind them, not hearing Rule's hoarse cry for her to come back.

The banisters of the staircase beckoned madly and the temptation was sugar sweet, but at the last moment a small piece of sanity returned and Cathryn refrained from simply dumping Ricky down the stairs. Ladies didn't do things like that, or that was what she told herself as she forced Ricky along the hall at a trot, handling the young woman with as much ease as if she were only a child. Ricky was yelling and wailing loudly enough to wake the dead, but Cathryn drowned her out with a roared, "Shut up!" as she rushed her into Ricky's own room.

"Sit down!" she bellowed, and Ricky sat. "I warned you! I told you to stay away from him. He's mine, and I won't tolerate you crawling all over him for another minute, do you hear? Get packed and get out!"

"Get out?" Ricky looked dazed, her mouth falling open. "Where to?"

"That's your problem!" Cathryn opened the closet and began hauling suitcases out. She threw them on the bed and opened them, then began pulling open drawers and dumping the contents into the bags, helter-skelter.

Ricky sprang to her feet. "Hey, don't blame it all on me! I wasn't exactly raping him, you know! One woman has never been enough for Rule—"

"It will be from now on! And don't try to make me believe that he invited you, because I don't believe it!"

Ricky glared at the tangle of clothing. "Damn it, quit throwing my clothes around like that!"

"Then pack them yourself!"

Abruptly Ricky bit her lip and tears slid down her cheeks. Cathryn stared at her in mingled disgust and amazement, wondering how anyone could cry and still look so lovely. No red and streaming nose, no blotched face, just diamond-bright tears sliding gracefully down.

"But I really don't have any place to go," Ricky whispered. "And I don't have any money."

The door opened and Monica came in, frowning her annoyance. "Must you two brawl through the house like wrestlers? What's going on?"

"She's trying to make me leave!" Ricky charged hotly, her tears drying up as if by magic. Cathryn stood silently, her hands on her hips and her expression implacable.

Monica glanced quickly at her stepdaughter and said in exasperation, "It's her house; I imagine she has the right to say who lives here."

"That's right, it's always been *her* house!"

"Stop that!" Monica said sharply. "Feeling sorry for yourself won't help anything. You must have known that eventually Cathryn would be coming back, and if you lacked the foresight to prepare yourself for the future, don't blame anyone else. Besides, do you really want to spend the rest of your life listening to the pitter-patter of someone else's kids?"

Evidently Monica observed a lot, even though she always seemed disinterested in anyone's concerns except her own. Cathryn pulled in a deep, calming breath. Of course! Life wasn't so complicated after all. It was really very simple. She loved Rule, she loved the ranch, and she wasn't about to give up either of them. Why tear herself up worrying about the depth of Rule's feelings? Whatever they were, they were there, and that was all that mattered.

With that thought full sanity returned. She sighed. "You don't have to leave right now," she told Ricky, rubbing her forehead to ease the tension that had begun to throb there. "I lost my temper when I saw... Anyway, you can take your time and make some plans. But you can't take forever," she warned. "I don't think you want to stay around for the wedding, anyway, do you?"

"Wedding?" Ricky turned pale; then two spots of color appeared on her cheeks. "You're awfully sure of yourself, aren't you?"

"I have reason to be," Cathryn replied evenly. "Rule asked me to marry him before he broke his leg. I'm accepting."

"Congratulations," Monica inserted with smooth precision. "I can see that we'll really be in the way, won't we? Ricky, dear, I've decided to take Cathryn up on her offer to use her apartment in Chicago. I suppose we can get along well enough for you to share the apartment with me, if you'd like. It *does* have two bedrooms, doesn't it?" she asked Cathryn hastily.

"Yes." It seemed a good idea to Cathryn. She looked at Ricky.

Ricky chewed her lip. "I don't know. I'll think about it."

"Don't think too long," advised Monica. "I'm making arrangements to leave by the end of the week."

"You said I was too old to live with Mommy," Ricky mimicked with a flash of resentment.

"Neither the arrangement nor the offer is a permanent one," snapped Monica. "For God's sake, make up your mind."

"All right." Ricky could look as sulky as a child when she tried, and she was really trying now, but Cathryn didn't care. She heaved a sigh of relief. When her temper cooled she would have felt guilty if she had thrown Ricky out of the house without giving her a chance to make some sort of arrangements. Now that she knew the time limit on Ricky's presence she felt better able to cope with it—so long as she didn't catch the woman touching Rule again.

Rule. Cathryn took another deep breath and prepared for the last battle. Rule Jackson's days as a bachelor were limited. It didn't matter if he didn't love her. She loved him enough for two, and she wasn't going to run away ever again. She was going to stay right there, and if he wanted the ranch he had to take her, too. One thing was certain: She couldn't bear the thought of any other woman thinking that he was unattached and jumping into his bed! She planned to attach him as soon as possible, and do it up right.

With the determination of a charging cavalry brigade, her dark eyes intent, she went down the hall to his room and thrust the door open.

She looked automatically at the bed and was stunned to find it empty. A chill ran down her back. She stepped into the room and at a movement to her right she turned her head. Aghast, she stared at him, a terrified cry of "Rule!" bursting from her throat.

He was out of the bed, struggling with the cast on his leg as he pulled on a pair of jeans. Somehow he had managed to tear open the seam of the left leg of the jeans so he could get them on over the cast. He was wavering precariously as he battled to dress himself, cursing between clenched teeth with every breath he drew, damning his own weakness, the cast on his leg, the throbbing of his head. He swung around clumsily at her cry and she nearly choked when she saw the raw despair that twisted his face, the tortured tears that streaked down his hard cheeks.

"Rule," she moaned, as he turned a look of such agony on her that she wanted to hide her eyes from it. He took a step toward her and lurched suddenly to one side when his broken leg was unable to take his weight. Wildly, Cathryn leapt across the room and caught him as he started to fall, holding him up with desperate strength.

"Oh, God," he groaned, wrapping his arms around her in a death grip, crushing her against his hard body. He bent his head to hers and harsh sobs shook him. "Don't go. God, baby, please don't go. I can explain. Just don't leave me again."

Cathryn tried to stiffen her legs, but she was slowly collapsing under the burden of his weight. "I can't hold you," she gasped. "You've got to get back in bed!"

"No," he refused thickly, his shoulders heaving. "I won't let you go. I couldn't get out of that damned bed, couldn't get my clothes on fast enough...I was so afraid you'd be gone before I could get to you, that I'd never see you again," he muttered brokenly.

Her throat closed at the thought of him battling his pain and injuries to reach her before she left. He couldn't walk, so how was he going to get to her? Crawl? Yes, she realized, he would have crawled if he had had to. The determination of this man was an awesome thing.

"I won't leave," she assured him through her tears. "I promise. I'll never leave you again. Please, darling, get back in bed. I can't hold you up much longer."

He sagged in her arms as some of the tension left him, and she felt her knees begin to buckle. "Please," she begged again. "You've got to get back in bed before you fall and break something else."

She was fortunate that the bed was only a few steps away, or she would never have made it. He was leaning heavily on her, sweat running down his face and mingling with the tears that wet it. He was almost at the end of his rope, and when she supported his head and shoulders as he lay back on the pillows he closed his eyes, his breath heaving in and out of his chest. He gripped her arm tightly, holding her beside the bed. "Don't leave," he said again, this time in little more than a whisper.

"I'm not leaving," she crooned. "Let me lift your leg up on the pillows. Oh, Rule, you shouldn't have tried to get up like that!"

"I had to stop you. You wouldn't have come back again." But he released her arm and she moved to the foot of the bed to lift his leg up. For a moment she stared at the gaping seam of his jeans, wondering how he had managed to tear the heavy-duty pants like that. She decided to get him out of the jeans while he was weak and unable to put up much of a fight, so she eased them down his hips and carefully drew them off. He lay limply, his eyes closed.

She wet a washcloth in cold water and wiped the sweat from his forehead, then the moisture from his cheeks. He opened his eyes and stared at her in fierce concentration, strength already returning to his magnificent body.

"I didn't invite Ricky in here," he said harshly. "I know what it looked like, but I was trying to make her stop. Maybe I wasn't pushing her away too hard, but I didn't want to hurt her—"

"I know," she assured him tenderly, placing her finger on his lips. "I'm not an idiot, at least not completely. I'd already warned her once before to stay away from you, and when I saw her crawling all over you like that I blew sky-high. She and Monica are leaving at the end of the week to take my apartment in Chicago. They can save me a trip," she added whimsically. "I left most of my clothes up there, and I need them. They can ship them to me."

He sucked in a deep breath, his dark eyes as bottomless as eternity. "You believe me?"

"Of course I believe you." She gave him an exquisite smile. "I trust you."

For a moment he looked stunned by her unquestioning faith; then a tiny scowl began to form between his brows. "You had no intention of leaving?"

"None."

"Then, damn it all," he said from between clenched teeth, "why did you go storming out of here and leave me lying in this bed screaming my guts out for you?"

Cathryn went very still, staring down at him. She hadn't realized it until this very moment, but his reaction said a lot. If he cared that much...was it possible? Did she dare dream...? She said carefully, "I never thought it would matter that much to you if I left or not, as long as the ranch stayed under your control."

He uttered a very explicit comment, then attacked fiercely. "Not matter! Do you think a man waits for a woman as long as I've waited for you if it doesn't matter to him whether she leaves or stays?"

"I didn't know you'd been waiting for me," she said simply. "I've always thought it was the ranch that meant the most to you."

His jaw tightened to granite. "The ranch does mean a lot to me. I can't deny that. I was almost at the bottom of a long downhill slide when Ward brought me here and saved my life, put me back together. I've worked myself half to death for years because this place meant salvation to me."

"Then why did you talk to Ira Morris?" she blurted, her dark eyes shadowed with the pain and shock she had felt at that betrayal. "Why did you tell him that I'd probably sell if the price was right? Why did you tell him how much the ranch is worth?'' She couldn't understand that, but then, there was so much about Rule that she didn't understand. He was so deep, hiding so much of himself. He'd have to learn to talk about himself, to share his thoughts with her. And he *was* learning, she thought hopefully.

He caught her hand, curling her fingers under his, and held it against his chest. A desperate look tightened his features before he looked away and deliberately wiped his face clear of expression. ''I was scared,'' he finally said in a strained voice. ''More scared than I ever was in Nam. At first I was furious at the thought that you might sell; then it really hit me and I was scared. But I was scared for myself, and what I might lose. Finally I realized that the ranch is yours, not mine, just like you've been telling me all along, and if you weren't happy here then the best thing for you would be to sell it and go somewhere where you could be happy. When Morris called I agreed to talk to him. I want you to be happy, honey. Whatever it takes, I want that for you.''

''I *am* happy,'' she assured him softly, turning her hand under his so she could feel the hard warmth of his body beneath her fingertips. She stroked the dark curls with absorbed delight. ''I'll never sell the Bar D. You belong here, and if this is where you are, then I'll be here, too.'' She caught her breath as soon as the words were out, unable to look at him as she waited in agony for his response. The seconds ticked by and still he was silent. She swallowed and forced herself to lift her gaze to him.

She hadn't expected him to shout hosannas, but neither was she expecting the way his eyes had narrowed, or the guarded expression that masked his face. "What are you saying?" he rumbled slowly.

It was now or never. She had to commit herself, had to take the first step, because if she backed off now she knew that Rule would, too. He had gone as far as he could go, this proud man of hers. She assured herself that it really wasn't that much of a gamble. She couldn't live without him—it was that simple. Cut and dried. She'd take him on any terms. "You asked me to marry you," she said carefully, choosing her words and watching the effect of each one on his expression. "I accept."

"Why?" he rapped out.

"Why?" she echoed, looking at him as if he had gone mad. Didn't he know? Did he really not understand? The horrible thought arose that he might have changed his mind. "Is...is the offer still open?" she stumbled, painful uncertainty evident in both her voice and her face. He reached up with his other hand and caught a handful of her hair, forcing her inexorably down to him. When their noses were almost bumping he stopped and regarded her with such intensity that she felt as if he were walking inside her mind.

"The offer is still open," he growled softly, the words whispering against her lips. "Just tell me why you're accepting it. Are you pregnant? Is that it?"

"No!" she denied, startled. "It isn't that. I mean, I don't know. How could I know yet? There hasn't been time."

"Then why are you agreeing to marry me?" he persisted. "Tell me, Cat."

He was pinning her down, refusing to let her hide behind anything, and suddenly she didn't want to hide. Serenity and inner strength flooded her. Let him have his confession. She could give it to him out of the richness of her love. She freed her hand from under his and cupped his face in both palms, her fingers lovingly molding the hard contours of his jaw. "Because I love you, Rule Jackson," she said with aching tenderness. "I've loved you for years...for what seems like forever. And it doesn't matter if you don't love me, if the ranch is all you care about. If you want the ranch, you have to take me. It's a package deal. So, Mr. Jackson, you'd better start learning how to be a husband."

He looked thunderstruck and his grip on her hair tightened. "Are you crazy?" he shouted. "What the hell are you talking about?"

"The ranch," she said steadily. "If you want it, you have to marry me to get it."

Raw fury began to form visibly on his face, in his eyes. He said something that didn't bear repeating, but it illustrated his feelings. His entire body shuddered as what little control he had left exploded, and he roared at her, "To hell with the ranch! Sell it! If that's what's been standing between us for all of these years, then get rid of it! If you want to live in Chicago, or Hong Kong, or Bangkok, then I'll live there with you, because *you're* what I've always wanted, not this damned ranch! My God, Cat, I've got a ranch of my own if that was what I wanted! Dad left everything to me when he died, you know." His hand swept over her body. "Did you think *this* was because I wanted the ranch? Sweet hell, woman, can't you tell that you make me crazy?"

Her blank expression told him that she had never even thought of it from that angle. He pulled her down on the bed beside him and clamped her to his side. "Listen to me," he said slowly, deliberately, every word separate and distinct. "I don't want the ranch. It's a good life and it saved me, and I'd miss it if we lived somewhere else, but I can live without it. What I can't live without anymore is you. I've tried. For eight years I got through life day by day, feeding myself on the memory of the one time I'd had you, hating myself for driving you away. When you finally came back I knew I'd never be able to let you go again. I'll do whatever it takes to keep you, honey, because if you walk out on me again I might as well stop living.''

Cathryn felt as if her heart had stopped beating. He hadn't actually said the words yet, but he was telling her that he loved her as desperately, as powerfully as she loved him. It was almost more than she could take in, more than she could allow herself to believe. ''I didn't know,'' she whispered dazedly. ''You never said...you never told me.''

''How could I tell you?'' he asked roughly. ''You were so young, too young for everything I wanted from you. I never meant for that day by the river to happen, but when it did I couldn't regret it. I wanted to do it again, over and over, until that terrified look in your eyes was gone and you looked at me with the same need I felt for you. But I didn't, and you ran. I regret that, because you met David Ashe and married him. It's a good thing you didn't come around for quite a while after that, Cat, because I've never wanted to take a man apart as badly as I did him.''

''You were jealous?'' She still couldn't make herself comprehend everything he was telling her, and she pinched herself surreptitiously; the small pain was real, and so was the man who lay beside her.

The look he gave her spoke volumes. ''Jealous isn't the word for it. I was insane with it.''

"You love me," she whispered in wonder. "You really love me. If only you'd told me! I had no idea!"

"Of course I love you! I *need* you, and I've never needed anyone before in my life. You were as wild and innocent as a foal, and I couldn't keep my eyes away from you. You made me feel alive again, made me forget the nightmares that jerked me up in bed. When I made love to you, we fit together perfectly. Everything was right, all the moves and reactions. You nearly burned me alive every time I touched you. I had to be with you, had to see you and talk to you, and you had no idea how I felt?"

He looked outraged, and Cathryn managed a small laugh as she snuggled closer to him. "It's that stone face of yours," she teased. "But I was so afraid of letting you know how I felt, afraid you didn't feel the same way."

"I feel the same," he said gruffly, then demanded, "Tell me again." He slid his palm up her side and cupped a breast. "Let me hear it again."

"I love you." She complied gladly, joyously with his demand. Saying the words aloud was a celebration, a benediction.

"Will you tell me that when we're making love?"

"As often as you want," she promised.

"I want. Now." His voice had roughened with desire and he pulled her to him, his mouth clinging to hers. The old familiar magic seared through her veins again and she melted against him, not noticing when he unbuttoned her shirt, only aware of the intense pleasure she felt when his hand touched her bare skin.

A dying glimmer of caution prompted her words. "Rule . . . we shouldn't. You need to rest."

"That's not what I need," he murmured in her ear. "Now, Cathryn. *Now.*"

"The door is open," she protested weakly.

"Then close it and come back to me. Don't make me chase you down."

He probably would, she thought, broken leg and all. She got up and closed the door, then came back to him. She couldn't touch him enough, couldn't satisfy her need to feel his hard, warm flesh beneath her fingers. She made love to him, lavishing him with her love, trailing kisses all over him and whispering "I love you" against his skin, imprinting him with the words. Now that she could say the words aloud, she found that she couldn't say them enough, and she made a litany of them as she loved him, lingering so long in her caresses that suddenly he couldn't take any more, lifting her bodily above him and fusing his flesh with hers in a quick, strong movement.

She danced the dance of passion with him, attacking and retreating, but always pleasuring. She was aware of nothing but him, the hot desire in his dark eyes, and something else, the glow of love returned.

"Don't stop saying it," he commanded, and she obeyed until the words wouldn't come, until all she could do was gasp his name and writhe against him. His powerful hands on her hips took over the motion, driving her higher and higher, until with an almost silent wail she collapsed, shuddering, on his chest.

In the quiet, sleepy aftermath he smoothed her tousled hair and held her tightly to him. "I'll need to hire more hands," he said drowsily.

"Mmmm," said Cathryn. "Why?"

"To take up the slack. I can tell right now that I won't be spending as much time on the range. I'll have a major problem just getting out of bed in the mornings. Taking care of a woman like you will be time-consuming, and I intend to do my best."

"I'll drink to that," she toasted, lifting an imaginary glass.

"We'll get married next week," he said, nuzzling his face into her hair.

"Next week?" She made a startled move away from him. "But you're still—"

"I'll be up by then," he soothed. "Trust me. And ask Monica if she and Ricky will stay for the wedding. Always mend your fences, honey."

She smiled. "I know. I don't want any bad feelings between us. And who knows? Lewis may keep Ricky here."

"Don't put any money on it. They both have too many hurts bottled up inside. He may want her, but I don't think he could live with her. Things don't always work out the way you want them to."

Silence fell again, and she felt herself slipping into sleep. A thought nagged at the edges of her consciousness, and she muttered, "I'm sorry about the tack room."

"It wasn't your fault," he comforted, his arms tightening about her.

"You called me stupid."

"I apologize. I panicked at the thought of you going into a burning stable, fighting with those horses to get them out. What if something had happened to you? I'd have gone mad."

"You don't blame me?" she whispered.

"I love you," he corrected. "I couldn't stand it if you were hurt."

She felt as if her heart would burst with happiness. So that tantrum had been purely because he didn't want her taking risks! She opened her eyes and looked up at him from where she lay with her head cradled on his powerful shoulder, and softly, as tenderly as a dream, she said, "I love you."

Rule's arms tightened around her even more, and he murmured, "I love you."

A moment later his deep voice drifted into the silence. "Welcome home, honey."

And at last she *was* home, in Rule's arms, where she belonged.

Take 3 of
"The Best of the Best™"
Novels FREE
Plus get a FREE surprise gift!

Special Limited-time Offer

Mail to The Best of the Best™

3010 Walden Avenue
P.O. Box 1867
Buffalo, N.Y. 14269-1867

YES! Please send me 3 free novels and my free surprise gift. Then send me 3 of "The Best of the Best™" novels each month. I'll receive the best books by the world's hottest romance authors. Bill me at the low price of $3.74 each plus 25¢ delivery and applicable sales tax, if any.* That's the complete price and a savings of over 10% off the cover prices—quite a bargain! I understand that accepting the books and gift places me under no obligation ever to buy any books. I can always return a shipment and cancel at any time. Even if I never buy another book from Harlequin, the 3 free books and the surprise gift are mine to keep forever.

183 BPA ANV9

Name	(PLEASE PRINT)	
Address		Apt. No.
City	State	Zip

This offer is limited to one order per household and not valid to current subscribers.
*Terms and prices are subject to change without notice. Sales tax applicable in N.Y.
All orders subject to approval.

UBOB-295   ©1990 Harlequin Enterprises Limited

Are you looking for more passionate stories by

LINDA HOWARD

Then order now for more romantic stories by one of MIRA's most popular authors: